Taha Hussein's

The Days

The Great Works of Arabic Literature: Guided Texts for Arabic Learners is a series of complete study packages intended for use in both Arabic literature courses and independent study. Each book in the series presents a complete guided study of one of the landmark works of modern Arabic literature, including the original text, a robust variety of comprehension and interpretation exercises, and guided discussions of the elements of literature and literary criticism. Each of these can be used as a major component of a curriculum, requiring no supplementation or adaptation. This series will be a great aid for teachers of Arabic and Arabic literature and for advanced learners who want to continue their study independently. Students in the fourth year of college-level Arabic study or higher are the main audience for these texts.

Taha Hussein's

The Days

A Guided Study for Arabic Learners

David DiMeo

The American University in Cairo Press
Cairo New York

First published in 2022 by
The American University in Cairo Press
113 Sharia Kasr el Aini, Cairo, Egypt
One Rockefeller Plaza, 10th Floor, New York, NY 10020
www.aucpress.com

ISBN 978 1 617 97131 0

Library of Congress Cataloging-in-Publication Data

Names: DiMeo, David Fred, author. | Husayn, Tãhã, 1889-1973. Ayyãm.
Title: Taha Hussein's The days: a guided study for Arabic learners / David DiMeo.
Identifiers: LCCN 2022027161 | ISBN 9781617971310 (paperback) | ISBN 9781649032379 (epub) | ISBN 9781649032386 (pdf)
Subjects: LCSH: Husayn, Tãhã, 1889-1973. Ayyãm.
Classification: LCC PJ7864.A35 A98 2022 | DDC 892.7/35--dc23/eng/20220727

1 2 3 4 5 26 25 24 23 22

Designed by David G. Hanna
Printed in the United States of America

Contents

Preface and Acknowledgments

Taha Hussein's *al-Ayam (The Days),* first serialized in 1926–27, is as much a story of an Egyptian society on the verge of seismic change as the (fictionalized) biography of one of the great leaders of that change. *The Days* would eventually become a three-volume chronicle, although the first volume, detailing the childhood of the protagonist, remains the most famous. It is that first volume that is presented here.

Born into a poor village in Middle Egypt, blinded as a child and placed into a dysfunctional educational system, Taha Hussein would rise to become rector of the University of Alexandria, minister of education, and one of the most influential authors in modern Egypt, nominated for the Nobel Prize fourteen times and known informally as the Dean of Arabic Literature. Taha Hussein's personal journey was Egypt's journey as well. The young man who refused to accept rote learning and adherence to tradition would be arguably the most influential figure in transforming Egypt's educational system, with a vision of modern, free education for all. If *The Days* is Egypt's story as much as Taha Hussein's, that is largely because he made it so.

The first modern Arabic novel widely known in the west, *The Days* has remained a literary masterpiece. Taha Hussein's innovative blending of fiction and autobiography cannot help but strike the reader from the first encounter with his protagonist curiously narrated in the third person and known as "our friend," rather than by a name. The author's relationship to this character, however, was more than just a stylistic innovation. Throughout a lifetime of reforming Egypt's education system—often against great resistance—Taha Hussein never lost touch with this character: the nine-year-old boy with boundless intellectual curiosity but no place to exercise it, the child-sheikh with a turban yet nothing to back it up. His ability to "know" this young man—his needs, his challenges, his aspirations—was a constant resource in his efforts to build an educational system to serve him.

It was no coincidence that the story that would become the first volume of *The Days* would appear in the journal *al-Hilal* at the same time the author was embroiled in the most bitter controversy in his life. Taha Hussein's book *Fi al-shi'r al-jahili* (On Pre-Islamic Poetry) created a firestorm by claiming, among other things, that parts of the Qur'an were fabricated and that much of pre-Islamic poetry was forged after the coming of Islam. The prime minister would remove him from his post as dean at Cairo University, and at least five books denouncing Hussein's text were published, including one by the sheikh of al-Azhar. Meanwhile, many leading Egyptian intellectuals supported Hussein. It was to intellectuals like these that he wrote in the avant-garde cultural journal the story of the curious young man who questioned tradition and blind obedience.

Taha Hussein would also stir controversy with his 1947 translation and commentary on Jean-Paul Sartre's concept of "committed literature" *(littérature engagée). Iltizam al-adib,* as Hussein dubbed it in Arabic, referring to the "duty" of the author to write for, and about, the masses, would come to dominate Arabic literature in the 1950s. *The Days* was already an example of what this movement sought: an eminently clear and touching picture of life for an underclass, disabled youth in a family struggling for survival, made vivid by the sensory and emotional picture that the narrative created. In it, Taha Hussein could relate the classical scholar Abu 'Ala' al-Ma'arri to the impoverished villager. This was very much a part of his ambition to make a world-class education available to every Egyptian, regardless of class or background.

Thus the study of *The Days* provides not only a picture of what life was like at a transitional moment in Egyptian history, but a view inside the mind of one who was determined to—and would—transform that society. That transformation is visible not only in the subject matter, but in the style of the novel, in its clear language, and in its objective approach to the examination of one's self. With this book, we hope to make that experience available to a wider audience.

This project would not have been possible without the generous cooperation of the Taha Hussein estate and Maha Aon. I am also, as always, extremely grateful to the amazing staff of the American University in Cairo Press: Nadine El-Hadi and Nadia Naqib, with whom it is an absolute joy to work. I would also like to thank my colleagues for their support, especially the wise counsel and advice of Ahmed Muhamed.

I hope that Taha Hussein will bring you as much joy as he has brought me.

How to Use This Book

This book is designed as a complete study unit, ready-made for classroom or individual use. The entire text of the first volume of Taha Hussein's trilogy *The Days* is included within these pages. We have structured the book to replicate the way the novel would be taught in an Arabic literature course by an experienced teacher. A course curriculum could use this book as it is presented, from first page to last, without supplemental materials or without reorganizing the text.

The learning objectives for this book are not simply to improve Arabic reading skills or appreciation of the novel, but to develop student understanding of literary criticism and analysis as a discipline and the important role of *The Days* in Egyptian literary and social history. This novel was part of, and a major force in, a social–political movement that changed Egypt permanently. The exercises in this book help to illuminate that connection.

The course is divided into ten units, each of which provides a series of activities from the level of reading comprehension through analysis up to presentational writing and speaking. Each unit breaks the text into five or six sections. As the chapters in the original novel vary greatly in length, the divisions in this text do not match those of Taha Hussein's chapters, although I have tried to adhere to those chapter divisions as much as possible. Based on the level of the reader and how a course is structured, a student could complete one or more sections per day, and a unit in one or two weeks. Each section is followed by comprehension questions. These are intended to ensure that students stay on track with the story. These will be especially helpful for independent learners, to ensure key points are not missed. At the end of each unit, students then complete more in-depth exercises in overall comprehension, interpretation, and analysis. At this point, they will analyze and discuss literary elements and techniques, cultural context and the major themes of the work. At the end of each unit, students complete either a medium-length writing assignment (two to three pages) or a speaking assignment (one to two minutes) on an overall theme of the novel.

This arrangement simulates an Integrated Performance Assessment (IPA) exercise in that students will fulfill three stages of activities for each unit:

- Stage 1: Interpretive Reading of a section of the novel with comprehension activities
- Stage 2: Interpersonal Speaking, to discuss interpretations of what they have read through guided activities
- Stage 3: Presentational Writing/Speaking, based on the preceding steps.

Unit Organization

The main divisions of this book are referred to as units, to avoid the confusion that the word "chapter" would cause, as the novel itself is arranged in chapters. Each unit contains:

- Author's Background. Rather than present a biography of Taha Hussein at the beginning of the book and not refer to it again, this book spreads the biography of the author across the ten units, tying each part to the themes that will be studied in the unit. This way, the author's background is an integral part of the analysis of every section.
- Reading. The reading is broken down into sections of approximately one to two pages in length, followed by comprehen

sion questions. The questions are designed to ensure students do not miss key plot points, and also to reinforce retention of the story. We believe putting comprehension questions only at the end of the book discourages readers from pausing to reflect on the text.

- Comprehension Exercise. These exercises are intended to reinforce key points from the entire unit and refresh students' familiarity with the story before moving on to interpretation.
- Interpreting the Text. Here, through a variety of activities, students are asked to think about the larger developments in the story, about what is implied, and about the author's (apparent) attitudes. These discussions will help students internalize the text and prepare for the final stages of analysis.
- Cultural and Historical Context. These notes are given in each unit to explain points that may not be familiar to today's reader, but would have been understood by Taha Hussein's original audience. They also give background to understand why Taha Hussein was writing and what issues the novel was attempting to address.
- Analyzing the Elements of Literature. This section is designed to strengthen readers' literary analysis and criticism skills and develop their capacity to analyze other works. The elements of literature are discussed in a separate section below.
- Themes. This is the synthesis and presentation stage of the unit. Here, students will develop and present a written or spoken interpretation of a key theme in the novel.
- Vocabulary Items. Although this is not intended as a vocabulary-building course, some vocabulary items will be needed to facilitate comprehension of the text. As a literary text, *The Days* uses a significant number of uncommon words and words outside of their familiar uses. The intent is not for stu-

dents to memorize or be tested on these words, as they are unlikely to encounter many of them again, but rather to facilitate reading. Vocabulary terms are presented in the order they appear in each unit.

Elements of Literature

Elements of literature are aspects that are common to all literary works. These are distinct from literary techniques, which may or may not be present in any given literary work. All stories, for example, are expected to have a setting, characters, and plot. A story may use irony or flashback as techniques, but may not.

In this book, students will analyze *The Days* in terms of its use of the elements of literature. This will aid students not only in understanding this novel but in developing their framework for literary analysis and familiarity with literary terminology. Each unit will examine a different element, beginning with a short explanation in Arabic about the element and then specific questions that apply it to the study of *The Days*. Although the exact delineation of literary elements differs among critics, those used in this book are representative of the most common.

Traditionally, the elements of literature (العَناصِر الأَدَبِيَّة) in Arabic have included:

- Characters (الشَّخْصِيات)
- Plot (الحِبْكَة)
- Style (الأسْلوب)
- Tone/Pace (جَرَس الصَوت/الوَتيرَة)
- Emotions (العَواطِف)

The introduction of European models of writing, of which Taha Hussein was a pioneer, in the early twentieth century, however, meant that criticism became rooted far more in European/western models than in traditional Arabic models. Therefore, this book will use the most common western elements of literature in its analysis, as would generally be the case in most classes on modern Arabic literature. For this study, we have adapted these to Arabic terms and explanations, but these are essentially western terms being translated into Arabic in most cases.

The elements of literature, then, used in this book are:

Genre (الجنْس الأَدَبي)

Genre refers to the general category of writing into which the work falls. The three traditional genres are prose, poetry, and drama, which are based on the type of language, but there are many other ways to categorize literary works. Among prose fiction writing, the short story and the novel are two important genres by length. Subject matter can be another distinction: historical fiction, science fiction, etc. Each genre has accepted (although often not written) rules and conventions that an author may follow or choose to violate. Identifying genre is important as it delineates what the expectations are for the literary work. Taha Hussein's *The Days*, it will be seen, straddles several generic boundaries and challenges some of their assumptions.

Fiction vs. non-fiction. The distinction between fiction and non-fiction is one of the trickiest in literary study, largely because authors have gone to great lengths to innovate with the distinction. Originally, non-fiction referred to true stories while fiction meant created stories, but authors have always blurred this distinction. Fictional stories may be heavily based on real events and real people, and supposedly non-fictional works are often very subjective and biased. A useful distinction is that fiction is meant to be subject to the interpretation of the reader, while non-fiction is not. A non-fiction text is at least ostensibly meant to convey factual truth as the writer understands it. A fictional work, no matter how heavily based in real events, still leaves the author the freedom to invent and change those events as desired.

The Days is a particularly famous example of a work that plays with the intersection of fiction and non-fiction and confounds traditional understanding of the difference.

Audience (القُرّاء)

Every work is written for a specific audience. The author will make assumptions about what information the audience would be expected to know, or how they would be expected to react to events. Taha Hussein's audience for *The Days* would recognize many of the institutions and customs that modern day readers might not be familiar with.

Setting (المكان وَالوَقْت)

The setting is the environment in which the story takes place, including its time and place. A setting may be real or imaginary and subject to different natural laws than those in real life. In socially engaged fiction, setting becomes much more important than in entertainment literature or literature focused on the self. Writers like Taha Hussein were part of a movement to use literature to critique the social problems around them and advocate for change. Thus, the social, political, and economic structures in which the characters live are often more important than the characters themselves. *The Days* is a sharp critique of the educational system in Egypt, which Taha Hussein spent much of his life trying to reform, although the medical system and organized religion are also highlighted.

Characters (الشَّخْصيات)

Character is probably the most familiar element of literature and the one needing the least explanation. The main character in the story is known as the protagonist, oftentimes referred to colloquially as the hero, although the main character need not be heroic. When one ex ists, the opponent of the protagonist is the antagonist. In socially engaged fiction, writers walked a delicate balance between portraying characters as individuals with personal choices and as constrained by their social and economic situation. Taha Hussein's use of character in this novel has been a source of interest and debate since its publication. That his protagonist is at least partly autobiographical, but yet treated as a different person than the author, blurs the lines between what is history and what may be fiction in the story.

Plot (الحَبْكَة)

The plot is the action of the story; what "happens" in the story. The plot will always differ to some extent from how it is reported (the narrative, see below). In some cases, this difference may be great. While writers of experimental and impressionist fiction intentionally create mystery around the actual details of the plots of their stories—in order to spark the reader's curiosity and imagination—writers of realism, of which Taha Hussein was a leader, tried to minimize the dissonance.

Structure (البُنْيَة)

Structure refers to how the story is presented. Though not a major issue in *The Days*, structure is a key component in many literary works. *The Arabian Nights (Alf lela wa-lela)* is famous for presenting a series of some two hundred stories told over a period of nights (the actual number varying from edition to edition) as part of a larger frame story. Many stories in the collection are embedded within other stories or carried across other stories, creating a very intricate structure.

Narration (السَّرْد)

Narration is one of the most important literary elements and can be broken down into many sub-elements, as will be done in the discussions in this book. Narration refers to *how* the story is told, as no narration can completely match the actual events. Some of the key components of narration are:

Narrator (السارد)

The narrator is the voice telling the story, which may or may not be associated with an actual person. In fiction, the narrator is distinct from the author, although the distance between them may vary. Statements made by the narrator may, in fact, go against the beliefs of the author. In experimental or abstract writing, this dissonance will be pronounced; in realist writing, the author will generally try to make the narrator sound as objective as possible. Narrators can be classified on several axes:

First- vs. Third-person. The most obvious distinction between narrating voices is whether the story is told about an "I" or a "He/She." First-person narration usually occurs when a character in the story is telling the story; third-person most often occurs when the narrating voice is outside the story, often presumed to be that of the author. This need not be the case, however, and Taha Hussein's *The Days* is a famous example of subverting the traditional conventions of first- and third-person narration, as will be studied in this book.

Omniscient vs. Limited. An omniscient narrator has complete knowledge of everything in the world of the story, even information not known to the characters. An omniscient, third-person narrator is common in realist writing as a way for the author to present the story as objectively and completely as possible. A limited narrator lacks some of this knowledge, such as what characters may be thinking. First-person narrators are generally limited.

Reliable vs. Unreliable. A reliable narrator is one that shares the values and beliefs of the author. The words of an unreliable narrator, by contrast, should not be taken at face value. They may obviously violate the author's beliefs, or may leave quite a bit of uncertainty. Naguib Mahfouz's novel *The Thief and the Dogs*, for example, is narrated by a wanted killer, Said Mahran, whose connection to reality is quite tenuous.

Point of View (وِجْهَة النَّظْر)

Point of view is sometimes treated as a sub-element of narration and sometimes as a separate element entirely. This term refers to the perspective from which we see the story. Even in an omniscient, third-person narrative, the events and information presented to the reader are limited to a certain perspective. Point of view may change many times in a written work. *The Days*, although a third-person narrative, generally takes the point of view of the main character, "Our Friend." The narrator's description of the village and its boundaries in the first chapters, for example, reflects the limited perspective of the protagonist, particularly in the sense of his being blind.

Themes (مَوْضُوعات)

Themes are the major issues or subjects the story addresses. Because of their importance, themes will be discussed in a separate section in every unit, and students will be given a longer writing or presentation assignment about a theme. Theme answers the question "what is this book about?" Themes can be as familiar as love, betrayal, or courage, but socially engaged writers focused largely on socio-economic themes. It will be very clear to the reader in a short time that education, poverty, and tradition are major themes in this book, but there are many others. A challenge that socially engaged writers faced was trying to make sure that social themes did not drown out individual themes, such that the characters also dealt with their internal issues and weaknesses, in addition to what the social and economic systems forced upon them.

Tone (جَرْس الصَّوْت)

Tone describes how the narrator's or author's attitude toward the subject is reflected in their choice of language. Often, the narrator's words are not meant to be taken at face value. The tone may be mocking, sarcastic, serious, anxious, nostalgic, and so on. Taha Hussein's narration of the protagonist's attempts to use magic spells, or the villagers' belief in superstitions presents these ideas as the characters themselves felt them, but in a way that shows he disagrees. Similarly, his descriptions of the young boy's boredom in the school or "Our Master's" reluctance to accept responsibility convey that the author does not share their attitude.

Language (اللُغَة)

Although closely related to tone, language refers to the actual type of language in which the work is written, such as the distinction between poetry (الشِّعْر) and prose (النَّثْر). A work will be written in some kind of register, such as a formal style or a conversational one. It could be also written in a regional dialect that may reflect the author's normal way of speaking or may be intended to mimic that of a character in the story. Modern Arab writers, especially those aiming to write for "the masses," have always faced the choice of using Standard Arabic or a Colloquial dialect. Taha Hussein was generally dismissive of Colloquial, considering it beneath the level of a language. Occasional phrases of Colloquial do appear in *The Days* although the work is overwhelmingly in Standard Arabic. Nonetheless, the work was praised for its clear and vivid language.

Unit One

Preparation for Reading

Author's Background

ولد طه حسين في قرية ريفية مصرية صغيرة في نهاية القرن التاسع عشر. خلال حياته، سافر إلى عواصم الثقافة العالمية، ودرس الفلسفة العربية والغربية في أهم مؤسسات التعليم في مصر وأوروبا، وحصل على شهادة الدكتوراه من جامعة السوربون، أشهر الجامعات الفرنسية. لا عجب، إذًا، أنه كان يعتبر فرص الدراسة والاكتشاف في القرية محدودة جدًا وأن تكون هذه المشاعر ملحوظة في أعماله الأدبية. انتبهوا لمؤشرات مشاعره تجاه قيود الحياة في القرية الموجودة في الرواية.

Reading

I

لا يذكر لهذا اليوم اسمًا، ولا يستطيع أن يضعه حيث وضعه الله من الشهر والسنة، بل لا يستطيع أن يذكر من هذا اليوم وقتًا بعينه، وإنما يقرّب ذلك تقريبًا.

وأكبر ظنه أن هذا الوقت كان يقع من ذلك اليوم في فجره أو في عشائه. ويرجح ذلك لأنه يذكر أن وجهه تلقى في ذلك الوقت هواءً فيه شيء من البرد الخفيف الذي لم تذهب به حرارة الشمس. ويرجح ذلك لأنه على جهله حقيقة النور والظلمة، يكاد يذكر أنه تلقى حين خرج من البيت نورًا هادئًا خفيفًا لطيفًا كأن الظلمة تغشي بعض حواشيه. ثم يرجح ذلك لأنه يكاد يذكر أنه حين تلقى هذا الهواءَ وهذا الضياء لم يأنس من حوله حركة يقظة قوية، وإنما آنس حركة مستيقظة من

نوم أو مقبلة عليه. وإذا كان قد بقي له من هذا الوقت ذكرى واضحة بيّنة لا سبيل إلى الشك فيها، فإنما هي ذكرى هذا السياج الذي كان يقوم أمامه من القصب، والذي لم يكن بينه وبين باب الدار إلا خطوات قصار. هو يذكر هذا السياج كأنه رآه أمس. يذكر أن قصب هذا السياج كان أطول من قامته، فكان من العسير عليه أن يتخطاه إلى ما وراءه. ويذكر أن قصب هذا السياج كان مقتربًا كأنما كان متلاصقًا، فلم يكن يستطيع أن ينسل في ثناياه. ويذكر أن قصب هذا السياج كان يمتد عن شماله إلى حيث لا يعلم له نهاية، وكان يمتد عن يمينه إلى آخر الدنيا من هذه الناحية. وكان آخر الدنيا من هذه الناحية قريبًا، فقد كانت تنتهي إلى قناة عرفها حين تقدمت به السن، وكان لها في حياته — أو قل في خياله — تأثير عظيم.

Comprehension Questions

١. كيف يميز الصبي أوقات اليوم؟

____

____

٢. ما الشيء الذي يتذكره بوضوح؟

____

____

٣. ما المادة التي صنع منها السياج؟

____

____

٤. إلى أي مدى امتد الجدار في مخيلة الشاب؟

____

____

٥. ماذا كان دور السياج في حياة الصبي من وجهة نظر الراوي[1]؟

____

____

II

يذكر هذا كله، ويذكر أنه كان يحسد الأرانب التي كانت تخرج من الدار كما يخرج منها، وتتخطى السياج وثبًا من فوق، أو انسيابًا بين قصبه، إلى حيث تقرض ما كان وراءه من نبت أخضر، يذكر منه الكرنب خاصة.

ثم يذكر أنه كان يحب الخروج من الدار إذا غربت الشمس وتعشّى الناس، فيعتمد على قصب هذا السياج مفكرًا مغرقًا في التفكير، حتى يردّه إلى ما حوله صوت الشاعر قد جلس على مسافة من شماله، والتف حوله الناس وأخذ ينشدهم في نغمة عذبة غريبة أخبار أبي زيد وخليفة دياب، وهم سكوت إلا حين يستخفهم الطرب أو تستفزهم الشهوة، فيستعيدون ويتمارون ويختصمون، ويسكت الشاعر حتى يفرغوا من لغطهم بعد وقت قصير أو طويل، ثم يستأنف إنشاده العذب بنغمته التي لا تكاد تتغير.

ثم يذكر أنه لا يخرج ليلة إلى موقفه من السياج إلا وفي نفسه حسرة لاذعة، لأنه كان يقدّر أن سيقطع عليه استماعه لنشيد الشاعر حين تدعوه أخته إلى الدخول فيأبى، فتخرج فتشده من ثوبه فيمتنع عليها، فتحمله بين ذراعيها كأنه الثمامة، وتعدو به إلى حيث تنيمه على

1. Narrator.

الأرض وتضع رأسه على فخذ أمه، ثم تعمد هذه إلى عينيه المظلمتين فتفتحهما واحدة بعد الأخرى، وتقطر فيهما سائلًا يؤذيه ولا يجدي عليه خيرًا، وهو يألم ولكنه لا يشكو ولا يبكي لأنه كان يكره أن يكون كأخته الصغيرة بكّاءً شكّاءً.

ثم يُنقل إلى زاوية في حجرة صغيرة، فتنيمه أخته على حصير قد بسط عليها لحاف، وتلقي عليه لحافًا آخر، وتذره وإن في نفسه لحسرات، وإنه ليمد سمعه مدًا يكاد يخترق به الحائط لعله يستطيع أن يصله بهذه النغمات الحلوة التي يرددها الشاعر في الهواء الطلق تحت السماء. ثم يأخذه النوم، فما يحس إلا وقد استيقظ والناس نيام، ومن حوله إخوته وأخواته يغطون فيسرفون في الغطيط، فيلقي اللحاف عن وجهه في خفية وتردد، لأنه كان يكره أن ينام مكشوف الوجه. وكان واثقًا أنه إن كشف وجهه أثناء الليل أو أخرج أحد أطرافه من اللحاف، فلا بد من أن يعبث به عفريت من العفاريت الكثيرة التي كانت تعمر أقطار البيت وتملأ أرجاءه ونواحيه، والتي كانت تهبط تحت الأرض ما أضاءت الشمس واضطرب الناس. فإذا أوت الشمس إلى كهفها، والناس إلى مضاجعهم، وأطفئت السرج، وهدأت الأصوات، صعدت هذه العفاريت من تحت الأرض وملأت الفضاء حركةً واضطرابًا وتهامسًا وصياحًا.

Comprehension Questions

١. لماذا يحسد الصبي الأرانب؟

____

____

٢. إلى ماذا كان الصبي يستمع في المساء؟

____

____

٣. كيف اعتادت أخته أن تنيمه بعد استماعه الى الشاعر؟

____

____

٤. ماذا كانت أم الصبي تفعل بعينيه في الليل؟

____

____

٥. لماذا رفض الصبي البكاء رغم آلامه؟

____

____

٦. ماذا كان الصبي يتوقع أن يجد خلال الليل؟

____

____

III

وكان كثيرًا ما يستيقظ فيسمع تجاوب الديكة وتصايح الدجاج، ويجتهد في أن يميز بين هذه الأصوات المختلفة، فأما بعضها فكانت أصوات ديكة حقًا، وأما بعضها الآخر فكانت أصوات عفاريت تتشكل بأشكال الديكة وتقلدها عبثًا وكيدًا. ولم يكن يحفل بهذه الأصوات ولا يهابها، لأنها كانت تصل إليه من بعيد، إنما كان يخاف الخوف كله أصواتًا أخرى لم يكن يتبينها إلا بمشقة وجهد، كانت تنبعث من زوايا الحجرة

نحيفة ضئيلة، يمثل بعضها أزيز المرجل يغلي على النار، ويمثل بعضها الآخر حركة متاع خفيف ينقل من مكان إلى مكان، ويمثل بعضها خشبًا ينقصم أو عودًا ينحطم.

وكان يخاف أشد الخوف أشخاصًا يتمثلها قد وقفت على باب الحجرة فسدّته سدًا، وأخذت تأتي بحركات مختلفة أشبه شيء بحركات المتصوفة في حلقات الذكر. وكان يعتقد أن ليس له حصن من كل هذه الأشباح المخوفة والأصوات المنكرة، إلا أن يلتف في لحافه من الرأس إلى القدم، دون أن يدع بينه وبين الهواء منفذًا أو ثغرة. وكان واثقًا أنه إن ترك ثغرة في لحافه فلا بد من أن تمتد منها يد عفريت إلى جسمه فتناله بالغمز والعبث.

لذلك كان يقضي ليله خائفًا مضطربًا؛ إلا حين يغلبه النوم، وما كان يغلبه النوم إلا قليلًا. كان يستيقظ مبكرًا، أو قل كان يستيقظ في السحر، ويقضي شطرًا طويلًا من الليل في هذه الأهوال والأوجال والخوف من العفاريت، حتى إذا وصلت إلى سمعه أصوات النساء يعدن إلى بيوتهن وقد ملأن جرارهن من القناة وهن يتغنين «الله يا ليل الله ...» عرف أن قد بزغ الفجر، وأن قد هبطت العفاريت إلى مستقرها من الأرض السفلى، فاستحال هو عفريتًا، وأخذ يتحدث إلى نفسه بصوت عال، ويتغنى بما حفظ من نشيد الشاعر، ويغمز من حوله من إخوته وأخواته، حتى يوقظهم واحدًا واحدًا. فإذا تم له ذلك، فهناك الصياح والغناء، وهناك الضجيج والعجيج، وهناك الضوضاء التي لم يكن يضع لها حدًا إلا نهوض الشيخ من سريره، ودعاؤه بالإبريق ليتوضأ.

حينئذ تخفت الأصوات وتهدأ الحركة، حتى يتوضأ الشيخ ويصلي ويقرأ ورده ويشرب قهوته ويمضي إلى عمله. فإذا أغلق الباب من دونه نهضت الجماعة كلها من الفراش، وانسابت في البيت صائحة لاعبة حتى تختلط بما في البيت من طير وماشية.

Comprehension Questions

١. هل كان الصبي ينام جيدًا؟

____

____

٢.ممَّ كان الصبي يخاف خلال الليل؟

____

____

٣. متى ينتهي عادة خوف الصبي خلال الليل؟

____

____

٤. ماذا كان الشيخ[2] يفعل كل صباح؟

____

____

IV

كان مطمئنًا إلى أن الدنيا تنتهي عن يمينه بهذه القناة التي لم يكن بينه وبينها إلا خطوات معدودة ... ولم لا؟ وهو لم يكن يرى عرض هذه القناة، ولم يكن يقدِّر أن هذا العرض ضئيل بحيث يستطيع الشاب النشيط أن

2. This term of respect for an elder or religious figure is used liberally throughout the novel, as in Egyptian society. Here, it refers to the boy's father.

يثب من إحدى الحافتين فيبلغ الأخرى، ولم يكن يقدِّر أن حياة الناس والحيوان والنبات تتصل من وراء هذه القناة على نحو ما هي من دونها، ولم يكن يقدِّر أن الرجل يستطيع أن يعبر هذه القناة ممتلئة دون أن يبلغ الماء إبطيه، ولم يكن يقدر أن الماء ينقطع من حين إلى حين عن هذه القناة، فإذا هي حفرة مستطيلة يعبث فيها الصبيان، ويبحثون في أرضها الرخوة عما تخلف من صغار السمك فمات لانقطاع الماء عنه.

لم يكن يقدِّر هذا كله، وإنما كان يعلم يقينًا لا يخالطه الظن أن هذه القناة عالم آخر مستقل عن العالم الذي كان يعيش فيه، تعمره كائنات غريبة مختلفة لا تكاد تحصى؛ منها التماسيح التي تزدرد الناس ازدرادًا، ومنها المسحورون الذين يعيشون تحت الماء بياض النهار وسواد الليل، حتى إذا أشرقت الشمس أو غربت طفوا يتنسمون الهواء، وهم حين يطفون خطر على الأطفال وفتنة للرجال والنساء. ومنها هذه الأسماك الطوال العراض التي لا تكاد تظفر بطفل حتى تزدرده ازدرادًا، والتي قد يتاح لبعض الأطفال أن يظفروا في بطونها بخاتم الملك، ذلك الخاتم الذي لا يكاد الإنسان يديره في إصبعه حتى يسعى إليه دون لمح البصر خادمان من الجن يقضيان له ما يشاء، ذلك الخاتم الذي كان يتختمه سليمان فيسخر له الجن والريح وما يشاء من قوى الطبيعة. وما كان أحب إليه أن يهبط في هذه القناة لعل سمكة من هذه الأسماك تزدرده فيظفر في بطنها بهذا الخاتم، فقد كانت حاجته إليه شديدة ... ألم يكن يطمع على أقل تقدير في أن يحمله أحد هذين الخادمين إلى ما وراء هذه القناة ليرى بعض ما هناك من الأعاجيب؟ ولكنه كان يخشى كثيرًا من الأهوال قبل أن يصل إلى هذه السمكة المباركة.

Comprehension Questions

١. في رأي الصبي، ما الذي يشكل حدود الدنيا؟

____

____

٢. ما هي بعض الأشياء لم يعرفها الصبي عن القناة ولكنها كانت واضحة للآخرين؟

____

____

٣. ما هي بعض الأخطار التي تخيلها في القناة؟

____

____

٤. لماذا كان الخاتم في بطن السمكة فريدًا من نوعه؟

____

____

٥. لماذا كان الصبي يقيم على جانب القناة وينتظر ظهور السمكة؟

____

____

V

على أنه لم يكن يستطيع أن يبلو من شاطئ هذه القناة مسافة بعيدة، فقد كان هذا الشاطئ محفوفًا عن يمينه وعن شماله بالخطر. فأما عن يمينه فقد كان هناك العَدوِيون[3]، وهم قوم من الصعيد[4] يقيمون في دار

3. A family name.
4. Upper (Southern) Egypt.

لهم كبيرة، يقوم على بابها دائمًا كلبان عظيمان لا ينقطع نباحهما، ولا تنقطع أحاديث الناس عنهما، ولا ينجو المار منهما إلا بعد عناء ومشقة. وأما عن شماله فقد كانت هناك خيام يقيم فيها «سعيد الأعرابي» الذي كان الناس يتحدثون بشره ومكره وحرصه على سفك الدماء، وامرأته «كوابس» التي كانت قد اتخذت في أنفها حلقة من الذهب كبيرة، والتي كانت تختلف إلى الدار، وتقبّل صاحبنا[5] من حين إلى حين، فيؤذيه خزامها ويروعه. وكان أخوف الأشياء إليه أن يتقدم عن يمينه فيتعرض لكلبي العدويين، أو يتقدم عن شماله فيتعرض لشر «سعيد» وامرأته «كوابس».

على أنه كان يجد في هذه الدنيا الضيقة القصيرة المحدودة من كل ناحية ضروبًا من اللهو والعبث تملأ نهاره كله.

ولكن ذاكرة الأطفال غريبة، أو قل إن ذاكرة الإنسان غريبة حين تحاول استعراض حوادث الطفولة، فهي تتمثل بعض هذه الحوادث واضحًا جليًا كأن لم يمض بينها وبينه من الوقت شيء، ثم يمحي منها بعضها الآخر كأن لم يكن بينها وبينه عهد.

Comprehension Questions

١. مم كان يتخوف الصبي من جيرانه على الشمال—سعيد وكوابس؟

____

____

١. كيف وصف الكاتب الجيران عن يمينه—العدويين؟

____

____

5. For the first time, the narrator is identifying the main character by the title he will use for the rest of the book—صاحبنا ("our friend").

٢. بصورة عامة، كيف يشعر الصبي بالعالم من حوله؟

____

____

٣. لماذا يشك الراوي في ذكريات صاحبنا؟

____

____

VI

يذكر صاحبنا السياج والمزرعة التي كانت تنبسط من ورائه، والقناة التي كانت تنتهي إليها الدنيا، و«سعيدًا» و«كوابس» وكلاب العدويين، ولكنه يحاول أن يتذكر مصير هذا كله فلا يظفر من ذلك بشيء. وكأنه قد نام ذات ليلة ثم أفاق من نومه فلم ير سياجًا ولا مزرعة ولا سعيدًا ولا كوابس، وإنما رأى مكان السياج والمزرعة بيوتًا قائمة وشوارع منظمة، تنحدر كلها من جسر القناة ممتدة امتدادًا قصيرًا من الشمال إلى الجنوب، وهو يذكر كثيرًا من الذين كانوا يسكنون هذه البيوت رجالا ونساءً، ومن الأطفال الذين كانوا يعبثون في هذه الشوارع.

وهو يذكر أنه كان يستطيع أن يتقدم يمينًا وشمالاً على شاطئ القناة دون أن يخشى كلاب العَدويين أو مكر سعيد وامرأته. وهو يذكر أنه كان يقضي ساعات من نهاره على شاطئ القناة سعيدًا مبتهجًا بما سمع من نغمات «حسن» الشاعر يتغنى بشعره في أبي زيد وخليفة ودياب، حين يرفع الماء بشادوفه ليسقي به زرعه على الشاطئ الآخر للقناة. وهو يذكر أنه استطاع غير مرة أن يعبر هذه القناة على كتف أحد إخوته دون أن يحتاج إلى خاتم الملك، وأنه ذهب غير مرة إلى حيث كانت تقوم وراء القناة شجرات من التوت فأكل من توتها ثمرات لذيذة. وهو يذكر أنه تقدم غير مرة عن يمينه على شاطئ القناة حتى وصل إلى حديقة المعلم وأكل فيها غير مرة تفاحًا، وقُطِف له فيها غير مرة

نعنـاع وريحـان. ولكنـه عاجـز كل العجـز أن يتذكـر كيـف اسـتحالت الحـال وتغيـر وجـه الأرض مـن طـوره الأول إلـى هـذا الطـور الجديـد.

Comprehension Questions

١. ما الذي حاول الصبي أن يتذكره؟

____

____

٢. في نهاية هذا النص، ما أهم شيء لا يستطيع صاحبنا أن يتذكره؟

____

____

٣. كيف عبر الصبي القناة في الماضي؟

____

____

٤. ما هي بعض الأكلات التي يتذكرها صاحبنا، وأين وجدها؟

____

____

٥. ماذا كان مصدر سعادة الصبي؟

____

____

Comprehension Exercise

Are the following statements true (صحيح) or false (خطأ) and why?

١. كان السياج مهمًا جدًا في ذكريات الصبي.

____

٢. حسد صاحبنا الأرانب لأنها كانت تأكل الخشب.

____

٣. شعر هذا الصبي بأنه يعيش في بيئة متميزة بالحرية غير المحدودة.

____

٤. لم ينم صاحبنا كثيرًا في الليل بسبب خوفه من الحرب العالمية الأولى.

____

٥. كان الصبي يؤمن بوجود مخلوقات سحرية تعيش في القناة.

____

٦. كان صاحبنا يحب أن يستمع إلى صوت الموسيقى من الراديو.

____

٧. لم يعبر الصبي القناة في حياته.

____

٨. لا يتذكر صاحبنا متى أو كيف تغير عالمه بالضبط.

____

Interpreting the Text

A. Answer the following questions in complete Arabic sentences, based on your interpretation of what you have read so far:

١. هل يشعر المؤلف بأن الذاكرة البشرية يعوّل عليها وواضحة؟

____

____

٢. هل كشف لنا المؤلف الأسباب وراء "تغير" حياة الصبي؟

____

____

٣. هل يبدو أن صاحبنا لديه خيال خصب؟

____

____

٤. ما هو أكثر شيء يريده الصبي في رأيكم؟

____

____

٥. كيف يجد صاحبنا سعادته في رأيكم؟

____

____

٦. قال الكاتب إن الصبي "جاهل حقيقة النور والظلمة." معنى هذا القول غير واضح الآن، ولكن كيف يمكن تفسير هذا التعبير؟

____

____

B. Predicting the direction of the story: The author has chosen so far to give only a partial revelation of the facts of the story, through the impressions of his character. Based on what you have read, what do you expect to discover as the story progresses?

١. كثير من ذكريات الصبي يعتمد على حاستي السمع واللمس، ما السبب في ظنكم؟

____

____

٢. يبدو أن حياة صاحبنا تختلف عن حيوات أخواته وأخوته أختلافًا كبيرًا. إلامَ يشير ذلك في رأيكم؟

____

____

٣. أشار الصبي إلى "تغير" في حياته. على أساس ما قرأتم في النص، ما الذي يمكن أن يكون سببًا لهذا التغيير؟

____

____

٤. من خلال ما يشير إليه النص عن شخصية الصبي، ما العوامل التي تتوقعون أن تلعب دورًا مهمًا في تشكيل مستقبله؟

____

____

Analyzing Elements of Literature

Narration (السرد): Point of View (وجهة النظر)

في أي قصة، يجب على المؤلف اختيار وجهة نظر يحكم من خلالها وتتحكم برؤيتنا وفهمنا للقصة، وهي تحدد كذلك مصدر الذكريات والأفكار والتصورات المطروحة أمام القارئ. وجدير بالذكر أن وجهة نظر القصة لا تكون بالضرورة وجهة نظر الراوي. إن وجهة النظر تلعب دورًا مهمًا في تشكيل التأثير العاطفي للقصة، والتي قد يستخدمها المؤلف أيضًا في تقييد معرفتنا أو التأثير على آرائنا بشأن أحداث القصة، وبمقدور الكاتب أيضا أن يغير وجهة نظر السرد أكثر من مرة خلال القصة.

A. Answer the following questions about the point of view of the narrative you have read so far:

١. هل نستطيع أن نحدد هوية راوي هذا النص؟ لماذا؟

____

____

٢. على من تعتمد وجهة النظر هذه في رأيكم؟

____

____

٣. ما هي بعض الدلالات على هذا؟

---

٤. ما الذي يقيد وجهة النظر هذه في النص؟

---

٥. ما هو رأي الراوي في صحة وجهة النظر هذه؟

---

٦. في رأيكم، ما هي مميزات وجهة النظر هذه؟ ولماذا اختارها الكاتب في رأيكم؟

Themes

Taha Hussein explores a number of important themes of his time in this novel. Consider the question below and prepare a two- to three-minute discussion of how this theme is presented in the excerpt you read.

يظهر صاحبنا كشخص ذي خيال خصب ونشيط ولكنه يشعر بقيود بيئته الضيقة. من الواضح أن فرصه للاكتشاف والتعلم محدودة جدًا. كيف يتناول المؤلف أهمية الحرية والخيال للأطفال وعدم توفر الاثنين في الريف المصري؟ هل تتوقعون أن تلعب هذه المشاكل دورًا في بقية القصة؟

Vocabulary Items

In reading novels, it is not necessary to know every word you encounter. In fact, it is very unlikely that you would recognize every word in a novel by Taha Hussein. In general, you will use context to get past unfamiliar words. In this text, however, some words are essential to the meaning of the story, and those are given here, in case some are unfamiliar to you. For nouns, the singular is given first, followed by the plural; for verbs, the past, followed by present, followed by the *masdar*:

hedge, fence, barrier of trees سِياج، أَسْياج

to cross, leap over تَخَطَّى، يَتَخَطَّى، تَخَطّ

sugar cane قَصَب

a fluid, liquid سائِل، سَوائِل

to irritate, hurt آذى، يُؤذّي، إيذاء

demon, spirit عِفْريت، عَفاريت

to assume a guise تَقَلَّدَ، يَتَقَلَّد، تَقَلُّد

to seize ظَفِرَ (بِـ)،يَظْفَر (بِـ)، ظَفَر

gap, space	ثُغْرَة، ثُغَر
blanket	لِحاف، لُحُف
to transform	اِسْتَحال، يَسْتَحيل، اِسْتَحالة
to play	عَبِثَ، يَعبَث، عَبَث
to swallow	اِزْدَرَدَ، يَزْدَرِد، اِزْدِراد
state, stage	طَوْر، أطْوار

Unit Two

Preparation for Reading

Author's Background

كمثل هذا الشاب في هذه الرواية، أصيب طه حسين بالعمى[6] في سن مبكرة. كان هذا نتيجة لعملية جراحية قام بها حلاق القرية. وكانت عادة شائعة في القرى الريفية في ذلك الوقت، الأمر الذي جعل طه حسين يدرك أهمية التدريب على الطب الحديث في مصر، بالإضافة إلى معرفته بسوء حالة التعليم المصري بشكل عام. نرى أيضًا أن الرواية تنقل لنا كيف كانت القرية المصرية غير مجهزة للتعامل مع احتياجات شاب من ذوي الاحتياجات الخاصة.[7]

Reading

I

كان سابع ثلاثة عشر من أبناء أبيه، وخامس أحد عشر من أشقته.[8] وكان يشعر بأن له بين هذا العدد الضخم من الشباب والأطفال مكانًا خاصًا يمتاز من مكان إخوته وأخواته. أكان هذا المكان يرضيه؟ أكان يؤذيه؟ الحق أنه لا يتبين ذلك إلا في غموض وإبهام، والحق أنه لا يستطيع الآن أن يحكم في ذلك حكمًا صادقًا. كان يحس من أمه رحمة

---

6. Blindness.
7. The term generally preferred these days over the word معوق, "disabled."
8. أشقة – siblings from the same mother and father. The connotation here is that his father had more than one wife. Children in polygamous families who shared the same mother typically have a closer bond than the half-siblings who are also living in the same household.

ورأفة، وكان يجد من أبيه لينًا ورفقًا، وكان يشعر من أخوته بشيء من الاحتياط في تحدثهم إليه ومعاملتهم له. ولكنه كان يجد إلى جانب هذه الرحمة والرأفة من جانب أمه شيئًا من الإهمال أحيانًا، ومن الغلظة أحيانًا أخرى. وكان يجد إلى جانب هذا اللين والرفق من أبيه شيئًا من الإهمال أيضًا، والازْوِرار من وقتٍ إلى وقت. وكان احتياط إخوته وأخواته يؤذيه، لأنه كان يَجد فيه شيئًا من الإشفاق مشوبًا بشيء من الازدراء.

على أنه لم يلبثٍ أن تبين سبب هذا كله، فقد أحس أن لغيره من الناس عليه فضلًا، وأن إخوته وأخواته يستطيعون ما لا يستطيع، وينهضون من الأمر لما لا ينهض له. وأحس أن أمه تأذن لإخوته وأخواته في أشياء تحظرها عليه، وكان ذلك يحفظه. ولكن لم تلبث هذه الحفيظة أن استحالت إلى حزن صامت عميق، ذلك أنه سمع إخوته يصفون ما لا علم له به، فعلم أنهم يرون ما لا يرى.

Comprehension Questions

١. كم عدد الأخوة والأخوات الذين كانوا أكبر أو أصغر منه سنًا؟

____

____

٢. كيف كان الصبي يشعر عندما يتذكر طفولته بصورة عامة؟

____

____

٣. كيف اختلفت معاملة الأم للصبي عن أسلوبها مع الأطفال الآخرين؟

___

___

٤. ما الذي يميز طريقة كلام الأولاد الآخرين في أثناء تعاملهم مع الشاب؟

___

___

٥. ماذا كانت الأخوات يقلن له أحيانًا ويجعله حزينًا؟

___

___

II

كان من أول أمره طلعَةً لا يحفل بما يلقى من الأمر في سبيل أن يستكشف ما لا يعلم. وكان ذلك يكلفه كثيرًا من الألم والعناء. ولكن حادثة واحدة حدّت ميله إلى الاستطلاع، وملأت قلبه حياءً لم يفارقه إلى الآن. كان جالسًا إلى العشاء بين إخوته وأبيه، وكانت أمه كعادتها تشرف على حفلة الطعام، ترشد الخادم وترشد أخواته اللائي كن يشاركن الخادم في القيام بما يحتاج إليه الطاعمون. وكان يأكل كما يأكل الناس. ولكن لأمر ما خطر له خاطر غريب! ما الذي يقع لو أنه أخذ اللقمة بكلتا يديه بدل أن يأخذها كعادته بيد واحدة؟ وما الذي يمنعه من هذه التجربة؟ لا شيء، وإذًا فقد أخذ اللقمة بكلتا يديه وغمسها من الطبق المشترك ثم رفعها إلى فمه. فأما إخوته فأغرقوا في الضحك. وأما أمه فأجهشت بالبكاء. وأما أبوه فقال في صوت هادئ حزين: ما هكذا تؤخذ اللقمة يا بني ... وأما هو فلم يعرف كيف قضى ليلته.

من ذاك الوقت تقيدت حركاته بشيء من الرزانة والإشفاق والحياء لا حدّ له. ومن ذلك الوقت عرف لنفسه إرادة قوية. ومَن ذلك الوقت حرم على نفسه ألوانًا من الطعام لم تبح له إلا بعد أن جاوز الخامسة والعشرين. حرم على نفسه الحساء والأرز، وكل الألوان التي تؤكل بالملاعق، لأنه كان يعرف أنه لا يحسن اصطناع الملعقة، وكان يكره أن يضحك إخوته، أو تبكي أمه، أو يعلمه أبوه في هدوء حزين.

هذه الحادثة أعانته على أن يفهم حقًا ما يتحدث به الرواة عن أبي العلاء[9] من أنه أكل ذات يوم دِبسًا، فسقط بعضه على صدره وهو لا يدري، فلما خرج إلى الدرسَ قال له بعض تلاميذه: يا سيدي أكلت دبسًا، فأسرع بيده إلى صدره، وقال: نعم، قاتل الله الشره! ثم حرم الدبس على نفسه طوال الحياة.

وأعانته هذه الحادثة على أن يفهم طورًا من أطوار أبي العلاء حق الفهم، ذلك أن أبا العلاء كان يتستر في أكله حتى على خادمه، فقد كان يأكل في نفق تحت الأرض، وكان يأمر خادمه أن يعدّ له طعامه في هذا النفق ثم يخرج، ويخلو هو إلى طعامه فيأخذ منه ما يشتهي. وقد زعموا أن تلاميذه تذاكروا مرة بطيخ حلب وجودته، فتكلف أبو العلاء وأرسل إلى حلب من اشترى لهم منه شيئًا، فأكلوا واحتفظ الخادم لسيده بشيء من البطيخ وضعه في النفق، وكأنه لم يضعه في المكان الذي تعود أن يضع فيه طعام الشيخ، وكره الشيخ أن يسأل عن حظه من البطيخ، فلبث البطيخ في مكانه حتى فسد ولم يذقه الشيخ.

Comprehension Questions

١. ما الذي فعله الصبي وجعل إخوته يضحكون عليه؟

____

____

9. The reference is to Abu 'Ala' al-Ma'arri, an eleventh-century Syrian writer.

٢. كيف كانت ردة فعل أمه تجاه ذلك؟

---

٣. لماذا حرم الصبي على نفسه تناول الأطعمة بالملعقة؟

---

٤. كيف عرف الطلاب في قصة أبي العلاء أنه قد أكل دبسًا؟

---

٥. كيف كان أبو العلاء يأكل بعد ذلك؟

III

فهم صاحبنا هذه الأطوار من حياة أبي العلاء حق الفهم لأنه رأى نفسه فيها. فكم كان يتمنى طفلاً لو استطاع أن يخلو إلى طعامه، ولكنه لم يكن يجرؤ على أن يعلن إلى أهله هذه الرغبة. على أنه خلا إلى بعض الطعام أحيانًا كثيرة، ذلك في شهر رمضان وفي أيام المواسم الحافلة. حين كان أهله يتخذون ألوانًا من الطعام حلوة، ولكنها تؤكل بالملاعق؛ فكان يأبى أن يصيب منها على المائدة. وكانت أمه تكره له هذا الحرمان،

فكانت تفرد له طبقًا خاصًا وتخلي بينه وبينه في حجرة خاصة، يغلقها هو من دونه حتى لا يستطيع أحدٌ أن يشرف عليه وهو يأكل.

على أنه عندما استطاع أن يملك أمر نفسه اتخذ هذه الخطة له نظامًا. بدأ بذلك حين سافر إلى أوروبا لأول مرة، فتكلف التعب وأبى أن يذهب إلى مائدة السفينة، فكان يحمل إليه الطعام في غرفته. ثم وصل إلى فرنسا فكانت قاعدته إذا نزل في فندق أو في أسرة أن يحمل إليه الطعام في غرفته دون أن يتكلف الذهاب إلى المائدة العامة. ولم يترك هذه العادة إلا حين خطب قرينته فأخرجته من عادات كثيرة كان قد ألفها.

هذه الحادثة أخذته بألوان من الشدة في حياته، جعلته مضرب المثل في الأسرة وبين الذين عرفوه حين تجاوز حياة الأسرة إلى الحياة الاجتماعية؛ كان قليل الأكل، لا لأنه كان قليل الميل إلى الطعام، بل لأنه كان يخشى أن يوصف بالشره أو أن يتغامز عليه إخوته. وقد آلمه ذلك أول الأمر، ولكنه لم يلبث أن تعوده حتى أصبح من العسير عليه أن يأكل كما يأكل الناس. كان يسرف في تصغير اللقمة، وكان له عم يغيظه منه كلما رآه فيغضب وينهره ويلح عليه في تكبير اللقمة، فيضحك إخوته. وكان ذلك سببًا في أن كره عمه كرهًا شديدًا. كان يستحي أن يشرب على المائدة مخافة أن يضطرب القدح من يده، أو ألا يحسن تناوله حين يقدم إليه، فكان طعامه جافًا ما جلس على المائدة، حتى إذا نهض عنها ليغسل يديه من حنفية كانت هناك، شرب من مائها ما شاء الله أن يشرب، ولم يكن هذا الماء نقيًا دائمًا، ولم يكن هذا النوع من ري الظمأ ملائمًا للصحة، فانتهى به الأمر إلى أن أصبح ممعودًا، وما استطاع أحد أن يعرف لذلك سببًا.

Comprehension Questions

١. بماذا كان يرغب الصبي سرًا؟

____

____

٢. كيف كانت عادته في تناول وجباته عندما سافر إلى أوروبا؟

---

٣. متى تغيرت هذه العادة، ولماذا؟

---

٤. لماذا لم يكن الصبي يأكل ويشرب مع الآخرين خلال وجبات الطعام؟

---

٥. لماذا غضب الصبي من عمه؟

IV

ثم حرم على نفسه من ألوان اللعب والعبث كل شيء، إلا ما لا يكلفه عناءً ولا يعرضه للضحك أو الإشفاق. فكان أحب اللعب إليه أن يجمع طائفة من الحديد وينتحي بها زَاوية من البيت، فيجمعها ويفرقها ويقرع بعضها ببعض، ينفق في ذلك ساعات، حتى إذ سئمه وقف على إخوته أو أترابه وهم يلعبون، فشاركهم في اللعب بعقله لا بيده. وكذلك عرف أكثر ألوان اللعب دون أن يأخذ منها بحظ. وانصرافه هذا عن العبث

حبب إليه لونًا من ألوان اللهو: هو الاستماع إلى القصص والأحاديث، فكان أحب شيء إليه أن يسمع إنشاد الشاعر، أو حديث الرجال إلى أبيه، والنساء إلى أمه. ومن هنا تعلم حسن الاستماع. وكان أبوه وطائفة من أصحابه يحبون القصص حبًا جمًا، فإذا صلوا العصر اجتمعوا إلى واحد منهم يتلو عليهم قصص الغزوات والفتوح، وأخبار عنترة والظاهر بيبرس،[10] وأخبار الأنبياء والنساك والصالحين، وكتبًا في الوعظ والسنن. وكان صاحبنا يقعد منهم مزجر الكلب وهم عنه غافلون، ولكنه لم يكن غافلاً عما يسمع، بل لم يكن غافلاً عما يتركه هذا القصص في نفوس السامعين من الأثر، فإذا غربت الشمس تفرق القوم إلى طعامهم، حتى إذا صلوا العشاء اجتمعوا فتحدثوا طرفًا من الليل، وأقبل الشاعر فأخذ ينشدهم أخبار الهلاليين والزناتيين،[11] وصاحبنا جالس يسمع في أول الليل كما كان يسمع في آخر النهار.

والنساء في قرى مصر لا يحببن الصمت ولا يملن إليه؛ فإذا خلت إحداهن إلى نفسها ولم تجد من تتحدث إليه، تحدثت إلى نفسها ألوانًا من الحديث، فغنت إن كانت فرحة، وعدّدت إن كانت محزونة. وكل امرأة في مصر محزونة حين تريد. وأحب شيء إلى نساء القرى إذا خلون إلى أنفسهن أن يذكرن آلامهن وموتاهن فيعدّدن، وكثيرًا ما ينتهي هذا التعديد إلى البكاء حقًا. وكان صاحبنا أسعد الناس بالاستماع إلى أخواته وهن يتغنين، وإلى أمه وهي تعدد. وكان غناء أخواته يغيظه ولا يترك في نفسه أثرًا؛ لأنه كان يجده سخيفًا لا يدل على شيء؛ في حين كان تعديد أمه يهزه هزًا عنيفًا، وكثيرًا ما كان يبكيه. وعلى هذا النحو حفظ صاحبنا كثيرًا من الأغاني، وكثيرًا من التعديد، وكثيرًا من جد القصص وهزله، وحفظ شيئًا آخر لم تكن بينه وبين هذا كله صلة؛ وهي الأوراد التي كان يتلوها جده الشيخ الضرير إذا أصبح أو أمسى.

---

10. These are the subjects of two of the most famous Arabic epic poems: Antar ibn Shaddad, a great warrior poet of the pre-Islamic period, and Baybars al-Bunduqdari, the greatest of the Medieval Mamluk warriors who ruled Egypt from 1250 to 1517.
11. Famous Arab Bedouin tribes about whom many epic poems circulate.

Comprehension Questions

١. كيف كان صاحبنا يقضي وقته عندما كان الأطفال الآخرين يلعبون؟

____

____

٢. ماذا كان يجب على الرجال فعله بعد صلاتهم في المساء؟

____

____

٣. ماذا كان رأيه في أغاني أخواته؟

____

____

٤. كيف أثر عليه تعديد والدته؟

____

____

٥. ماذا تعلم الصبي من جده؟

____

____

V

كان جده هذا ثقيل الظل بغيضًا إليه، وكان يقضي في البيت فصل الشتاء من كل سنة، وكان قد صلح ونسك حين اضطرته الحياة إلى الصلاح والنسك، فكان يصلي الخمس لأوقاتها، ولم يكن لسانه يفتر عن ذكر الله. وكان يستيقظ آخر الليل ليقرأ «ورد السّحر» وكان ينام في ساعة متأخرة بعد أن يصلي العشاء ويقرأ ألوانًا من الأوراد والأدعية. وكان صاحبنا ينام في حجرة مجاورة لحجرة هذا الشيخ، فكان يسمعه وهو يتلو، وكان يحفظ ما يتلو حتى حفظ من هذه الأوراد والأدعية شيئًا كثيرًا. وكان أهل القرية يحبون التصوف ويقيمون الأذكار،[12] وكان صاحبنا يحب منهم ذلك، لأنه كان يلهو بهذا الذكر، وبما ينشده المنشدون أثناءه. ولم يبلغ التاسعة من عمره حتى كان قد وعى من الأغاني والتعديد والقصص وشعر الهلاليين والزناتيين والأوراد والأدعية وأناشيد الصوفية جملة صالحة، وحفظ إلى ذلك كله القرآن.

Comprehension Questions

١. متى كان الجد يزور بيت الصبي عادة؟

____

____

٢. ماذا كان برنامج الجد اليومي؟

____

____

12. التصوّف – Sufism, folk Islam very popular particularly in rural areas of Egypt. الذكر is an important part of Sufi practice, in which prayers or phrases, such as the name of God, are chanted by the group as a means of reaching the mental state of spiritual connection with God.

٣. ماذا كان رأي الصبي في جده بشكل عام؟

____

____

٤. لماذا أحب الصبي تقاليد القرية الصوفية؟

____

____

٥. ما هي نتيجة الاستماع إلى الأوراد القرآنية؟

____

____

Comprehension Exercise

Are the following statements true (صحيح) or false (خطأ) and why?

١. كان الصبي يحب الاشتراك في ألعاب إخوته وأخواته.

____

٢. كان صاحبنا الابن الوحيد لأمه ولكن أبوه كان له أبناء آخرون من زوجته الأولى.

____

٣. كان الصبي يشعر بالخجل الشديد عندما يأكل مع الأسرة.

---

٤. الاستماع إلى القصص والتعديد والأوراد وغيرها كانت هوايته المفضلة.

---

٥. بقي صاحبنا أعزبًا طوال حياته.

---

٦. كانت هناك صلة صداقة قوية بين الصبي وجده.

---

٧. تأثر صاحبنا بحياة الكاتب أبو العلاء تأثرًا عميقًا.

---

٨. أهمل جد الصبي واجباته الدينية.

Interpreting the Text

A. Answer the following questions in complete Arabic sentences, based on your interpretation of what you have read so far:

١. ماذا قصد المؤلف بقوله إن الصبي "علم أنهم يرون ما لا يرى"؟

---

٢. لماذا كان تناول الطعام يسبب صعوبات لصاحبنا؟

---

٣. ما هو الأثر العام الذي يبدو أن الزواج سيتركه على الصبي؟

---

٤. لماذا يجد صاحبنا في الاستماع متعةً وسرورًا لا يجدهما في أنشطة أخرى؟

---

٥. كيف ترون بيئة القرية من حيث تأثيرها على طفل من ذوي الاحتياجات الخاصة مثل هذا الصبي؟

B. Predicting the direction of the story: This section of the novel has revealed more facts about the main character and some of the events of his life. Based on what you have read, what can you conclude about the hero's life and what do you expect will happen as the story progresses?

١. من خلال ذكريات الصبي عن صعوباته في الأكل نعرف بعض الأشياء عن حياته، ولكن ما الذي يمكننا أن نتنبأ به بخصوص مستقبله، على الأقل؟

____

____

٢. ما المهنة المناسبة لصاحبنا طبقا لهواياته وأنشطته؟ ماذا سيدرس لاحقًا في ظنكم؟

____

____

٣. من خلال معرفتكم بالأحوال والفرص المتوفرة في القرية، هل تتوقعون أن يبقى الصبي هناك مدة طويلة؟

____

____

٤. هل تظنون أن شعور صاحبنا بالعزلة سيستمر طوال حياته؟

____

____

Cultural and Historical Background

Blindness was a common affliction in Egyptian society at the time, partially due to poor medical care, which lagged far behind that in Europe. Taha Hussein was blinded by an unsafe operation performed by the village barber, who typically served as the closest thing to a surgeon in rural areas, with predictably disastrous results. This particular issue, and its larger implications for Egypt's modernization, were at the heart of another of the great transformational Egyptian novels—Yahya Haqqi's *The Lamp of Umm Hashim*. The traumatic, first-hand experience would be one factor that shaped Hussein's passion for educational reform.

Occupations for the blind were extremely limited at the time, as they had been during the previous centuries. Because Muslim society had a long tradition of primarily oral education, based heavily in memorization and recitation, and a great respect for oral communication of all forms—poetry, storytelling, preaching, and so on—opportunities for the blind in these fields were much greater than in others. As a result, some of the greatest intellectuals and religious figures in Muslim culture were blind.

In section II, the main character makes reference to Abu 'Ala' al-Ma'arri, an eleventh-century blind Syrian writer. Here, the youth has empathy for al-Ma'arri because of the practical difficulties of being blind, but his reference to al-Ma'arri by his first name and the character's awareness of such minor anecdotes reflect the special affinity that Taha Hussein had for al-Ma'arri. Beyond these similarities, al-Ma'arri was also a very controversial writer who attacked Islamic orthodoxy and promoted rationalism, much like Taha Hussein would do later on. Taha Hussein would write his doctoral dissertation on al-Ma'arri.

Analyzing Elements of Literature

Emotion (العاطفة)

أحد الأسباب الرئيسية لجاذبية هذا العمل الأدبي هو التأثير العاطفي والشعوري الذي يتركه على القارئ، والذي يمكننا من خلاله فهم وجهات نظر مختلفة، واكتساب نظرة ثاقبة لمشاكل الآخرين والتعاطف معها. في الواقع، غياب العواطف في سرد القصة يمكن أن يكون له صلة بموقف ووجهة نظر المؤلف أيضًا.

يكشف لنا طه حسين في هذه القصة عن مشاعر الشخصية الرئيسية ببالغ التفهم والتعاطف، ويدعونا إلى لمس التحديات الخاصة بالشاب وأحاسيسه ككفيف في قرية مصرية تقليدية.

In the following questions, discuss how the author evokes and expresses emotion in his description of the experiences of his character.

١. كيف تعبر عبارة صاحبنا عن ذكريات مشاعره المتضاربة حول طفولته؟

____

____

٢. ماذا تكشف لنا حادثة ''اللقمة'' عن شخصية الصبي؟ كيف تؤثر ردود أفعال الآخرين عليه؟ ما مدى عمق التأثير ومدته؟

____

____

٣. كيف تساعد لحظات السعادة القليلة في ذكريات الصبي في التعاطف معه؟

____

____

٤. في رأيكم، ما هي العواطف السائدة في القصة؟

____

____

Themes

الوحدة والعزلة

Feelings of isolation and alienation are a very common theme in modern novels. Prepare a one- to two-page written answer to the questions below, based on what you have read so far.

مشاعر الغربة والعزلة شائعة جدًا في الروايات الحديثة. لا شك في أن الشخصية الرئيسية في هذه القصة—''صاحبنا''—قد مرت بمثل هذه المشاعر. كيف جعلنا الكاتب نفهم عزلة الصبي؟ إلى أي حد يختلف

عالمه عن عالم إخوته؟ ما هي بعض الاختلافات الجوهرية التي تميزه عنهم؟ ما هي بعض الأفكار والعواطف التي يحفظها في الداخل ولا يعرفها سائر أفراد أسرته؟

Vocabulary Items

Here are some important words that will help you understand the story:

obscurity, lack of clarity	إبْهام
kindness, pity	رَأْفَة
gentleness, kindness	لِين
roughness	غِلْظَة
pity	إِشْفاق
scorn	ازْدِراء
curious, inquisitive	طلعَة
to concern oneself with	حَفَلَ بِـ، يَحْفِل بِـ، حَفْل
shyness	حَياء
to part with	فارَقَ، يُفارِق، مُفارَقة
morsel	لُقْمَة، لُقَم
to dip, dunk	غَمَسَ، يَغْمِس، غَمْس

gravity, composure	اَلرَّزانَة
syrup	دِبْس
to be alone, isolate oneself	خَلا، يَخْلُو، خَلاء
a bunch	طائِفَة، طَوائِف
to separate oneself, go off	انْتَحَى، يَنْتَحِي، انْتَحاء
entertainment	لَهْو
lamenting (lamentation)	عَدَّدَ، يُعَدِّد، تَعْدِيد
to exasperate	غاظَ، يَغِيظ، غَيْظ
sections of the Qur'an recited daily as units	وِرْد، أَوْراد
odious	بَغِيض
to be pious	صَلَحَ، يَصْلُح، صَلاح
to be an ascetic	نَسَكَ، يَنْسُك، نُسك

Unit Three

Preparation for Reading

Author's Background

مثل صاحبنا، أصبح طه حسين "شيخًا" في عمر مبكر بفضل حفظه القرآن، ويتذكره لمدة قصيرة، على الأقل. ولكنه سيصبح ناقدًا قويًا لنظام التعليم في مصر. لم يقتصر انتقاده على المرحلة الابتدائية ولا على مستوى الكُتّاب فقط، بل تضمن كل المراحل، خاصة الجامعية. كعميد كلية الآداب ووزير للمعارف في مصر قاد حركة الإصلاح في التعليم المصري، ولذلك واجه معارضة قوية من بعض الجهات الإسلامية. انعكس كل هذه على أعماله الأدبية، وخاصة رواية سيرته الذاتية "الأيام".

Reading

I

ولكنه لا يعرف كيف حفظ القرآن، ولا يذكر كيف بدأه، ولا كيف أعاده، وإن كان يذكر من حياته في الكُتّاب مواقف كثيرة، منها ما يضحكه الآن، ومنها ما يحزنه؛ يذكر أوقاتًا كان يذهب فيها إلى الكُتّاب محمولًا على كتف أحد أخويه، لأن الكُتّاب كان بعيدًا، ولأنه كان أضعف من أن يقطع ماشيًا تلك المسافة. ثم لا يذكر متى بدأ يسعى إلى الكُتّاب. ويرى نفسه في ضحى يوم جالسًا على الأرض بين يدي «سيِّدنا» ومن حوله طائفة من النعال؛ كان يعبث ببعضها، وهو يذكر ما كان قد ألصق بها من الرقع. وكان «سيِّدنا» جالسًا على دكة من الخشب صغيرة ليست بالعالية ولا بالمنخفضة قد وضعت على يمين الداخل من باب الكُتّاب بحيث يمر كل داخل «بسيِّدنا». وكان «سيِّدنا» قد تعود متى دخل الكُتّاب

أن يخلـع عباءتـه، أو بعبـارة أدق «دفَّيَّتَـهُ» ويلفهـا لفًا يجعلهـا فـي شـكل المخـدة ويضعهـا عـن يمينـه، ثـم يخلَع نعلـه ويتربـع علـى دكتـه، ويشـعل سيجارته، ويبـدأ فـي نـداء الأسـماء. وكان «سـيِّدنا» لا يعفـي نعليـه إلا إذا لـم يجد مـن ذلك بـدًا، كان يرقعهمـا مـن اليمـين ومـن الشـمال ومـن فـوق ومـن تحـت. وكان إذا أخلـت بـه إحـدى نعليـه دعـا أحـد صبيـان الكُتّـاب وأخـذ النعـل بيـده وقـال لـه: تذهـب إلـى «الحزيِّـن» وهـو هنـا قريـب، فتقـول لـه: «يقـول لك سـيِّدنا إن هـذه النعل فـي حاجـة إلـى لـوزة مـن الناحيـة اليمنـى»، انظـر أتـرى؟ هنـا حيـث أضـع أصبعـي، فيقـول لك «الحزيِّـن»: «نعـم سـأضع هـذه اللـوزة»، فتقـول لـه: «يقـول لـك سـيِّدنا: يجـب أن تتخيـر الجلـد متينًـا غليظًـا جديـدًا، وأن تحسـن الرقـع بحيـث لا يظهـر، أو بحيـث لا يـكاد يظهـر». فيقـول لـك: «نعـم سـأفعل هـذا»، فتقـول لـه: «ويقـول لـك سـيدنا: إنـه عميلـك منـذ زمـن طويـل، فاسـتوص بالأجـر خيـرًا» ومهمـا يقـل لـك فـلا تقبـل منـه أكثـر مـن قـرش، ثـم عـد إلـيَّ مسـافة مـا أغمـض عينـي ثـم أفتحهـا. وينطلـق الصبـي ويلهـو عنـه سـيدنا، ثـم يعـود وقـد أغمـض سـيدنا عينـه وفتحهـا مـرة ومـرة ومـرات.

Comprehension Questions

١. كيف كان صاحبنا يقضي وقته في الكُتّاب؟

____

____

٢. لماذا كان يرسل "سيدنا" الطلاب إلى "الحزيِّن"؟

____

____

٣. كم سيدفع المعلم لإصلاح حذائه؟

____

____

٤. كيف يشعر صاحبنا تجاه ذكرياته عن الكُتّاب؟

____

____

٥. ماذا يتذكر صاحبنا عن الحذاء؟

____

____

II

على أن الرجل كان يستطيع أن يغمض عينه ويفتحها دون أن يرى أو يكاد يرى شيئًا، فقد كان ضريرًا إلا بصيصًا ضئيلًا جدًا من النور في إحدى عينيه، يمثل له الأشباح دون أن يمكنه أن يتميزها. وكان الرجل سعيدًا بهذا البصيص الضئيل ... وكان يخدع نفسه ويظن أنه من المبصرين ... ولكن ذلك لم يكن يمنعه من أن يعتمد في طريقه إلى الكُتّاب وإلى البيت على اثنين من تلاميذه، يبسط ذراعيه على كتفي كل واحد منهما، ويمشي الثلاثة في الطريق هكذا! قد أخذوها على المارة، حتى إنهم ليتنحون لهم عنها.

وكان منظر سيدنا عجبًا في طريقه إلى الكُتّاب وإلى البيت صباحًا ومساءً. كان ضخمًا بادنًا وكانت دفيته تزيد في ضخامته وكان كما قدمنا يبسط ذراعيه على كتفي رفيقيه. وكانوا ثلاثتهم يمشون وإنهم ليضربون الأرض بأقدامهم ضربًا. وكان سيدنا يتخير من تلاميذه لهذه

المهمة أنجبهم وأحسنهم صوتًا؛ ذلك أنه كان يحب الغناء، وكان يحب أن يعلم تلاميذه الغناء، وكان يتخير الطريق لهذا الدرس. فكان يغني ويأخذ رفيقيه بمصاحبته حينًا، والاستماع له حينًا آخر، أو يأخذ واحدًا منهما بالغناء على أن يصاحبه هو والرفيق الآخر. وكان سيدنا لا يغني بصوته ولسانه وحدهما، وإنما يغني برأسه وبدنه أيضا، فكان رأسه يهبط ويصعد، وكان رأسه يلتفت يمينًا وشمالاً. وكان سيدنا يغني بيديه أيضا. فكان يوقع الأنغام على صدر رفيقه بأصابعه. وكان سيدنا يعجبه «الدّور» أحيانًا؛ ويرى أن المشي لا يلائمه فيقف حتى يتمه. وأبدع من هذا كله أن سيدنا كان يرى صوته جميلا. وما يظن صاحبنا أن الله خلق صوتًا أقبح من صوته. وما قرأ صاحبنا قول الله عز وجل «إِنَّ أَنكَرَ الْأَصْوَاتِ لَصَوْتُ الْحَمِيرِ»[13] إلَّا ذكر سيدنا وهو يوقع أبياتًا مَن «البردة» في طَريقه إلى الجَامع منطلقًا لصلاة الظهر، أو في طريقه إلى البيت منصرفا من الكتّاب.

Comprehension Questions

١. لماذا احتاج "سيّدنا" إلى المرافقة عندما كان يمشي من وإلى الكُتّاب؟

____

____

٢. ماذا كان "سيّدنا" يحب أن يفعل خلال سيره من الكُتّاب؟

____

____

13. The Qur'an 31:19.

٣. من كان "سيّدنا" يختار لمرافقته في طريقه من الكُتّاب؟

____

____

٤. ماذا كان رأي صاحبنا في صوت "سيّدنا"؟

____

____

٥. في الآية القرآنية التي ذكرها صاحبنا، بمَ يذكره صوت المعلم؟

____

____

III

يرى صاحبنا نفسه كما قدمنا، جالسًا على الأرض يعبث بالنعال من حوله، وسيدنا يقرئه سورة الرحمن، ولكنه لا يذكر أكان يقرؤها بادئًا أم معيدًا.

وكأنه يرى نفسه مرة أخرى جالسًا لا على الأرض ولا بين النعال، بل على يمين سيدنا على دكة أخرى طويلة، وسيدنا يقرئه: «أَتَأْمُرُونَ النَّاسَ بِالْبِرِّ وَتَنسَوْنَ أَنفُسَكُمْ وَأَنتُمْ تَتْلُونَ الْكِتَابَ أَفَلَا تَعْقِلُونَ»،[14] وأكبر ظنه أنه كان قد أتم القرآن بدءًا وأخذ يعيده. وليس غريبًا أن ينسى صاحبنا كيف حفظ القرآن فقد أتم حفظه ولما يتم التاسعة من عمره. وهو يذكر في وضوح وجلاء ذلك اليوم الذي ختم فيه القرآن، ذلك أن سيدنا كان يتحدث إليه قبل هذا اليوم بأيام عن ختم القرآن، وعن أن أباه سيبتهج

14. The Qur'an 2:44.

بـه. وكان يضـع لذلـك شـروطًا ويطالـب بحقوقـه.[15] ألـم يكـن قـد علـم قبـل صاحبنـا أربعـة مـن إخوتـه ذهـب واحـد منهـم إلـى الأزهـر،[16] والآخـرون إلـى المـدارس، وصاحبنـا هـو الخامـس ... فكـم لسـيدنا علـى الأسـرة مـن حقـوق! وحقـوق سـيدنا علـى الأسـرة كانـت تتمثـل دائمًـا طعامًـا وشـرابًا وثيابًـا ومـالًا. فأمـا الحقـوق التـي كان يقتضيهـا إذا ختـم صاحبنـا القـرآن فعشـوة دسـمة قبـل كل شـيء، ثـم جبـة وقفطـان، وزوج مـن الأحذيـة وطربوش مغربـي وطاقيـة مـن القمـاش الـذي تتخـذ منـه العمائـم وجنيـه أحمـر،[17] لا يرضـى بشـيء دون ذلـك ... فـإذا لـم يـؤدَّ إليـه هـذا كلـه فهـو لا يعـرف الأسـرة،[18] ولا يقبـل منهـا شـيئًا، ولا صلـة بينـه وبينهـا، وهـو يقسـم علـى ذلك بمحرجـات الأيْمـان. وكان هـذا اليـوم يـوم أربعـاء. وكان سـيدنا قـد أنبأ فـي الصبـاح بـأن صاحبنـا سـيختم القـرآن فـي هـذا اليـوم. وأقبلـوا فـي العصـر؛ يمشـي سـيدنا معتمـدًا علـى رفيقيـه، ويمشـي صاحبنـا مـن ورائـه يقـوده يتيـم مـن أيتـام القريـة. حتـى إذا بلغـوا البيـت دفـع سـيدنا البـاب دفعًـا، وصـاح صيحتـه المعتـادة: «يـا سـتَّار»،[19] واتجـه إلـى المنظـرة فـإذا فيهـا الشـيخ قـد انفتـل مـن صـلاة العصـر وهـو يقـرأ شـيئًا مـن الأدعيـة كعادتـه، فاسـتقبلهم مبتسـمًا مطمئنًـا، وكان صوتـه هادئـًا، وكان صـوت سـيدنا عاليًـا، وكان صاحبنـا لا يقـول شـيئًا، وكان اليتيـم مبتهجًـا. أجلـس الشـيخ سـيدنا ورفيقيـه، ووضـع فـي يـد اليتيـم قطعـة مـن فضـة، ودعـا الخـادم وأمـره أن يأخـذ هـذا اليتيـم إلـى حيـث يصيـب شـيئًا مـن الطعـام، ومسـح علـى رأس ابنـه وقـال: «فتـح اللـه عليـك، انصـرف إلـى أمـك، وقـل لهـا إن سـيدنا هنـا».

Comprehension Questions

١. كم كان عمر صاحبنا عندما ختم القرآن؟

____

____

15. That is, his payment.
16. Al-Azhar University, the leading Islamic university in Egypt.
17. A guinea, a gold coin.
18. Meaning he would disavow them.
19. A traditional greeting.

٢. ماذا كان سيّدنا يتوقع من أسرة صاحبنا نتيجةً لنجاحه في تعلّم القرآن؟

____

____

٣. كم من إخوة صاحبنا درسوا مع سيدنا؟

____

____

٤. ماذا وعد سيدنا نفسه قبل الذهاب إلى بيت صاحبنا؟

____

____

٥. من رافق سيدنا في سيره إلى بيت صاحبنا؟

____

____

IV

وكانت أمه قد سمعت صوت سيدنا، وكانت قد أعدت له ما لا بد منه في مثل هذا الوقت، وهو كوز ضخم طويل من السكر المذاب لا شيء عليه. أخرج إلي سيدنا هذا الكوز فعبه عبًا، وشرب رفيقاه كوبين من السكر المذاب أيضا. ثم أخرجت القهوة فشربها سيدنا مع الشيخ. وكان سيدنا يلحّ على الشيخ في أن يمتحن الصبي فيما حفظ من القرآن، وكان الشيخ يجيب: «دعه يلعب إنه صغير». ثم نهض سيدنا لينصرف، فقال

له الشيخ: «نصلي المغرب معًا إن شاء الله». وكانت هذه هي الدعوة إلى العشاء. وما أحسب أن سيدنا نال شيئًا آخر أجرًا على ختم صاحبنا للقرآن، فقد كان يعرف الأسرة منذ عشرين سنة، وكان له فيها عادات غير مقطوعة، وكانت الكلفة بينه وبينها مرفوعة، وكان واثقًا أن الحظ إن يخطئه معها هذه المرة فلن يخطئه مرة أخرى.

منذ هذا اليوم أصبح صبينا شيخًا وإن لم يتجاوز التاسعة لأنه حفظ القرآن، ومن حفظ القرآن فهو شيخ مهما تكن سنه. دعاه أبوه شيخًا، ودعته أمه شيخًا، وتعوَّد سيدنا أن يدعوه شيخًا أمام أبويه، أو حين يرضى عنه، أو حين يريد أن يترضاه لأمر من الأمور. فأما فيما عدا ذلك فقد كان يدعوه باسمه، وربما دعاه «الواد». وكان شيخنا الصبي[20] قصيرًا نحيفًا شاحبًا زريَّ الهيئة على نحو ما، ليس له من وقار الشيوخ ولا من حسن طلعتهم حظ قليل أو كثير. وكان أبواه يكتفيان من تمجيده وتكبيره بهذا اللفظ الذي أضافاه إلى اسمه كبرًا منهما وعجبًا لا تلطفًا به ولا تحببًا إليه. أما هو فقد أعجبه هذا اللفظ في أول الأمر، ولكنه كان ينتظر شيئًا آخر من مظاهر المكافأة والتشجيع. كان ينتظر أن يكون شيخًا حقًا، فيتخذ العمّة ويلبس الجبّة والقفطان، وكان من العسير إقناعه بأنه أصغر من أن يحمل العمة ومن أن يدخل في القفطان ... وكيف السبيل إلى إقناعه بذلك وهو شيخ قد حفظ القرآن! وكيف يكون الصغير شيخًا! وكيف يكون من حفظ القرآن صغيرًا! هو إذا مظلوم ... وأي ظلم أشد من أن يحال بينه وبين حقه في العمة والجبة والقفطان! ...

Comprehension Questions

١. ماذا قدمت الأم إلى سيدنا في زيارته إلى البيت؟

____

____

20. To distinguish him from his father, whom the author also refers to as الشيخ.

٢. ماذا طلب سيدنا من أبي صاحبنا؟

____

____

٣. لماذا رفض الأب أن يمتحن الشاب؟

____

____

٤. كيف تغيرت حال صاحبنا بعد أن يصبح شيخًا؟

____

____

٥. بماذا دعاه أبوه وأمه بعد ذلك؟

____

____

V

وما هي إلا أيام حتى سئم لقب الشيخ، وكره أن يدعى به، وأحس أن الحياة مملوءة بالظلم والكذب، وأن الإنسان يظلمه حتى أبوه، وأن الأبوة والأمومة لا تعصم الأب والأم من الكذب والعبث والخداع.

ثم لم يلبث شعوره هذا أن استحال إلى ازدراء للقب الشيخ، وإحساس بما كان يملأ نفس أبيه وأمه من الغرور والعجب، ثم لم يلبث أن نسي هذا كله فيما نسي من الأشياء.

على أنه في حقيقة الأمر لم يكن خليقًا أن يدعى شيخًا، وإنما كان خليقًا رغم حفظه للقرآن أن يذهب إلى الكُتّاب كما كان يذهب مهمل الهيئة، على رأسه طاقيته التي تنظف يومًا في الأسبوع، وفي رجليه حذاء يجدّ مرة في السنة، ولا يدعه حتى لا يحتمل شيئًا، فإذا تركه فليمش حافيًا أسبوعًا أو أسابيع حتى يأذن الله له بحذاء جديد. كان خليقًا بهذا كله؛ لأن حفظه للقرآن لم يدم طويلًا ... أكان وحده ملومًا في ذلك؟ أم كان اللوم مشتركًا بينه وبين سيدنا؟ الحق أن سيدنا أهمله حينًا وعني بغيره من الذين لم يختموا القرآن. أهمله ليستريح، وأهمله لأنه لم يتقاض أجرًا على ختمه للقرآن. واستراح صاحبنا إلى هذا الإهمال، وأخذ يذهب إلى الكُتّاب يقضي فيه طوال النهار في راحة مطلقة، ولعب متصل، ينتظر أن تنتهي السنة ويأتي أخوه الأزهري من القاهرة، حتى إذا انتهت الإجازة وعاد إلى القاهرة، اصطحبه ليُصبح شيخًا حقًا، وليجاور في الأزهر.

Comprehension Questions

١. كيف تغير شعور صاحبنا تجاه لقب "شيخ" بصورة عامة؟

____

____

٢. هل حفظ صاحبنا القرآن حفظًا جيدًا، وهل حافظ على ما حفظه؟

____

____

٣. لماذا أهمل سيدنا تدريس الشاب؟

٤. ماذا كان الشاب يفعل عادة عندما يبلى حذائه؟

٥. لماذا كان صاحبنا ينتظر نهاية السنة؟

VI

ومضى على هذا شهر وشهر وشهر. يذهب صاحبنا إلى الكُتّاب ويعود منه في غير عمل، وهو واثق بأنه قد حفظ القرآن، وسيدنا مطمئن إلى أنه حفظ القرآن، إلى أن كان اليوم المشئوم ... كان هذا اليوم مشئومًا حقًا، ذاق فيه صاحبنا لأول مرة مرارة الخزي والذلة والضعة وكره الحياة. عاد من الكُتّاب عصر ذلك اليوم مطمئنًا راضيا، ولم يكد يدخل الدار حتى دعاه أبوه بلقب الشيخ، فأقبل عليه ومعه صديقان له. فتلقاه أبوه مبتهجًا، وأجلسه في رفق، وسأله أسئلة عادية، ثم طلب إليه أن يقرأ «سورة الشعراء». وما هي إلا أن وقع عليه هذا السؤال وقع الصاعقة، ففكر وقدّر، وتحفّز واستعاذ بالله من الشيطان الرجيم، وسمّى الله الرحمن الرحيم.[21] ولكنه لم يذكر من سورة الشعراء إلا أنها

21. These are all phrases recited as the traditional opening to reciting the Qur'an, meaning here that he recited the standard opening.

إحدى سور ثلاث، أولها (طسم)،[22] فأخذ يردّد (طسم) مرة ومرة ومرة، دون أن يستطيع الانتقال إلى ما بعدها. وفتح عليه أبوه بما يلي هذه الكلمة من سورة الشعراء، فلم يستطع أن يتقدم خطوة. قال أبوه: فاقرأ سورة النمل. فذكر أن أول سورة النمل، كأول سورة الشعراء (طس) وأخذ يردد هذا اللفظ، وفتح عليه أبوه، فلم يستطع أن يتقدم خطوة أخرى ... قال أبوه: فاقرأ سورة القصص، فذكر أنها الثالثة، وأخذ يردّد (طسم)، ولم يفتح عليه أبوه هذه المرة، ولكنه قال له في هدوء: قم؛ فقد كنت أحسب أنك حفظت القرآن. قام خجلا يصبب عرقًا، وأخذ الرجلان يعتذران عنه بالخجل وصغر السن، ولكنه مضى لا يدري أيلوم نفسه لأنه نسي القرآن، أم يلوم سيدنا لأنه أهمله، أم يلوم أباه لأنه امتحنه ...؟

ومهما يكن من شيء، فقد أمسى هذا اليوم شرَّ مساء، ولم يظهر على مائدة العشاء، ولم يسأل عنه أبوه، ودعته أمه في إعراض إلى أن يتعشى معها، فأبى. فانصرفت عنه ونام.

ولكن هذا المساء المنكر كان في جملته خيرًا من الغد. ذهب إلى الكُتّاب، فإذا سيدنا يدعوه في جفوة: ماذا حصل بالأمس؟ وكيف عجزت عن أن تقرأ سورة الشعراء؟ وهل نسيتها حقا؟ اتلها عليَّ! فأخذ صاحبنا يردد (طسم) ... وكانت له مع سيدنا قصة كقصته مع أبيه. قال سيدنا: عوضني الله خيرًا فيما أنفقت معك من وقت، وما بذلت في تعليمك من جهد، فقد نسيت القرآن ويجب أن تعيده. ولكن الذنب ليس عليك ولا عليّ، وإنما هو على أبيك؛ فلو أنه أعطاني أجري يوم ختمت القرآن لبارك الله له في حفظك، ولكنه منعني حقي فمحا الله القرآن من صدرك.

ثم بدأ يقرئه القرآن من أوله، شأنه مع من لم يكن شيخًا ولا حافظا.

22. The sura begins with these three letters, which is all the youth can remember.

Comprehension Questions

١. كيف كان صاحبنا يقضي وقته في الكُتّاب بعدما أصبح شيخًا؟

____

____

٢. ماذا طلب أبو صاحبنا من الشاب عند رجوعه من الكُتّاب؟

____

____

٣. ماذا تذكر الشاب من سورة الشعراء؟

____

____

٤. كيف كانت ردّة فعل أبي صاحبنا تجاه فشله في حفظ القرآن؟

____

____

٥. على من ألقى سيدنا باللوم لفشل صاحبنا في حفظ القرآن؟

____

____

Comprehension Exercise

Are the following statements true (صحيح) or false (خطأ) and why?

١. كان سيدنا معلّمًا مجتهدًا.

____

٢. نسي صاحبنا معظم ما تعلّمه في الكُتّاب.

____

٣. منهج الكُتّاب يشجع على التفكير المستقل والفهم العميق.

____

٤. كانت العلاقة بين سيدنا وأسرة الشاب جيدة لفترة طويلة.

____

٥. كان الأب يزور المجلس مع أصدقائه ليتفاخر بولده.

____

٦. تقاليد المجتمع تتطلب من الناس أن يحترموا أي شخص حفظ القرآن، مهما كان عمره.

____

٧. لام سيدنا نفسه لفشل الشاب.

____

٨. حصل سيدنا على مكافآت كثيرة نتيجة لنجاح صاحبنا في حفظ القرآن.

____

Interpreting the Text

A. Answer the following questions in complete Arabic sentences, based on your interpretation of what you have read so far:

١. لماذا رفض أبو الشاب أن يمتحن ابنه خلال زيارة سيدنا في ظنكم؟

____

____

٢. هل ترون أن لقب "الشيخ" لم يكن مناسبًا لصاحبنا؟

____

____

٣. ما مدى التزام صاحبنا بدراسته للقرآن؟

____

____

٤. ما رأي الكاتب في مصداقية لقب "الشيخ" بصورة عامة؟

____

____

٥. لو أن أباه امتحنه، هل كان صاحبنا سيحتفظ بلقب الشيخ لوقتٍ طويل؟

____

____

B. Interpretation: What are the implications (both obvious and implied) in the following lines from the text:

١. من حفظ القرآن فهو شيخ مهما تكن سنه.

____

____

٢. كيف يكون الصغير شيخًا! وكيف يكون من حفظ القرآن صغيرًا!

____

____

٣. على رأسه طاقيته التي تنظف يومًا في الأسبوع، وفي رجليه حذاء يجدّ مرة في السنة.

---

٤. الذنب ليس عليك ولا عليّ، وإنما هو على أبيك؛ فلو أنه أعطاني أجري يوم ختمت القرآن لبارك الله له في حفظك.

---

٥. وكان واثقًا أن الحظ إن يخطئه معها هذه المرة فلن يخطئه مرة أخرى.

Cultural and Historical Background

1. The custom of one becoming a "sheikh" and gaining the distinctive emblems of that rank upon memorizing the Qur'an is genuine. Although Taha Hussein clearly means to mock this practice with the image of a nine-year-old sheikh who has forgotten everything, the story is true.
2. The letters at the beginning of the Qur'anic suras that the boy recites are known as the *muqatta'at* (حروف مُقَطَّعات). These combinations of disjointed letters appear at the beginning of 29 of the 114 suras of the Qur'an. Although interpretations of

their meanings have been advanced, no one knows the purpose or meaning of these mysterious letters. The fact that of all he has supposedly memorized, the boy only remembers parts of the suras he, by definition, cannot understand, further highlights the lack of any real learning this "sheikh" has gained.

Analyzing Elements of Literature

Imagery (التصوير الأدبي)

يقصد المؤلف أحيانًا استدعاء الصور — سواء كانت مرئية أو صوتية أو إحساس أو غير ذلك — في ذهن القارئ من أجل تحفيز ردّ فعل عاطفي بعينه. قد يكون الهدف من هذا خلق التعاطف مع الشخصية أو التأثير على رأي القارئ في الشخصية أو إثارة الاهتمام بالقصة.

في هذه الرواية، يستخدم طه حسين صورة الشيخ الصغير في نقده للنظام التعليمي الذي يكرهه. من الواضح أن هذا اللقب لا يليق بصاحبنا بسبب صغر عمره، لكنه يثير التساؤل حول الفرق بينه وبين أي شيخ آخر.

Answer the following questions about the use of the image of the young sheikh in this story:

١. يرتدي الشاب ثياب الشيخ الديني، رغم افتقاره إلى المعرفة الصحيحة بالقرآن. هل ينتقد المؤلف قيمة هذه الرموز الدينية بشكل عام؟

____

____

٢. ذكر المؤلف الأحذية مرارًا. من الواضح أن القرية تعاني من الفقر. في القسم، كيف يختلف الاهتمام بطاقية صاحبنا عن الاهتمام بأحذيته؟ إلى ماذا يشير الفرق بين الطاقية النظيفة والأحذية البالية بالنسبة لأولويات مجتمعه؟

Themes

التعليم

The critique of the educational system in Egypt is one of the main themes of Hussein's novel, never more vividly presented than in the sections above. Prepare a one- to two-page analysis in Arabic of the effectiveness of the author's critique by answering the question below:

صاحبنا، في دوره الجديد "كشيخ" يمثل رمزًا لفشل النظام التعليمي الإسلامي التقليدي. ما هي بعض مشاكل هذا النظام التي يعكسها الرمز المتمثل بالشيخ؟

Vocabulary Items

The following words are particularly useful in following Taha Hussein's narrative in this section:

a religious primary school, teaching primarily memorization of the Qur'an	كُتَّاب، كَتاتيب
part of the day before noon	ضُحَى

wooden bench	دَكَّة، دِكَك
shoes	نَعْل، نِعال
piaster	قِرْش، قُرُوش
to wink, blink	أَغْمَضَ، يغمِض، إِغْماض
blind	ضَرير
glimpse, glimmer	بَصِيص
most excellent, outstanding	أَنْجَب
does not suit	لم يُلائِمْ، لا يُلائِمُ
left side	شِمال
to be delighted, rejoice	ابْتَهَجَ، يَبْتَهَج، ابْتِهاج
dinner	عَشْوَة
traditional items of men's clothing: a loose outer garment, a robe or caftan, a fez, and a brimless cap made of fabric	جُبَّة، جُبَب – قُفْطان، قفاطِين – طَرْبُوش، طرابِيش – طاقِيَّة، طواقٍ
afternoon	عَصْر، عَصارٍ
orphan	يَتِيم، أَيْتام

jug	كُوز، أَكْواز
ceremony, formality	كُلْفَة، كُلَف
to commit an error	أَخْطَأَ، يُخْطِئ، إِخْطاء
pale, emaciated	شاحِب
gravity, dignity	وَقار
turban	عِمَّة
tired, bored	سَئِم
did not hesitate, did not take long	لَمْ يَلْبَث
worthy, suitable	خَلِيق، خُلَقاء

Unit Four

Preparation for Reading

Author's Background

بالرغم من وجود مدارس حكومية مؤسسة على نظام أوروبي حديث في مصر، فإن فرص التعليم أمام معظم المصريين كانت قليلة بسبب الرسوم المطلوبة فيها. بما أن طه حسين ينحدر من أسرة فقيرة أنجبت أولاد كثار، يعمل أبوهم في درجة وظيفية صغيرة، كان السبيل الوحيد إلى التعليم أمامه هو نظام حلقة الكُتّاب القديم، أي المدرسة التقليدية لحفظ القرآن. بسبب عدم قدرته على الالتحاق بمدرسة حكومية، أصر طه حسين خلال عمله كمُصلح تعليمي وكوزير للمعارف على أن يكون التعليم مجانيًا وعنصرًا أساسيًا في المجتمع.

Reading

I

وليس من شك في أنه حفظ القرآن بعد ذلك حفظًا جيدًا في مدة قصيرة جدًا. فهو يذكر أنه عاد من الكُتّاب ذات يوم مع سيدنا، وكان سيدنا في هذا اليوم حريصًا على أن يعود معه، حتى إذا وصلوا إلى الدار عطف عليها سيدنا فدفع الباب فاندفع له، وصاح صيحته المألوفة «يا ستار!» وكان الشيخ كعادته في المنظرة قد فرغ من صلاة العصر. فلما استقر سيدنا في مجلسه، قال للشيخ: «زعمت أن ابنك قد نسي القرآن، ولمتني في ذلك لومًا شديدًا، وأقسمت لك إنه لم ينس وإنما خجل، فكذبتني وعبثت بلحيتي هذه، وقد جئت اليوم لتمتحن ابنك أمامي، وأنا أقسم: لئن ظهر أنه لا يحفظ القرآن، لأحْلِقَنَّ لحيتي هذه

ولأصبحن معرة الفقهاء في هذا البلد.» قال الشيخ: «هوّن عليك! وما لك لا تقول: إنه نسي القرآن ثم أقرأته إياه مرةً أخرى؟» قال: «أقسم بالله ثلاثًا ما نسيه ولا أقرأته، وإنما استمعت له القرآن، فتلاه عليَّ كالماء الجاري، لم يقف ولم يتردّد.»

وكان صاحبنا يسمع هذا الحوار، وكان مقتنعًا أن أباه محق وأن سيدنا كاذب، ولكنه لم يقل شيئا، ولبث منتظرًا الامتحان.

وكان الامتحان عسيرًا شاقًا، ولكن صاحبنا كان في هذا اليوم نجيبًا بارعًا، لم يُسأل عن شيء إلا أجاب في غير تردّد وقرأ في إسراع، حتى كان الشيخ يقول له: «على مهلك فإن الكرَّ في القرآن خطيئة.» حتى إذا أتم الامتحان قال له أبوه: «فتح الله عليك، اذهب إلى أمك فقل لها إنك حفظت القرآن حقًا.» ذهب إلى أمه ولكنه لم يقل لها شيئًا ولم تسأله هي عن شيء. وخرج سيدنا في ذلك اليوم، ومعه جبة من الجوخ خلعها عليه الشيخ.

Comprehension Questions

١. لماذا أصر سيدنا على مرافقة الصبي إلى بيته؟

____

____

٢. هل نجح صاحبنا في الامتحان هذه المرة؟

____

____

٣. كيف فسر سيدنا فشل الصبي خلال امتحانه السابق؟

____

____

٤. هل صدق صاحبنا كلام المعلم لأبيه؟

____

____

٥. ماذا كانت مكافأة الأب لسيدنا؟

____

____

II

وأقبل سيدنا إلى الكُتّاب مِن الغد مسرورًا مبتهجًا، فدعا الشيخ الصبيّ بلقب الشيخ هذه المرة قائلًا: أمّا اليوم، فأنت تستحق أن تدعى شيخًا، فقد رفعت رأسي وبيضت وجهي وشرفت لحيتي أمس، واضطر أبوك إلى أن يعطيني الجبّة. ولقد كنت تتلو القرآن أمس كسلاسل الذهب، وكنت على النار مخافة أن تزل أو تنحرف، وكنت أحصنك بالحي القيوم الذي لا ينام؛[23] حتى انتهى هذا الامتحان. وأنا أعفيك اليوم من القراءة، ولكن أريد أن آخذ عليك عهدًا، فعدني بأن تكون وفيًا. قال الصبي في استحياء: لك عليّ الوفاء. قال سيدنا: فأعطني يدك. وأخذ بيد الصبي. فما راع الصبي إلا شيء في يده غريب، ما أحس مثله قط، عريض يترجرج، ملؤه شعر تغور فيه الأصابع، ذلك أن سيدنا قد وضع يد

23. The living one who never sleeps; a reference to God.

الصبـي علـى لحيتـه وقـال: هـذه لحيتـي أسـلمك إيّاهـا، وأريـد إلاّ تهينهـا، فقـل: «واللـه العظيـم» ثلاثـا «وحـق القـرآن المجيـد لا أهينهـا» وأقسـم الصبـي كمـا أراد سـيدنا. حتـى إذا فـرغ مـن قسـمه؛ قـال لـه سـيدنا: كـم فـي القـرآن مـن جـزء؟ قـال: ثلاثـون، قـال سـيدنا: وكـم[24] نشـتغل فـي الكُتّـاب مـن يـوم؟ قـال الصبـي: خمسـة أيـام. قـال سـيدنا: فـإذا أردت أن تقـرأ القـرآن مـرة فـي كل أسـبوع، فكـم تقـرأ مـن جـزء كل يـوم؟ فكـر الصبـي قليـلاً ثـم قـال: سـتة أجـزاء. قـال سـيدنا: فتقسـم لتتلـونَّ علـى العريـف سـتة أجـزاء مـن القـرآن فـي كل يـوم مـن أيـام العمـل، ولتكونـنَّ هـذه التـلاوة أول مـا تأتـي بـه حـين تصـل إلـى الكُتّـاب. فـإذا فرغـت منهـا فـلا جنـاح عليـك أن تلهـو وتلعـب، علـى ألاَّ تصـرف الصبيـان عـن أعمالهـم. أعطـى الصبـي علـى نفسـه هـذا العهـد. ودعـا سـيدنا العريـف فأخـذ عليـه عهـدًا مثلـه، ليسـمعنَّ للصبـي فـي كل يـوم سـتة أجـزاء مـن القـرآن، وأودعـه شـرفه، وكرامـة لحيتـه، ومكانـة الكُتّـاب فـي البلـد، وقبـل العريـف الوديعـة. وانتهـى هـذا المنظـر وصبيـان الكُتّـاب ينظـرون ويعجبـون.

Comprehension Questions

١. ما كان شعور سيدنا وهو في طريقه إلى الكُتّاب بعد امتحان صاحبنا؟

____

____

٢. ماذا طلب سيدنا من الصبي؟

____

____

24. Meaning كم يومًا؟.

٣. كم جزء من القرآن وعد صاحبنا بأن يقرأ كل يوم؟

____

____

٤. من كلفه سيدنا بالاستماع إلى قراءة الصبي؟

____

____

٥. على ماذا أقسم الصبي؟

____

____

III

من ذلك اليوم انقطعت صلة الصبي التعليمية «بسيدنا»، واتصلت بالعريف. ولم يكن العريف أقل غرابة من سيدنا. كان شابًا طويلًا نحيفًا أسود فاحمًا، أبوه سوداني، وأمه مولدة، وكان سيئ الحظ، لم يوفق في حياته إلى خير، جرب الأعمال كلها فلم يفلح في شيء منها. أرسله أبوه عند كثير من الصناع ليتعلم صنعة فلم يفلح. وحاول أن يجد له في معمل السكر؛ شغل العامل أو الخفير أو البواب أو الخادم، فلم يفلح في شيء من هذا. وكان أبوه ضيق الصدر به، يمقته ويزدريه، ويؤثِر عليه إخوته الذين يعملون جميعًا ويكسبون. وكان قد ذهب إلى الكُتّاب في صباه فتعلم القراءة والكتابة، وحفظ سورًا من القرآن لم يلبث أن نسيها. فلما ضاقت به الحياة وضاق بها أقبل إلى سيدنا فشكا إليه أمره، قال له سيدنا: فتعال هنا فكن عريفًا. عليك أن تعلم الصبيان القراءة والكتابة وتلاحظهم وتمنعهم من العبث، وتقوم مقامي متى غبت،

وعلـيّ أن أقرئهـم القـرآن وأحفظهـم إيّـاه. وعليـك أن تفتـح الكُتّـاب قبـل أن تطلـع الشـمس، وتشـرف علـى تنظيفـه قبـل أن يحضـر الصبيـان، وعليـك أن تغلـق الكُتّـاب متـى صليـت العصـر، وتأخـذ مفتاحـه، وعليـك مـع هـذا كلـه؛ أن تكـون يـدي اليمنـى. ولـك ربـع مـا يأتـي بـه الكُتّـاب مـن نقـد، تقتضـي ذلـك فـي كل أسـبوع أو فـي كل شـهر. وتم هـذا العقـد بـين الرجلـين وقـرأا عليـه الفاتحـة، وبـدأ العريـف عملـه.

وكان العريـف يبغـض سـيدنا بغضًـا شـديدًا ويزدريـه، ولكنـه يصانعـه. وكان سـيدنا يكـره العريـف كرهًـا عنيفًـا ويحتقـره، ولكنـه يتملقـه.

فأمـا العريـف فـكان يكـره سـيدنا؛ لأنـه أثـر غشـاش كـذاب، يخفـي عليـه بعـض مـوارد الكُتّـاب، ويسـتأثر[25] بخيـر مـا يحمـل الصبيـان معهـم مـن طعـام. ويزدريـه؛ لأنـه كان ضريـرًا يتكلـف الإبصـار، وكان قبيـح الصـوت، يتكلـف حسـن الصـوت. وأمـا سـيدنا فـكان يكـره العريـف؛ لأنـه مـكار داهيـة، ولأنـه يخفـي عليـه كثيـرًا ممـا ينبغـي أن يعلمـه، ولأنـه سـارق؛ يسـرق مـا يوضـع بـين يديهمـا مـن الطعـام وقـت الغـداء، ويختلـس أطاييـه، ولأنـه يأتمـر مـع كبـار الصبيـان فـي الكُتّـاب، ويعبـث معهـم علـى غفلـة منـه، فـإذا صليـت العصـر وأغلـق الكُتّـاب كان بينـه وبينهـم مواعيـد هنـاك عنـد شـجر التـوت، أو عنـد «القنطـرة» أو فـي «معمـل السـكر».

ومـن غريـب الأمـر أن الرجلـين كانـا صادقـين مصيبـين، وأنهمـا كانـا مضطريـن إلـى أن يتعاونـا علـى كـره ومضـض؛ أحدهمـا محتـاج إلـى أن يعيـش، والآخـر محتـاج إلـى مـن يدبـر لـه أمـور الكُتّـاب.

Comprehension Questions

١. هل نجح العريف في الكثير من محاولاته المهنية؟

____

____

25. To monopolize.

٢. لماذا فضل أبو العريف أبناءه الآخرين عليه؟

____

____

٣. هل كان العريف يحفظ القرآن حفظًا جيدًا؟

____

____

٤. ما هي مسؤوليات العريف في الكُتّاب؟

____

____

٥. هل كانت العلاقة بين سيدنا والعريف جيدة؟

____

____

IV

اتصل صبينا بالعريف، وأخذ يتلو القرآن بين يديه، ستة أجزاء في كل يوم. ولكن ذلك لم يستمر ثلاثة أيام، ضاق الصبي بهذه التلاوة منذ اليوم الأول، وضاق العريف بها منذ اليوم الثاني، وتكاشفا بهذا الضيق في اليوم الثالث، واتفقا منذ اليوم الرابع على أن يتلو الصبي في سره، ستة أجزاء بين يدي العريف، حتى إذا أحس اضطرابًا، أو غاب عنه لفظ، سأل عنه العريف. وأخذ الصبي يأتي في كل يوم، فيسلم

على العريف، ويجلس على الأرض بين يديه، ويحرك شفتيه مهمهمًا كأنه يقرأ القرآن، ويسأل العريف من حين إلى حين عن كلمة، فيجيبه مرة، ويتثاقل عنه مرة أخرى. ويأتي سيدنا في كل يوم قبيل الظهر؛ فإذا سلم وجلس، كان أول عمل يأتيه أن يدعو الصبي فيسأله: أقرأت؟ — نعم — من أين إلى أين؟

وكان الصبي يجيب: من البقرة إلى «لتجدنَّ» في يوم السبت، ومن «لتجدنَّ» إلى «وما أبرئ» في يوم الأحد ...[26] وكذلك قسم القرآن ستة أقسام اصطلح عليها الفقهاء، وخص لكل يوم من الأيام الخمسة، قسما من هذه الأقسام يخبر به سيدنا متى سأله.

ولكن العريف لم يكن ليكتفي بهذا الاتفاق الذي يريحه ويريح الصبي، وإنما كان يطمع في أن يستفيد من موقف الصبي بين يديه، وكان ينذر الصبي من حين إلى حين، بأنه سيخبر سيدنا، أنه قد وجد بعض السور «متعتعة» سيئة الحفظ عند الصبي: «سورة هود»، أو «سورة الأنبياء»، أو «سورة الأحزاب»، وإذ كان القرآن كله «متعتعا» عند الصبي، لأنه أهمل قراءته منذ أشهر، فقد كان يكره أن يمتحنه سيدنا، ويشتري صمت العريف بكل شيء. وكم دفع إلى العريف ما كان يملأ جيبه من خبز، أو فطير، أو تمر ... وكم دفع إليه هذا القرش الذي كان يعطيه إياه أبوه من حين إلى حين، والذي كان يريد أن يشتري به أقراص النعناع. وكم احتال على أمه، ليأخذ منها قطعة ضخمة من السكر، حتى إذا وصل إلى الكُتّاب دفعها إلى العريف، وإنه ليشتهيها كلها أو بعضها، فيأخذها العريف ويدعو بالماء يغمس فيه السكر، ثم يمصه مصا شديدًا، ثم يزدرد السكر وقد ذاب أو كاد ... وكم نزل عن طعامه الذي كان يحمل إليه من البيت ظهر كل يوم، وإنه لشديد الجوع، ليأكل العريف مكانه؛ ولا يخبر سيدنا بأن القرآن عنده متعتع ...

على أن هذه الصِّلات المستمرة لم تلبث أن ضمنت له مودة العريف، فقد اتخذه العريف صديقًا، وأخذ يصطحبه إلى الجامع بعد الغداء ليصلي معه الظهر، ثم أخذ يعتمد عليه، ويثق به، ويطلب إليه أن يُقرئ القرآن بعض الصبيان، أو يسمعه من بعض الذين أخذوا يعيدون ويحفظون. وهنا كان صاحبنا يسلك مع تلاميذه مسلك العريف معه

26. البقرة: The second and longest sura in the Qur'an. لتجدنَّ and وما أبرئ mark the beginnings of parts seven and thirteen respectively.

بالدقـة، كان يُجلس الصبيـان بـين يديـه، ويأخذهـم بالتـلاوة ثـم يتشـاغل عنهـم بالحديثٍ مـع أترابـه، حتـى إذا فـرغ مـن حديثـه، التفـت إليهـم، فـإذا آنس منهـم عبثـا أو إبطـاء أو اضطرابًـا ، فالنذيـر ، ثـم الشـتم، ثـم الضـرب، ثـم إخبار العريـف. والحـق أنـه لـم يكـن أحسـن حفظـا للقرآن مـن تلاميذه، ولكـن العريـف قد اتخـذ معـه هـذه الخطـة، فيجـب أن يكـون هـو عريفـا حقـًا. وإذا كان العريـف لا يشـتمه ولا يضربـه، ولا يرفـع أمـره إلـى سـيدنا ، فذلـك لأنـه يدفـع ثمـن ذلـك كلـه غاليًـا . وقـد فهـم الصبيـان هـذا فأخـذوا يدفعـون لـه الثمـن غاليًـا أيضًـا ، وأخـذ هـو يسـترد بالرشـوة مـا كان يدفـع إلـى العريـف. علـى أن رشـوته كانـت متنوعـة، فلـم يكـن محرومًـا فـي بيتـه، ولـم يكـن فـي حاجـة إلـى الخبـز ولا إلـى التمـر ولا إلـى السـكر، ولـم يكـن يسـتطيع أن يقبـل «الفلـوس». ومـاذا يصنـع بالفلـوس وهـو لا يسـتطيع أن ينفقهـا وحـده؟ فهـو إن قبلهـا دلَّ علـى نفسـه، وافتضـح أمـره. وإذًا فقـد كان عسـيرًا وكان إرضـاؤه شـاقًا . وكان الصبيـان يتفننـون فـي إرضائـه فيشـترون لـه أقـراص النعنـاع و«السـكر النبـات» و«اللـب» و«الفـول السـوداني»، وكان يتفضـل بكثيـر مـن ذلـك علـى العريـف.

Comprehension Questions

١. كم يومًا استمر صاحبنا في القراءة أمام العريف؟

____

____

٢. هل كان الصبي يقرأ القرآن حقًا عندما جلس أمام العريف؟

____

____

٣. عن ماذا كان سيدنا يسأل صاحبنا عادة، وكيف كان صاحبنا يجيب؟

____

____

٤. لماذا هدد العريف بالقول للمعلم إن صاحبنا لم يحفظ بعض السور حفظًا مقبولاً؟

____

____

٥. على ماذا اتفق صاحبنا والعريف بخصوص الطلاب الآخرين؟

____

____

V

ولكن لونًا من الرشوة خاصًا كان يعجبه ويفتنه، ويشجعه على أن يهمل واجبه أشنع إهمال، وهذا اللون هو القصص والحكايات والكتب. فإذا استطاع الصبي أن يقص عليه أحدوثة، أو يشتري له كتابًا من هذا الرجل الذي يتنقل بالكتب في قرى الريف، أو يتلو عليه فصلاً من قصة «لزير سالم» أو «أبي زيد»، فهو واثق بما شاء من رضاه، ورفقه ومحاباته، وكان أمهر تلاميذه في هذه، صبية مكفوفة البصر، يقال لها نفيسة. أرسلها أهلها إلى الكُتّاب لتحفظ القرآن فحفظته، وأتقنت حفظه، ووكلها سيدنا إلى العريف ووكلها العريف إلى صاحبنا، وأخذ صاحبنا يسلك معها مسلك العريف معه. وكان أهل هذه الفتاة أغنياء، ولكنهم من المحدثين. كان أبوها حمَّارًا ثم أصبح تاجرًا مثريًا، وكان ينفق على أهله من غير حساب، ويسبغ عليهم سعة غريبة من العيش. فلم تكن

تنقطع الفلوس من يد نفيسة. وكانت أقدر الصبيان على تخير الرِّشا، ثم كانت أحفظهم للقصص، وأقدرهم على الاختراع، وأحفظهم لألوان الغناء المفرح، والتعديد المبكي، وكانت تحسن الغناء والتعديد معًا. وكانت غريبة الأطوار، في عقلها شيء من الاضطراب، فكانت تلهي صاحبنا أكثر وقته بحديثها وتعديدها، وأقاصيصها وألوان رشوتها. وبينما كان صاحبنا يرشو ويرتشي، ويخدع ويُخدع، كان القرآن يمحى من صدره آية آية وسورة سورة، حتى كان اليوم المحتوم ... ويا له من يوم!

كان يوم الأربعاء، وكان صاحبنا قد قضاه فرحًا مسرورًا. زعم لسيدنا في أول النهار أنه قد أتم الختمة، ثم فرغ بعد ذلك لاستماع القصص والأحاديث، وعبث آخر النهار.

فلما انصرف من الكُتّاب لم يذهب إلى البيت، وإنما ذهب مع جماعة من أصحابه إلى الجامع ليصلي العصر. وكان يحب الذهاب إلى الجامع، والصعود في المنارة، والاشتراك مع المؤذن في التسليم (وهو النداء الذي يلي الأذان الشرعي).

ذهب في ذلك اليوم وصعد في المنارة، واشترك في الأذان وصلى. وأراد أن يعود إلى البيت، ولكنه افتقد نعله فلم يجدها. كان قد وضعها إلى جانب المنارة، فلما فرغ من الصلاة ذهب يلتمسها فإذا هي قد سرقت. أحزنه ذلك بعض الشيء، ولكنه كان فرحًا مبتهجًا هذا اليوم، فلم يجزع ولم يقدّر للأمر عاقبة، وعاد إلى البيت حافيًا. وما كان أبعد المسافة بين البيت والجامع! ولكن ذلك لم يرعه فكثيرًا ما مشي حافيًا.

دخل البيت، وإذا الشيخ في المنظرة كعادته يدعوه: وأين نعلاك؟ فيجيب: نسيتهما في الكُتّاب. فلا يحفل الشيخ بهذا الجواب، ثم يهمل الصبي حينًا ريثما يدخل فيتحدث إلى أمه وإخوته قليلا، ويأكل كسرة من الخبز؛ كان من عادته أن يأكلها متى عاد من الكُتّاب. ثم يدعوه الشيخ، فيسرع إلى إجابته. فإذا استقر به مكانه، قال له أبوه: ماذا تلوت اليوم من القرآن؟ فيجيب: ختمته وتلوت الأجزاء الستة الأخيرة. قال الشيخ: ومازلت تحفظه حفظًا جيدًا؟ قال: نعم. قال الشيخ: فاقرأ لي سورة سبأ. وكان صاحبنا قد نسي سورة سبأ، كما نسي غيرها من السور، فلم يفتح الله عليه بحرف. قال الشيخ: فاقرأ سورة فاطر، فلم يفتح الله عليه بحرف. قال الشيخ في هدوء وسخرية: وقد زعمت أنك مازلت تحفظ القرآن؟ فاقرأ سورة يس. ففتح الله عليه بالآيات

الأولى من هذه السورة، ولكن لسانه لم يلبث أن انعقد، وريقه لم يلبث أن جف، وأخذته رعدة منكرة تصبب على أثرها في وجهه عرق بارد. قال الشيخ في هدوء: قم واجتهد في أن تنسى نعليك كل يوم، فما أرى إلا أنك أضعتهما كما أضعت القرآن، ولكن لي مع سيدك شأنًا آخر.

Comprehension Questions

١. أي نوع من الرشوة يفضل صاحبنا؟

____

____

٢. لماذا أصبحت نفيسة مفضلة بين الطلاب في رأي الصبي؟

____

____

٣. كيف كان المستوى المادي لعائلة نفيسة؟

____

____

٤. ماذا حدث لنعلي الصبي؟

____

____

٥. لماذا غضب أبو صاحبنا منه مرة أخرى؟

____

____

Comprehension Exercise

Are the following statements true (صحيح) or false (خطأ) and why?

١. اعترف سيدنا بأن طالبه قد نسي ما كان يحفظه من القرآن.

____

٢. وعد صاحبنا المعلم بأنه سيقرأ جزءًا من القرآن كل يوم.

____

٣. بالرغم من حفظه نص القرآن حفظًا سليمًا، فشل صاحبنا في امتحان أبيه بسبب خجله.

____

٤. نجح العريف في بعض المهن قبل توظفه في الكُتّاب.

____

٥. حفظ العريف القرآن حفظًا جيدًا.

____

٦. هدد العريف صاحبنا بإخبار سيدنا بضعفه في حفظ بعض سور القرآن من أجل الحصول على رشوة منه.

---

٧. عامل صاحبنا الطلاب الآخرين بنفس الطريقة التي عامله بها العريف.

---

٨. يفضل صاحبنا الحكايات والكتب على كل أنوا ع الرشوة الأخرى.

---

٩. كانت نفيسة طالبة مفضلة بسبب معرفتها بنص القرآن.

---

١٠. غضب أبو الصبي على سيدنا مرة أخرى نتيجة لإهماله المستمر في مسؤولياته كمعلم.

Interpreting the Text

A. Answer the following questions in complete Arabic sentences, based on your interpretation of what you have read so far:

١. لماذا تعتقد أن العريف وصل إلى الكُتّاب بعد فشله في العثور على وظيفة؟

____

____

٢. لماذا استمر سيدنا والعريف في العمل معًا بالرغم من الكراهية المتبادلة بينهما؟

____

____

٣. ما هو موقف سيدنا من واجباته التعليمية؟ هل تعتقد أنه يقدر أن يصبح معلمًا فعلاً؟

____

____

٤. نظرًا لفشل نظام الكُتّاب الكامل في هدفه الرسمي، ما دوره الحقيقي في القرية؟

____

____

٥. لماذا لم يتوقع صاحبنا الامتحان من أبيه ولم يستعد له رغم تجربته السابقة؟

____

____

B. Predicting the direction of the story: This section of the novel has revealed more facts about the main character and some of the events of his life. Based on what you have read, what can you conclude about the protagonist's life and what do you expect will happen as the story progresses?

١. هل تظنون أن صاحبنا سيحفظ القرآن حقًا؟

____

____

٢. ماذا سيفعل أبو الصبي بسيدنا بعد فشل ابنه مرة أخرى؟

____

____

٣. هل تتوقعون أي تغير في نظام الكُتّاب وأساليبه الأساسية؟

____

____

٤. هل سيرجع صاحبنا إلى الكُتّاب مرة أخرى؟

____

____

٥. هل ستستمر الصداقة بين صاحبنا والعريف بعد الأحداث الأخيرة؟

____

____

Cultural and Historical Background

1. By the time of Taha Hussein's writing, educational reform was already well underway in Egypt. The modern Cairo University, patterned on a European model, was opened in 1908, initially called the Egyptian University. Muhammad 'Abduh led controversial reforms to the venerable al-Azhar, oldest university in Egypt and one of the oldest in the world, against much resistance. Primary and secondary schools, built on European models, were being established in the larger cities of Egypt. None of these reforms had filtered down to the small village in the Minya Governorate of Upper Egypt where Taha Hussein spent his childhood. The old, now neglected and corrupt education system still persisted there.
2. The decision to relegate the incompetent *'arif* to the village *kuttab* after numerous failures at finding an occupation was fairly typical. This was often the place for those who had no other employment or educational opportunities. The fact that three characters in this small village school, at the least, are identified

as blind—"Our Friend," "Our Master," and Nafisa—is also not a coincidence. Memorizing the Qur'an had long been the only occupation available in a society with little to no accommodations for the disabled. Nonetheless, a great many blind children placed in the Islamic school system—Taha Hussein among them—would go on to become great scholars.

Analyzing Elements of Literature

Narration (السرد): Narrator (الراوي)

الراوي هو الشخص الذي تروى القصة بصوته. في بعض الأحيان، قد يكون شخصية رئيسية في القصة، أو شخصية ثانوية لها علاقة بأحد أبطال القصة. في أوقات أخرى، لا تتحدد هوية الراوي في الرواية، ولا يُكشف عن هوية الشخص الذي يروي القصة وسبب روايته لها حتى نهاية القصة. في الأدب الإنجليزي، هناك نوعان رئيسيان من الرواة:

First-person (سرد بضمير المتكلم): هذا يعني أن الشخصية، عادة الشخصية الرئيسية، تروي القصة. يتميز هذا النوع باستخدام ضمير المتكلم "أنا" كثيرًا. هذا الأسلوب يبدو أكثر ذاتيةً عادة.

Third-person (سرد بضمير الغائب):[27] في هذه الحالة، يكون الراوي بعيدًا عن أحداث القصة، وعادة ما يشير إلى الشخصيات بضمير الغائب، مثلًا هو وهي وهم. عادة ما يبدو السرد بضمير الغائب أكثر موضوعية.

Taha Hussein's decision to narrate his largely autobiographical story in the third-person mode was innovative and has been the subject of much discussion and analysis. In this regard, answer the following

27. The Arabic terms المتكلم and الغائب—literally "the speaker" and "the absent one"—are grammatical in origin, not a categorization based on whether the narrator was "present" at the events, as Taha Hussein's third-person narrator is revealed to have been. These refer instead to the types of pronouns and verbs that are used by the narrator, who in this case refers to his autobiographical character as "he," rather than "I."

questions about his narration based on what you have read so far:

١. هل نستطيع أن نحدد هوية راوي هذا النص؟ لماذا؟

____

____

٢. على أي وجهة نظر تعتمد هذه القصة؟

____

____

٣. ما هي بعض الإشارات إلى وجهة النظر هذه؟

____

____

٤. ما هو رأي الكاتب في صحة وجهة النظر هذه؟

____

____

٥. ما هي مميزات وجهة النظر هذه من ناحية السرد؟ لماذا اختارها الكاتب في رأيكم؟

____

____

Themes

العمى

كان العمى من الإعاقات الشائعة في الريف المصري في القرن التاسع عشر وبداية القرن العشرين بسبب سوء الصرف الصحي وضعف نظام الصحة العامة. لم يكن هناك الكثير من المهن المتاحة للمكفوفين، باستثناء الدراسة والتدريس. وطالما حظيت مهنة التدريس بالكثير من الاحترام في الثقافة العربية والإسلامية نظرًا لمكانة اللغة العربية، وخاصة القرآن، في هذه المجتمعات. وإن كنا حتى الآن لم نر سوى سلبيات نظام التدريس في الكُتّاب في القرى بالرواية، إلا أن نجاح المؤلف طه حسين في مساره المهني في حد ذاته يدل على توفر الفرص في هذا المجال.

In view of all you have read so far, prepare a two- to three-minute presentation on the following question:

كيف تتخيلون شكل الحياة بالنسبة لشخص مكفوف في المجتمع الريفي الذي يصوره لنا الكاتب؟ ما هي فرص الاستمتاع التي تتوفر أمامه بعيدًا عن الدراسة والمهنة؟

Vocabulary Items

to call someone a liar   كَذَّبَ، يُكَذِّب، تَكْذيب

to swear (an oath)	أَقْسَمَ، يَقْسِم، إِقْسام
indeed, if …	لَئِن
shame	مَعَرَّة
slow down!	عَلَى مَهْلَك
(here) garble	كَرَّ، يَكُرّ، كُرُور
felted wool	جُوخ، أَجْواخ
to bestow upon	خلع على
to entrust	أَحْصَنَ، يُحْصِن، إِحْصان
assistant, monitor (usually an older student)	عَرِيف، عُرَفاء
not ever	ما … قَطُّ
to try	جَرَّبَ، يُجَرِّب، تَجْريب
of mixed race	مُوَلَّد، مُوَلَّدون
to get angry	ضاقَ، يَضِيق الصَّدْر
to approach	أَقْبَل، يُقْبِل، إِقْبال عَلَى
to flatter	مَلِقَ، يَمْلَق، مَلَق

a cheat	غَشاش
to appropriate, take	اسْتَأْثَر، يَسْتَأْثِر، اسْتِئثار
to pretend	تَكَلَّفَ، يَتَكَلَّف، تَكَلُّف
distress	مَضَض
to reveal (to each other)	تَكاشَفَ، يَتَكاشَف، تَكاشُف
to give rest to, be comfortable for	أَرَاحَ، يُرِيح، إِراحَة
faltering (i.e., not being recited properly)	مُتَعْتَع
fondness	مَوَدَّة
blind	مَكْفُوفـ/ـة، مَكفوفون/مكفوفات
to assign, to entrust	وَكَلَ، يَكِل، وُكول
unalterable	مَحْتُوم
refers here to those classes newly successful; new money	مُحدَث، مُحدَثون/مُحدَثات

Unit Five

Preparation for Reading

Author's Background

نشرت رواية الأيام أولًا في مجلة أدبية تدعى "الهلال" على مدار عام واحد، وكانت هذه المجلة واحدة من أهم المجلات الأدبية والثقافية الرائدة في العالم العربي، (وما زالت تصدر حتى الآن). كان قراء المجلة في ذلك الوقت من النخبة المثقفة والمؤثرة، ولهذا فقد كان من المتوقع أن تتفق غالبية القراء مع وجهة نظر طه حسين التي تنتقد نظام التعليم في ريف مصر. بالإضافة الى ذلك، كانت الرواية تنشر على أجزاء شهرية، الأمر الذي أتاح للقراء وقتًا كافيًا لمناقشة كل جزء والتنبؤ بالجزء الذي يليه في الشهر القادم. ونحن من خلال الأنشطة المقدمة في هذه الدروس نتبع نفس الطريقة التي وصلت عبرها الرواية الى القراء في ذلك الوقت.

Reading

I

خرج صاحبنا من المنظرة منكس الرأس مضطربًا يتعثر، ومضى في طريقه حتى وصل إلى الكرار — والكرار حجرة في البيت كانت تدخر فيها ألوان من الطعام، وكان يربى فيها الحمام — وكانت في زاوية من زواياها القُرْمة — وهي قطعة ضخمة عريضة من الخشب كأنها جذع شجرة — كانت أمه تقطع عليها اللحم. وكانت تدع على هذه القرمة طائفة من السكاكين؛ منها الطويل، ومنها القصير، ومنها الثقيل ومنها الخفيف.

مضى صاحبنا حتى وصل إلى الكرار، وانعطف إلى الزاوية التي فيها القرمة، وأهوى إلى الساطور، وهو أغلظ ما كان عليها من سكين وأحدّه وأثقله، فأخذه بيمناه وأهوى به إلى قفاه ضربًا! ثم صاح، وسقط الساطور من يديه، وأسرعت أمه إليه، وكانت قريبة منه لم تحفل به حينما مرّ بها، فإذا هو واقف يضطرب والدم يسيل من قفاه! والساطور ملقى إلى جانبه … وما أسرع ما ألقت أمه نظرة إلى الجرح! وما أسرع ما عرفت أنه ليس شيئًا! وما هي إلاّ أن أنهالت عليه شتمًا وتأنيبًا، ثم جذبته من إحدى يديه حتى انتهت به إلى زاوية من زوايا المطبخ، فألقته فيها إلقاءً، وانصرفت إلى عملها. ولبث صاحبنا في مكانه لا يتحرك ولا يتكلم، ولا يبكي ولا يفكر كأنه لا شيء. وإخوته وأخواته من حوله يضطربون ويلعبون، لا يحفلون به ولا يلتفت هو إليهم.

وقربت المغرب، وإذا هو يدعى ليجيب أباه، فخرج خزيان متعثرًا حتى انتهى إلى المنظرة. فلم يسأله أبوه عن شيء، وإنما ابتدره سيدنا بهذا السؤال: ألم تقرأ عليّ اليوم الأجزاء الستة من القرآن؟ قال: بلى. قال: ألم تقرأ عليّ أمس سورة سبأ؟ قال: بلى. قال: فما بالك لم تستطع أن تقرأها اليوم؟ فلم يجب. قال سيدنا: فاقرأ سورة سبأ. فلم يفتح الله عليه منها بحرف. قال أبوه: فاقرأ السَّجْدة. فلم يحسن شيئًا. هنا اشتد غضب الشيخ، ولكن على سيدنا لا على الصبي. قال: وإذا فهو يذهب إلى الكُتّاب لا ليقرأ ولا ليحفظ، ولا لتعنى به أو تلتفت إليه، وإنما هو لعب وعبث! ولقد عاد اليوم حافيًا، وزعم أنه نسي نعليه في الكُتّاب … وما أظن عنايتك بحفظه للقرآن، إلا كعنايتك بمشيه حافيًا أو ناعلاً …

Comprehension Questions

١. ماذا فعل صاحبنا بعد الامتحان في المطبخ وخافت أمه بسببه؟

____

____

٢. هل كان جرح الصبي خطيرًا؟

____

____

٣. كيف تعاملت الأم مع الصبي بعد أن فحصت جرحه؟

____

____

٤. ماذا سأل أبو صاحبنا ابنه بعد فشله في الامتحان؟

____

____

٥. على من غضب أبو الصبي؟

____

____

II

قال سيدنا: أقسم بالله العظيم ثلاثًا ما أهملته يومًا، ولولا أني خرجت اليوم من الكُتّاب قبل انصراف الصبيان، لما رجع حافيًا. وإنه ليقرأ علي القرآن مرة في كل أسبوع: ستة أجزاء في كل يوم، أسمعها منه متى وصلت في الصباح. قال الشيخ: لا أصدق من هذا شيئًا. قال سيدنا: امرأتي طالق ثلاثًا ما كذبتك قط، وما أنا بكاذب الآن، وإني لأسمع له القرآن مرة في كل أسبوع. قال الشيخ: لا أصدق. قال سيدنا: أفتظن

أن ما تدفع إليَّ في كل شهر أحب إليَّ من امرأتي؟ أم تظن أنيٍ في سبيل ما تدفع إليَّ أستحل الحرام، وأعيش مع امرأة طلقتها ثلاثًا بين يديك؟ قال الشيخ: ذلك شيء لا شأن لي به، ولكن هذا الصبي لن يذهب إلى الكُتّاب منذ غد. ثم نهض فانصرف، ونهض سيدنا فانصرف كئيبًا محزونًا. وظل صاحبنا في مكانه لا يفكر في القرآن ولا فيما كان، وإنما يفكر في مقدرة سيدنا على الكذب، وفي هذا الطلاق المثلث الذي ألقاه كما يلقي سيجارته متى فرغ من تدخينها!!

ولم يظهر الصبي في هذه الليلة على المائدة. ومكث ثلاثة أيام يتجنب مجلس أبيه ويتجنب المائدة. حتى إذا كان اليوم الرابع دخل أبوه عليه في المطبخ حيث كان يحب أن ينزوي إلى جانب الفرن؛ فما زال يكلمه في دعابة وعطف ورفق، حتى أنس الصبي إليه، وانطلق وجهه بعد عبوسه، وأخذه أبوه بيده فأجلسه مكانه من المائدة، وعني به أثناء الغداء عناية خاصة. حتى إذا فرغ الصبي من طعامه ونهض لينصرف، قال أبوه هذه الجملة في مزاح قاس لم ينسه قط، لأنه أضحك منه إخوته جميعًا، ولأنهم حفظوها له، وأخذوا يغيظونه بها من حين إلى حين—قال: «أحفظت القرآن؟»

وانقطع الصبي عن الكُتّاب، وانقطع سيدنا عن البيت، والتمس الشيخ فقيهًا آخر يختلف إلى البيت في كل يوم؛ فيتلو فيه سورة من القرآن مكان سيدنا. ويقرئ الصبي ساعة أو ساعتين. وظل الصبي حرًا يعبث ويلعب في البيت متى انصرف عنه الفقيه الجديد. حتى إذا كان العصر أقبل عليه أصحابه ورفاقه منصرفهم من الكُتّاب، فيقصون عليه ما كان في الكُتّاب، وهو يلهو بذلك، ويعبث بهم وبكُتّابهم، وبسيدنا وبالعريف. وكان قد خيل إليه أن الأمر قد انبت بينه وبين الكُتّاب ومن فيه، فلن يعود إليه، ولن يرى الفقيه ولا العريف. فأطلق لسانه في الرجلين إطلاقًا شنيعًا، وأخذ يظهر من عيوبهما وسيئاتهما ما كان يخفيه، وأخذ يلعنهما أمام الصبيان ويصفهما بالكذب والسرقة والطمع. ويتحدث عنهما بأشياء منكرة؛ كان يجد في التحدث بها شفاءً لنفسه، ولذة لهؤلاء الصبيان. وما له لا يطلق لسانه في الرجلين، وليس بينه وبين السفر إلى القاهرة إلا شهر واحد؟ فسيعود أخوه الأزهري من القاهرة بعد أيام؛ حتى إذا قضى إجازته اصطحبه إلى الأزهر، حيث يصبح مجاورًا، وحيث تنقطع عنه أخبار الفقيه والعريف.

الحق أنه كان سعيدًا في هذه الأيام؛ كان يشعر بشيء من التفوق على رفاقه وأترابه، فهو لا يذهب إلى الكتّاب كما يذهبون، وإنما يسعى إليه الفقيه سعيًا. وسيسافر إلى القاهرة حيث الأزهر، وحيث «سيدنا الحسين» وحيث «السيدة زينب»[28] وغيرهما من الأولياء. وما كانت القاهرة عنده شيئًا آخر، إنما كانت مستقر الأزهر، ومشاهد الأولياء والصالحين.

Comprehension Questions

١. بماذا أقسم سيدنا؟

____

____

٢. لماذا ذكر سيدنا طلاق زوجته مرارًا؟

____

____

٣. ما أكثر شيء أدهش الصبي في كلام المعلم؟

____

____

28. Two famous mosques in Cairo.

٤. كيف استمتع الصبي بوقته مع الآخرين بعد أن توقف عن الذهاب إلى الكُتّاب؟

---

٥. ماذا كان يتوقع صاحبنا؟

III

ولكن هذه السعادة لم تدم إلا ريثما يعقبها شقاء شنيع؛ ذلك أن سيدنا لم يطق صبرًا على هذه القطيعة، ولم يستطع أن يحتمل انتصار الشيخ عبد الجواد عليه، فأخذ يتوسل بفلان وفلان إلى الشيخ. وما هي إلا أن لانت قناة الشيخ، وأمر الصبي بالعودة إلى الكُتّاب متى أصبح. عاد كارهًا مقدرًا ما سيلقاه من سيدنا وهو يقرئه القرآن للمرة الثالثة، ولكن الأمر لم يقف عند هذا الحد، فقد كان الصبيان ينقلون إلى الفقيه والعريف كل ما يسمعون من صاحبهم. ولله أوقات الغداء طوال هذا الأسبوع! وما كان سيدنا ينال به الصبي من لوم! وما كان العريف يعيد عليه من ألفاظه؛ تلك التي كان يطلق بها لسانه مقدرًا أنه لن يرى الرجلين!

في هذا الأسبوع تعلم الصبي الاحتياط في اللفظ، وتعلم أن من الخطل والحمق، الاطمئنان إلى وعيد الرجال، وما يأخذون أنفسهم به من عهد. ألم يكن الشيخ قد أقسم ألا يعود الصبي إلى الكُتّاب أبدًا؟ وها هو ذا قد عاد. وأيّ فرقٍ بين الشيخ يقسم ويحنث! وبين سيدنا يرسل الطلاق والأيمان إرسالا، وهو يعلم أنه كاذب؟ وهؤلاء الصبيان يتحدثون إليه، فيشتمون له الفقيه والعريف، ويغرونه بشتمهما، حتى إذا ظفروا منه بذلك، تقربوا به إلى الرجلين وابتغوا به إليهما الوسيلة.

وهـذه أمّـه تضحك منـه، وتغري بـه سـيدنا حـين أقبل يتحـدث إليها بمـا نقـل إليـه الصبيـان. وهـؤلاء إخوتـه يشـمتون بـه، ويعيـدون عليـه مقالـة سـيدنا مـن حـين إلـى حـين، يغيظونـه ويثيـرون سـخطه. ولكنـه كان يحتمـل هـذا كلـه فـي صبـر وجلد. ومـا لـه لا يصبـر ولا يتجلـد، وليـس بينـه وبـين فـراق هـذه البيئـة كلهـا، إلا شـهر أو بعـض شـهر!

Comprehension Questions

١. كيف أقنع سيدنا الأب بإرسال ابنه إلى الكُتّاب مرة أخرى؟

____

____

٢. بم أخبر الأولاد سيدنا والعريف؟

____

____

٣. ما الدرس المستفاد الذي تعلمه صاحبنا بعد رجوعه إلى الكُتّاب؟

____

____

٤. هل فقد صاحبنا أمله خلال الأيام الصعبة في الكُتّاب؟

____

____

٥. كيف كان الصبي يصبّر نفسه على الصعوبات التي واجهها؟

____

____

IV

ولكن الشهر مضى، ورجع الأزهري إلى القاهرة، وظل صاحبنا حيث هو كما هو، لم يسافر إلى الأزهر، ولم يتخذ العمة، ولم يدخل في جبة أو قفطان.

كان لا يزال صغيرًا، ولم يكن من اليسير إرساله إلى القاهرة، ولم يكن أخوه يحب أن يحتمله، فأشار بأن يبقى حيث هو سنة أخرى، فبقي ولم يحفل أحد برضاه أو غضبه.

على أن حياته تغيرت بعض الشيء، فقد أشار أخوه الأزهري بأن يقضي هذه السنة في الاستعداد للأزهر، ودفع إليه كتابين يحفظ أحدهما جملة، ويستظهر من الآخر صحفًا مختلفة.

فأما الكتاب الذي لم يكن بدّ من حفظه كله فألفية ابن مالك.[29] وأما الكتاب الآخر فمجموع المتون. وأوصى الأزهري قبل سفره بأن يبدأ بحفظ "الألفية"، حتى إذا فرغ منها وأتقنها إتقانًا، حفظ من الكتاب الآخر أشياء غريبة، بعضها يسمى الجوهرة، وبعضها يسمى الخريدة، وبعضها يسمى السراجية، وبعضها يسمى الرَّحبيّة، وبعضها يسمى لاميّة الأفعال. وكانت هذه الأسماء تقع من نفس الصبي مواقع تيه وإعجاب، لأنه لا يفهم لها معنى، ولأنه يقدر أنها تدل على العلم، ولأنه يعلم أن أخاه الأزهري قد حفظها وفهمها فأصبح عالما وظفر بهذه المكانة الممتازة في نفس أبويه وإخوته وأهل القرية جميعًا. ألم يكونوا جميعًا يتحدثون بعودته قبل أن يعود بشهر، حتى إذا جاء أقبلوا إليه فرحين مبتهجين متلطفين؟ ألم يكن الشيخ يشرب كلامه شربًا، ويعيده على الناس في إعجاب وفخار؟ ألم يكن أهل القرية يتوسلون إليه أن يقرأ لهم درسًا في التوحيد أو الفقه؟ وماذا عسى أن يكون التوحيد؟ وماذا

29. A thirteenth-century book of Arabic grammar, taught in rhyme.

عسى أن يكون الفقه؟ ثم ألم يكن الشيخ يتوسل إليه، ملحًّا مستعطفًا مسرفًا في الوعد، باذلا ما استطاع وما لم يستطع من الأماني، ليلقي على الناس خطبة الجمعة؟ ثم هذا اليوم المشهود يوم مولد النبي.[30] ماذا لقي الأزهري من إكرام وحفاوة، ومن تجلّة وإكبار؟ كانوا قد اشتروا له قفطانًا جديدًا، وجبة جديدة وطربوشًا جديدًا، و«مركوبًا» جديدًا. وكانوا يتحدثون بهذا اليوم وما سيكون منه قبل أن يظلهم بأيام. حتى إذا أقبل هذا اليوم وانتصف، أسرعت الأسرة إلى طعامها فلم تصب منه إلا قليلا، ولبس الفتى الأزهري ثيابه الجديدة، واتخذ في هذا اليوم عمامة خضراء، وألقى على كتفيه شالا من الكشمير، وأمه تدعو وتتلو التعاويذ، وأبوه يخرج ويدخل جذلان مضطربًا. حتى إذا تم للفتى من زيه وهيئته ما كان يريد، خرج فإذا فرس ينتظره بالباب، وإذا رجال يحملونه فيضعونه على السرج، وإذا قوم يكتنفونه من يمين ومن شمال وآخرون يسعون بين يديه، وآخرون يمشون من خلفه، وإذا البنادق تطلق في الفضاء، وإذا النساء يزغردن من كل ناحية، وإذا الجو يتأرّج بعرف البخور، وإذا الأصوات ترتفع متغنية بمدح النبي، وإذا هذا الحفل كله يتحرك في بطء وكأنما تتحرك معه الأرض وما عليها من دور. كل ذلك لأن هذا الفتى الأزهري قد اتخذ في هذا اليوم خليفة،[31] فهو يطاف به في المدينة وما حولها من القرى في هذا المهرجان الباهر، وما باله اتخذ خليفة دون غيره من الشبان؟ لأنه أزهري قد قرأ العلم وحفظ الألفية والجوهرة والخريدة!

فلم لا يبتهج الصبي حين يرى أن سيقرأ من العلم ما قرأ أخوه، وأن سيمتاز من رفاقه وأترابه بحفظ الألفية والجوهرة والخريدة؟

Comprehension Questions

١. هل ذهب صاحبنا إلى القاهرة كما كان يتوقع؟

____

____

30. Holiday celebrating the birth of the Prophet.
31. I.e., to be the leader of the procession.

٢. ماذا أعطى الأزهري الصبي؟

٣. ما نصيحة الأزهري لأخيه؟

٤. كيف تعامل أهل القرية مع الأزهري في احتفال مولد النبي؟

٥. في رأي صاحبنا، لماذا احتفل أهل القرية بأخيه؟

V

وكم كان فرحًا مختالًا حين غدا إلى الكُتَّاب يوم السبت، وفي يده نسخة من "الألفية"! لقد رفعته هذه النسخة درجات، وإن كانت هذه النسخة ضئيلة قذرة سيئة الجلد؛ ولكنها على ضآلتها وقذارتها، كانت تعدل عنده خمسين مصحفًا من هذه المصاحف التي كان يحملها أترابه.

المصحف! لقد حفظ ما فيه فما أفاد من حفظه شيئًا. وكثير من الشبان يحفظونه فلا يحفل بهم أحد، ولا ينتخبون خلفاء يوم المولد النبوي.

ولكن الألفية ... وما أدراك ما الألفية؟ وحسبك أن سيدنا لا يحفظ منها حرفًا. وحسبك أن العريف لا يحسن أن يقرأ الأبيات الأولى منها. والألفية شعر، وليس في المصحف شعر.

الحق أنه ابتهج بهذا البيت:

قال محمد هو ابن مالك   أحمد ربي الله خير مالك

ابتهاجًا لم يشعر بشيء مثله أمام أي سورة من سور القرآن.

وكيف لا يبتهج وقد أحسّ منذ اليوم الأول أنه ارتفع درجات؛ فأصبح «سيدنا» لا يستطيع أن يشرف على حفظه للألفية، ولا أن يقرئه إيّاها، بل ضاق الكُتّاب كله بالألفية، وكلف الصبي أن يذهب في كل يوم إلى المحكمة الشرعية؛ ليقرأ على القاضي ما يريد أن يحفظه من الألفية. القاضي عالم من علماء الأزهر، أكبر من أخيه الأزهري، وإن كان أبوه لا يؤمن بذلك، ولا يرى أن القاضي يكافئ ابنه. هو على كل حال عالم من علماء الأزهر، وهو قاضي الشرع (بقاف ضخمة وراء مفخمة) وهو في المحكمة لا في الكُتّاب. وهو يجلس على دكة مرتفعة، وقد وضعت عليها الطنافس والوسائد، لا تقاس إليها دكة سيدنا، وليس حولها نعال مرقعة. وعلى بابه رجلان يقومان مقام الحاجب، ويسميهما الناس هذا الاسم البديع، الذي لم يكن يخلو من هيبة: «الرسل».

نعم! كان يجب على الصبي أن يذهب إلى المحكمة في كل صباح، فيقرأ على القاضي بابًا من أبواب الألفية. وكم كان القاضي يحسن القراءة! وكم كان يملأ فمه بالقاف والراء! وكم كان صوته يتهدج بقول ابن مالك:

كلامنا لفظ مفيد كاستقم   واسم وفعل ثم حرف الكلم
واحِدُه كلمة والقول عمّ   وكلمة بها كلام قد يُؤَم

ولقد استطاع القاضي أن يؤثِّر في نفس الصبي، ويملأه تواضعًا حين قرأ هذه الأبيات:

وتقتضي رضًا بغير سُخط	فائقةً ألفيّة ابن معطي
وهو بسبق حائز تفضيلا	مستوجب ثنائي الجميلا
والله يقضي بهبات وافرة	لي وله في درجات الآخرة

قرأ القاضي هذه الأبيات بصوت يحطمه البكاء حطمًا، ثم قال للصبي: من تواضع لله رفعه، أتفهم هذه الأبيات؟

قال الصبي: لا.

قال القاضي: إن المؤلف رحمه الله تعالى، عندما بدأ في نظم ألفيته اغترّ وأخذه الكبر فقال: «فائقة ألفية ابن معطي»،[32] فلما كان الليل رأى فيما يرى النائم، أن ابن معطي قد أقبل يعاتبه عتابًا شديدًا، فلما أفاق من نومه أصلح من هذا الغرور وقال: «وهو بسبق حائز تفضيلا».

وكم كان الشيخ مبتهجًا فرحًا حين عاد إليه الصبي عصر ذلك اليوم؛ فقص عليه ما سمع من القاضي، وقرأ عليه الأبيات الأولى من الألفية! فكان يقطع هذه الأبيات بهذه الكلمة التي يعبر بها الناس عن الاستحسان: «الله! الله».

Comprehension Questions

١. هل استطاع سيدنا أن يدرّس الصبي كتاب الألفية؟

____

____

32. Another grammarian, who wrote before Ibn Malik.

٢. إلى من ذهب صاحبنا لتعلم الألفية؟

____

____

٣. كيف قارن الصبي بين أهمية كتاب الألفية والقرآن؟

____

____

٤. ماذا كان عيب ابن مالك في الحكاية التي نقلها القاضي إلى الصبي؟

____

____

٥. كيف فسر ابن مالك أهمية ابن معطي وعمله في القصة التي رواها القاضي؟

____

____

Comprehension Exercise

Are the following statements true (صحيح) or false (خطأ) and why?

١. كاد يموت الصبي متأثرًا بجراحه الخطيرة بسبب الساطور.

______

٢. أفراد عائلة صاحبنا عاملوه بكل تعاطف ولطف بعد حادثة الساطور.

______

٣. بدأ صاحبنا ينتقد سيدنا والعريف أمام الأولاد الآخرين لأنه اعتقد أنه لن يعود إلى الكُتّاب أبدًا.

______

٤. أقنع سيدنا الأب بإرسال ابنه للكتّاب مرة أخرى.

______

٥. كان صاحبنا يحترم سيدنا بسبب صدقه ونزاهته.

______

٦. كان أخو صاحبنا وهو طالب في الأزهر، شخصًا محترمًا في القرية بفضل دراساته.

______

٧. افتخر صاحبنا كثيرًا بكتاب تعليم قواعد اللغة الذي أهداه أخوه إليه.

---

٨. سرعان ما نسي صاحبنا كل ما تعلمه من كتاب الألفية كما نسي حفظه للقرآن من قبل.

---

٩. لم يكن فهم القاضي لكتاب الألفية مقتصرًا على الحفظ فقط، وإنما جعل يفهم معاني كلمات الكتاب وتاريخه.

---

١٠. تعلم صاحبنا من تجربة الكتاب أن يقول الحقيقة دائمًا ويبدي آرائه الحقيقية للناس.

Interpreting the Text

A. Answer the following questions in complete Arabic sentences, based on your interpretation of what you have read so far:

١. كيف تختلف طريقة تدريس القاضي عن طريقة سيدنا؟

---

٢. ما الذي يبدو أنه السبب الأساسي في تفضيل الشاب لكتاب الألفية على القرآن؟

____

____

٣. ما هي دوافع صاحبنا في الذهاب إلى الأزهر للدراسة؟

____

____

٤. ما هي طبيعة العلاقة بين سيدنا ومعظم الطلاب في الكتّاب؟ هل كانت تقوم على الاحترام المتبادل؟

____

____

٥. ماذا يمكن أن يكون رأي المؤلف في الحفظ كشكل من أشكال التعلم بشكل عام؟

____

____

B. Predicting the direction of the story: This section of the novel contains hints about the future for the main character. Based on what you have read, what can you conclude about the hero's life and what do you expect will happen as the story progresses?

١. هل تعتقدون أن الشاب سيذهب إلى الأزهر فعلا كما يخطط؟ إذا كان الأمر كذلك، كيف تتوقعون أن يكون شكل تجربته هناك؟[33]

____

____

٢. هل انقطعت علاقة الصبي بسيدنا أخيرًا؟ هل تتوقعون أنه سيعود تحت إشراف سيدنا مرة أخرى؟

____

____

٣. كيف سيكون تأثير القاضي على صاحبنا في رأيكم؟

____

____

٤. هل سيكمل صاحبنا دراسة الألفية كلها؟

____

____

33. In fairness to the reader, this question is not fully answered until the second book of this trilogy, but predicting the direction based on what we know of the protagonist's personality so far will go a long way to forming a solid opinion of his character.

٥. هل تعتقدون أن الأزهري سيعود إلى القرية مرة أخرى؟ وهل تظنون أنه سيأخذ أخاه إلى القاهرة معه؟

____

____

Cultural and Historical Background

1. The book that the youth is memorizing is *al-Alfiya* by Ibn Malik, a thirteenth-century grammarian from al-Andalus. Until the twentieth century, it was often the second or third book memorized by students in Islamic schools. As the title suggests, it is a thousand-line poem that helps students remember Arabic grammar. The poem is not an explanation of grammar rules, but illustrates their use. As an example, the first two lines the boy recites require correct application of grammatical case to make the lines rhyme. As this alone is not sufficient to understand the rules, there have been numerous commentaries on *al-Alfiya*, which are also studied. Here, as in his previous memorization of the Qur'an, he does not have the commentaries and is only memorizing text without understanding it, as his conversations with the *qadi* reveal.
2. The celebration described, Mawlid al-Nabi, which marks the Prophet's birthday, is one of the largest popular festivals in Egypt and many other Muslim countries. These events are usually led by large Sufi orders. The practice is not without controversy, as some conservative Muslim states, such as Saudi Arabia and Qatar, ban it because, unlike 'Id al-Fitr and 'Id al-Adha, it is not part of the Sunna, or the traditions and practices of the Prophet.

Analyzing Elements of Literature

Audience (القارئ)

كل عمل أدبي له وضع معين ويستهدف نوع بعينه من القراء، وهذا عامل مهم يجب وضعه في الاعتبار عند تحليل النص؛ فمثلاً يمكننا أن نسأل: ما الافتراضات التي يشترك بها الكاتب مع القارئ؟ هل هناك خلفية ثقافية مشتركة بينهما؟ هل توقع الكاتب أن القراء سوف يتفاعلون بطريقة معينة مع بعض الأحداث في القصة؟

نُشر كتاب "الأيام" في مصر على مدار سنتين، ١٩٢٦ و ١٩٢٧، وفي هذا الوقت كان الكثير من الأوضاع التي تذكرها الرواية—مثل الكُتّاب والأعياد والفقر الريفية—مألوفا بالنسبة لمعظم المصريين الذين قرأوا الرواية. لذلك توقع الكاتب قدر كبير من التفاعل والفهم من القراء.

You may have encountered a number of references in the reading so far that are not familiar to you, but which the author seems to have expected his audience to recognize. Based on what you have read and your understanding of the context in which this novel was published, answer the following questions:

١. إلى أي مدى كان دور "الخليفة" مهمًا في الاحتفال بالمولد؟ هل تعتقدون أن هذا الدور مشهور في المجتمع المصري؟

____

____

٢. يحمل اسم الأزهر أهمية كبيرة لدى الصبي. ما هي بعض دلالات أهمية هذه الجامعة؟

____

____

٣. ما التوقعات التي تعكسها دراسة الشاب تحت إشراف وتدريس القاضي مع وضع حدود قدرة الكُتّاب التعليمية بعين الاعتبار؟

____

____

٤. كان التعليم في مصر في بداية القرن العشرين يعتمد بشدة على حفظ النصوص التراثية. ما هي بعض الإشارات في الرواية التي تدل على ذلك؟

____

____

Themes

الصدق

صدم صاحبنا من مدى سهولة الكذب على لسان سيدنا خاصة في قسمه أن يطلق زوجته. ولكن عدم صدقه لم يؤثر كثيرًا على قرار أبوه أن يرسل ابنه إليه مرة أخرى. في الحقيقة، صدم صاحبنا أيضًا من عدم جدوى وعود أبيه. وبالإضافة إلى فقدان ثقته في القسم الذي يعطيه الناس، فإن تجاربه محت أي ثقة كانت لديه في بعض المؤسسات مثل الكُتّاب.

Based on what you have read, prepare a one- to two-page answer to the following question:

كيف ستؤثر تجارب صاحبنا مع الكذب والصدق في القرية على مستقبله كطالب وكاتب في ظنكم؟

Vocabulary Items

with bowed head	مُنَكَّس (الرَّأس)
cleaver	ساطُور، سَواطِير
sharpest	أَحَدّ
back of the head, neck	قَفا، أَقْفاء
to anticipate, forestall, preempt	ابْتَدَرَ، يَبْتَدِر، ابْتِدار
to treat as lawful that which is forbidden	اسْتَحَلَ، يَسْتَحِل، اسْتِحلال الحَرام
downcast, dejected	كَئِيب
joking, humor	دُعابَة
frown	عَبُوس
joke	مُزاح
to request, seek	الْتَمَس، يَلْتَمِس، الْتِماس

horrible	شَنيع
The Azharite (student of al-Azhar University)	الأَزْهَرِي
peers, contemporaries	تِرْب، أَتْراب
(here) holy person (people)	وَليّ، أَوْلِيَاء
(here) until	رَيْثَما
hardship	شِقَّة، شِقَق
to curry favor, ingratiate oneself	تَوَسَّلَ، يَتَوَسَّل، تَوَسُّل
"so-and-so," a term used in place of a name when the name is not important	فُلان
when morning comes	مَتَى أَصْبَحَ، يَصْبِح
to give, dish out	نالَ، يَنول، نَوْل
foolishness	خَطَل
promises	وَعْد، وَعِيد
to break one's oath	حَنِثَ، يَنْحَث، حِنْث
to spur on, encourage	أَغْرَى، يُغْري، إِغْراء

to exasperate	أَغاظَ، يُغِيظ، إغاظة
to bear	تَجَلَّدَ، يَتَجَلَّد، تَجَلُّد
resentment	سُخُط
to memorize	اسْتَظْهَرَ، يَسْتَظْهِر، اسْتِظْهار
pride	تِيه
to surround	اكْتَنَفَ، يَكْتَنِف، اكْتِناف
to make the zaghruda, a trilling sound of celebration	زَغْرَدَ، يُزَغْرِد، زَغْرَدَة
to be fragrant	تَأَرَّجَ، يَتَأَرَّج، تَأَرُّج
a physical copy of the Qur'an	مُصْحَف، مَصاحِف
lines of poetry	بَيْت، أَبيات
to tremble	تَهَدَّجَ، يَتَهَدَّج، تَهَدُّج
to become haughty, dazzled by self	اغْتَرَّ، يَغْتَرّ، اغْتِرار
to rebuke, censure	عَتَبَ، يَعْتِب، عَتْب
humility	تَواضُع

Unit Six

Preparation for Reading

Author's Background

كما هو الحال مع بطل روايته، كان طه حسين يحلم بالدراسة في جامعة الأزهر، وتحقق هذا الحلم عندما كان عمره ثلاثة عشر عامًا. ولكنه وجد بيئة الأزهر مظلمة وغير مناسبة للتفكير المستقل والحر. ولذلك انتقل إلى الجامعة المصرية (المعروفة الآن باسم جامعة القاهرة)، والتي تأسست عام ١٩٠٨ على غرار نموذج التعليم العالي الأوروبي. حصل طه حسين على أول شهادة دكتوراه من هذه الجامعة في سنة ١٩١٤، وكان موضوع رسالته ''الأعمى المتشكك: أبي العلاء المعري''. بعد ذلك درس التاريخ في جامعة مونبلييه في فرنسا وأصبح أول مصري حاصل على الدكتوراه من السوربون في باريس. حقق طه حسين كل هذه الإنجازات بالرغم من فقره، ولذلك كان مناصرًا قويًا للتعليم المجاني ودعم الحكومة للتعليم.

Reading

I

على أن لكل شيء حدًا. فقد مضى صاحبنا في حفظ ''الألفية'' فرحًا مبتهجًا حتى انتهى إلى باب المبتدأ، ثم فترت همته، وكان أبوه يسأله عصر كل يوم: هل ذهبت إلى المحكمة؟

فيجيب: نعم.

فكم حفظت؟ فيقرأ له ما حفظ.

ولكن الأمرِ ثقل عليه منذ باب المبتدأ، فأخذ يحفظ ويذهب إلى المحكمة متثاقلًا متباطئًا، حتى وصل إلى باب المفعول المطلق،[34] ثم لم يستطع أن يتقدم خُطوة قصيرة ولا طويلة. ولبث يذهب إلى المحكمة في كلِ يوم، ويقرأ على القاضي فصلًا من فصول الألفية، حتى إذا عاد إلى الكتّاب ألقى الألفية في ناحية، وانصرف إلى عبثه ولعبه، وإلى قراءة القصص والأحاديث.

فإذا كان العصر وسأله أبوه: هل ذهبت إلى المحكمة؟ أجاب: نعم.

وكم حفظت من بيت؟

أجاب: عشرين.

من أيّ باب؟

من باب الإضافة، أو من باب النعت، أو من باب جمع التكسير.

فإذا قال له: اقرأ عليّ ما حفظت، قرأ عليه عشرين بيتًا من المائتين الأولين، مرة من المعرب والمبني، وأخرى من النكرة والمعرفة، وثالثة من المبتدأ والخبر، والشيخ لا يفهم شيئًا، ولا يلاحظ أن ابنه يخدعه! وإنما يكتفي بأن يسمع كلامًا منظومًا، وهو مطمئن إلى القاضي. ومن غريب الأمر أن الشيخ لم يفكر مرة واحدة في أن يفتح الألفية، ويقابل على الصبي وهو يقرأ. ولو قد فعل يومًا من الأيام، لكانت للصبي قصة كقصته مع سورة الشعراء، أو سبأ، أو فاطر ...

على أن الصبي تعرض لهذا الخطر مرة. ولولا أن أمه شفعت فيه لكان له مع أبيه موقف مشهود.

كان له أخ يختلف إلى المدارس المدنية، فعاد من القاهرة ليقضي فصل الصيف واتفق أنه حضر هذا الامتحان اليومي أيامًا متصلة؛ فسمع الشيخ يسأل الصبي: أيّ باب قرأت؟ فيجيب الصبي: باب العطف (مثلًا). فإذا طلب إليه أن يعيد ما قرأ، أعاد عليه باب العلم أو باب الصّلة والموصول.

34. المفعول المطلق، الإضافة، النعت، جمع التكسير، النكره والمعرفة، المبتدأ والخبر، العطف، العَلَم، الصّلة والموصول – these are all grammatical concepts that are taught in *al-Alfiya*. The youth is referring to sections of the book.

سكت الشاب[35] في أول يوم، وفي اليوم الذي يليه، فلما كثر ذلك انتظر حتى انصرف الشيخ، وقال للصبي أمام أمه: إنك تخدع أباك وتكذب عليه، وتلعب في الكتّاب، ولا تحفظ من الألفية شيئًا ...

قال الصبي: إنك كاذب! وما أنت وذاك! وإنما الألفية للأزهريين لا لأبناء المدارس! وسل القاضي ينبئك بأني أذهب إلى المحكمة في كل يوم.

قال الشاب: أيّ باب حفظت اليوم؟

قال الصبي: باب كذا.

قال الشاب: ولكنك لم تقرأ هذا الباب على أبيك، وإنما قرأت عليه باب كذا، وهات نسخة الألفية أمتحنك فيها. بُهت الصبي وظهر عليه الوجوم، وهمّ الشاب أن يقص القصة على الشيخ، ولكنّ أمه توسلت إليه! وكان الشاب رفيقًا بأمّه رءوفًا بأخيه، فسكت. وظل الشيخ على جهله حتى عاد الأزهري. فلما عاد امتحن الصبي، وما هي إلا أن عرف جلية الأمر، فلم يغضب ولم ينذر ولم يخبر الشيخ، وإنما أمر الصبي أن ينقطع عن الكتّاب والمحكمة. وأحفظه الألفية كلها في عشرة أيام.

Comprehension Questions

١. في أي باب من كتاب الألفية بدأت صعوبات صاحبنا؟

____

____

35. Taha Hussein's use of generic terms, rather than names, to identify his characters causes some confusion. In this scene, الشاب refers to the boy's older brother who studied in a secular school. The brother from al-Azhar is called here الأزهري. In section III below, however, the Azharite is also called الشاب. This is a constant feature of the narrative and requires the reader to bear the context in mind to determine to whom a term refers.

٢. لماذا كان سؤال الشيخ للصبي كل يوم؟

____

____

٣. من اكتشف أن صاحبنا كان يكذب على أبيه؟

____

____

٤. لماذا لم يخبر الشاب الشيخ بما فعل الصبي؟

____

____

٥. ماذا أمر الأزهري الصبي بفعله؟

____

____

II

للعلم في القرى ومدن الأقاليم جلال ليس له مثله في العاصمة ولا في بيئاتها العلمية المختلفة. وليس في هذا شيء من العجب ولا من الغرابة، وإنما هو قانون العرض والطلب، يجري على العلم كما يجري على غيره مما يباع ويشترى. فبينما يروح العلماء ويغدون في القاهرة لا يحفل بهم أحد، أو لا يكاد يحفل بهم أحد، وبينما يقول العلماء فيكثرون في القول، ويتصرفون في فنونه، دون أن يلتفت إليهم أحد غير تلاميذهم

فـي القاهـرة، تـرى علمـاء الريـف، وأشـياخ القـرى ومـدن الأقاليـم، يغـدون ويروحـون فـي جـلال ومهابـة، ويقولـون فيسـتمع لهـم النـاس مـع شـيء مـن الإكبـار مؤثـر جـذاب. وكان صاحبنـا متأثـرًا بنفسـية الريـف، يكبـر العلمـاء كمـا يكبرهـم الريفيـون، ويـكاد يؤمـن بأنهـم فطـروا مـن طينـة نقيـة ممتـازة، غيـر الطينـة التـي فطـر منهـا النـاس جميعًـا.

وكان يسـمع لهـم وهـم يتكلمـون، فيأخـذه شـيء مـن الإعجـاب والدهـش، حـاول أن يجـد مثلـه فـي القاهـرة أمـام كبـار العلمـاء، وجلة الشـيوخ فلـم يوفق.

كان علمـاء المدينـة ثلاثـة أو أربعـة؛ قـد تقسـموا فيمـا بينهـم إعجـاب النـاس ومودتهـم. فأمـا أحدهـم فـكان كاتبًـا فـي المحكمـة الشـرعية، قصيـرًا ضخمًـا، غليـظ الصـوت جهوريـه، يمتلـئ شـدقه بالألفـاظ حـين يتكلـم؛ فتخـرج إليـك هـذه الألفـاظ ضخمـة كصاحبهـا، غليظـة كصاحبهـا، وتصدمـك معانيهـا كمـا تصدمـك مقاطعهـا. وكان هـذا الشـيخ[36] مـن الذيـن لـم يفلحـوا فـي الأزهـر؛ قضـى فيـه مـا شـاء أن يقضـي مـن السـنين، فلـم يوفـق إلـى العالميـة ولا للقضـاء، فقنـع بمنصـب الكاتـب فـي المحكمـة، علـى حـين كان أخـوه قاضيًـا ممتـازًا، قـد جعـل إليـه قضـاء أحـد الأقاليـم. ولـم يكـن هـذا الشـيخ يسـتطيع أن يجلـس فـي مجلـس إلا فخـر بأخيـه، وذم القاضـي الـذي هـو معـه. كان حنفـي[37] المذهـب، وكان أتبـاع أبـي حنيفـة فـي المدينـة قليلـين، أو لـم يكـن لأبـي حنيفـة فـي المدينـة أتبـاع؛ فـكان ذلـك يغيظـه ويحنقـه علـى خصومـه العلمـاء الآخريـن، الذيـن كانـوا يتبعـون الشـافعي أو مالـكًا، ويجـدون فـي أهـل المدينـة صـدى لعلمهـم، وطلابًـا للفتـوى عندهـم. فـكان لا يـدع فرصـة إلا مجـد فيهـا فقـه أبـي حنيفـة، وغـض فيهـا مـن فقـه مالـك والشـافعي.

36. The author's use of the same terms to refer to different characters can be confusing. الشيخ has been used so far to refer to the protagonist's father. Beginning at this point, it also refers to the other *ulema* of the village and the leaders of the Sufi orders. The context makes it clear to whom he refers.

37. Hanifi, one of the four main schools of Sunni law. Abu Hanifa is the founder of the school. Two other schools, the Shaf'i and Maliki are also mentioned here.

Comprehension Questions

١. هل كان المتعلمون يتمتعون باحترام أكبر في القرية أم بين أهل المدن الكبرى؟

٢. كم كان عدد العلماء في هذه القرية؟

٣. كيف حصل الكاتب في المحكمة على وظيفته؟

٤. بماذا افتخر الكاتب؟

٥. ما الاختلاف بين مذهب الكاتب ومذهب معظم الناس في القرية؟

III

وأهل الريف مكرة أذكياء، فلم يكن يخفى عليهم أن الشيخ إنما يقول ما يقول، ويأتي ما يأتي من الأمر، متأثرًا بالحقد والموجدة، فكانوا يعطفون عليه، ويضحكون منه. وكانت المنافسة شديدة عنيفة بين هذا الشيخ وبين الفتى الأزهري. كان ينتخب خليفة في كل سنة، فغاظه أن ينتخب هذا الفتى خليفة دونه. ولما تحدث الناس أن الفتى سيلقي خطبة الجمعة سمع الشيخ هذا الحديث ولم يقل شيئًا. حتى إذا كان يوم الجمعة وامتلأ المسجد بالناس؛ وأقبل الفتى يريد أن يصعد المنبر، نهض الشيخ حتى انتهى إلى الإمام، وقال في صوت سمعه الناس: إن هذا الشاب حديث السن، وما ينبغي له أن يصعد المنبر ولا أن يخطب، ولا أن يصلي بالناس وفيهم الشيوخ وأصحاب الأسنان، ولئن خليت بينه وبين المنبر والصلاة لأنصرفن. ثم التفت إلى الناس وقال: ومن كان منكم حريصًا على ألاّ تبطل صلاته فليتبعني. سمع الناس هذا فاضطربوا، وكادت تقع بينهم الفتنة لولا أن نهض الإمام فخطبهم وصلى بهم، وحيل بين الفتى وبين المنبر هذا العام. ومع ذلك فقد كان الفتى أجهد نفسه في حفظ الخطبة واستعد لهذا الموقف أيامًا متصلة، وتلا الخطبة على أبيه غير مرة، وكان أبوه ينتظر هذه الساعة أشد ما يكون إليها شوقًا، وأعظم ما يكون بها ابتهاجًا. وكانت أمه مشفقة تخاف عليه العين،[38] فما كاد يخرج إلى المسجد ذلك اليوم، حتى نهضت إلى جمر وضعته في إناء وأخذت تلقي فيه ضروبًا من البخور، وتطوف به البيت حجرة حجرة، تقف في كل حجرة لحظات وتهمهم بكلمات. وظلت كذلك حتى عاد ابنها، فإذا هي تلقاه من وراء الباب مبخرة مهمهمة، وإذا الشيخ مغضب يلعن هذا الرجل الذي أكل الحسد قلبه، فحال بين ابنه وبين المنبر والصلاة.

وكان في المدينة عالم آخر شافعي. كان إمام المسجد، وصاحب الخطبة والصلاة، وكان معروفا بالتقى والورع، يذهب الناس في إكباره وإجلاله إلى حدّ يشبه التقديس، كانوا يتبركون به، ويلتمسون عنده شفاء مرضاهم وقضاء حاجاتهم. وكأنه كان يرى في نفسه شيئًا من الولاية. وظل أهل المدينة بعد موته سنين يذكرونه بالخير، ويتحدثون مقتنعين بأنه عندما أنزل في قبره قال بصوت سمعه المشيعون جميعًا:

38. Refers to the "evil eye"; the curse of an envious person.

اللهم اجعله منزلًا مباركًا. وكانوا يتحدثون بما رأوا فيما يرى النائم من حظ هذا الرجل عند الله، وما أعدّ له في الجنة من نعيم.

وشيخ ثالث كان في المدينة، وكان مالكي المذهب، ولم يكن ينقطع للعلم ولا يتخذه حرفة، وإنما كان يعمل في الأرض، ويتجر، ويختلف إلى المسجد فيؤدى الخمس، ويجلس إلى الناس من حين إلى حين، فيقرأ لهم الحديث، ويفقههم في الدين متواضعًا غير تيّاه ولا فخور، ولم يكن يحفل به إلا الأقلون عددًا.

Comprehension Questions

١. لماذا اعترض الشيخ على صعود الشاب الأزهري منبر المسجد؟

____

____

٢. ما هو السبب الحقيقي لحقد الشيخ على الأزهري؟

____

____

٣. ماذا سيحدث لأهل المسجد إذا تبعوا الشاب في الصلاة حسب قول الشيخ؟

____

____

٤. إلى أي درجة احترم أهل القرية أئمة المساجد؟

___

___

٥. كيف وصف المؤلف شخصية الشيخ الثالث؟

___

___

IV

هؤلاء هم العلماء. ولكن علماء آخرين كانوا منبثين في هذه المدينة وقراها وريفها. ولم يكونوا أقل من هؤلاء العلماء الرسميين تأثيرًا في دهماء الناس وتسلطا علي عقولهم، منهم هذا الحاج ... الخياط الذي كان دكانه يكاد يقابل الكتّاب، والذي كان الناس مجمعين على وصفه بالبخل والشح، والذي كان متصلا بشيخ من كبار أهل الطرق.[39] والذي كان يزدري العلماء جميعًا، لأنهم يأخذون علمهم من الكتب لا عن الشيوخ، والذي كان يرى أن العلم الصحيح إنما هو العلم اللدني، الذي يهبط على قلبك من عند الله دون أن تحتاج إلى كتاب؛ بل دون أن تقرأ أو تكتب.

ومنهم هذا الشيخ ... الذي كان في أول أمره حمّارًا ينقل للناس بضائعهم وأمتعتهم، ثم أصبح تاجرًا، واقتصرت حمره على نقل تجارته، والذي كان الناس مجمعين على أنه أكل أموال اليتامى، وأثرى على حساب الضعفاء، والذي كان يكثر من ترديد هذه الآية وتفسيرها «إن الذين يأكلون أموال اليتامى ظلمًا إنما يأكلون في بطونهم نارًا وسيصلَوْن سعيرًا»[40] والذي كان يكره الصلاة في المسجد الجامع، لأنه

39. Sufi orders.
40. The Qur'an 4:10.

كان يكره الإمام ومن إليه من العلماء، ويؤثر الصلاة في جامع صغير لا قيمة له ولا مكانة.

ومنهم هذا الشيخ ... الذي لم يكن يقرأ ولا يكتب ولا يحسن قراءة الفاتحة، ولكنه كان شاذليًا[41] من أصحاب الطريق، كان يجمع الناس إلى الذكر، ويفتيهم في أمور دينهم ودنياهم.

ثم منهم الفقهاء الذين كانوا يقرءون القرآن ويقرئونه للناس، والذين كانوا يُميزون أنفسهم من العلماء ويتسَمَّوْن «حملة كتاب الله» والذين كانوا يتصلون بدهماء الناس والنساء منهم خاصة. كانت جمهرتهم من المكفوفين، فكانوا يدخلون البيوت يتلون فيها القرآن، وكان النساء يتحدثن إليهم، ويستفتينهم في أمور الصوم والصلاة وما إلى ذلك من أمورهن. وكان لهؤلاء الفقهاء علم مخالف كل المخالفة لعلم العلماء، الذين يأخذون علمهم من الكتب، والذين بينهم وبين الأزهر سبب قوي أو ضعيف. وكان علمهم مخالفًا أيضًا لعلم أصحاب الطرق وأهل العلم اللدني. كانوا يأخذون علمهم من القرآن مباشرة، يفهمونه كما يستطيعون، لا كما هو ولا كما ينبغي أن يفهم. يفهمونه كما كان يفهمه سيدنا، وكان من أذكى الفقهاء، وأشدهم علمًا وأقدرهم على التأويل. سأله الصبي ذات يوم: ما معنى قول الله تعالى «وخلقكم أطوارًا؟»[42] فأجاب هادئًا مطمئنًا: خلقناكم كالثيران لا تعقلون شيئًا. أو يفهمونه كما يفهمه جدّ هذا الصبي نفسه، وكان من أحفظ الناس للقرآن، وأبرعهم في فهمه وتفسيره وتأويله. سأله حفيده ذات يوم عن قول الله تعالي: «ومن الناس من يعبد الله على حرف فإن أصابه خير اطمأن به وإن أصابته فتنة انقلب على وجهه خسر الدنيا والآخرة»[43] فقال: «على حرف دكة، على حرف مصطبة ... فإن أصابه خير فهو مطمئن في مكانه، وإن أصابه شر انكفأ على وجهه».

وكان صبينا يختلف بين هؤلاء العلماء جميعًا، ويأخذ عنهم جميعًا، حتى اجتمع له من ذلك مقدار من العلم ضخم مختلف مضطرب متناقض، ما أحسب إلا أنه عمل عملا غير قليل في تكوين عقله الذي لم يخل من اضطراب واختلاف وتناقض.

41. A leader of a Sufi group.
42. The Qur'an 71:14.
43. The Qur'an 22:11.

Comprehension Questions

١. لماذا ازدرى الخياط العلماء الآخرين في القرية؟

---

٢. كيف حصل الشيخ التاجر على ثروته في رأي أهل القرية؟

---

٣. لماذا كان الشيخ الذي لايعرف القراءة والكتابة محترمًا في القرية رغم افتقاره إلى التعليم؟

---

٤. ماذا الذي كان يفعله "حملة كتاب الله"؟

---

٥. بماذا تفوق سيدنا على معظم فقهاء القرية؟

V

وشيوخ الطريق، وما شيوخ الطريق؟ كانوا كثيرين منبثين في أقطار الأرض، لا تكاد تخلو منهم المدينة أسبوعًا.

وكانت مذاهبهم مختلفة، وكانوا قد تقسموا الناس فيما بينهم فجعلوهم شيعًا، وفرقوا أهواءهم تفريقًا عظيمًا. وكانت المنافسة حادة في الإقليم بين أسرتين من أصحاب الطريق، لإحداهما أعلاه وللأخرى أسفله.[44]

وإذا كان أهل الإقليم ينتقلون ولا يأبون على أنفسهم الهجرة من قرية إلى قرية، ومن مدينة إلى مدينة داخل الإقليم، فقد كان يتفق أن ينزل أتباع إحدى الأسرتين حيث تتسلط الأسرة الأخرى. وكان زعماء الأسرتين يتنقلون في الإقليم يزورون أتباعهم وأشياعهم. ولله ما كان يحدث من الخصومات يوم يهبط صاحب[45] العالية إلى السافلة، أو يصعد صاحب السافلة إلى العالية! وكان أبو الصبي من أتباع صاحب العالية، أخذ عنه العهد، وأخذ عنه أبوه من قبل. وكانت أم الصبي من أتباع صاحب العالية أيضًا، بل كان أبوها من أنصاره وحوارييه المقربين إليه. ومات صاحب العالية وخلفه على الطريق ابنه الحاج ... وكان أنشط من أبيه، وأقدر على الكيد واللؤم، وأنهض للخصومة. كان أقرب من أبيه إلى الدنيا، وأبعد من أبيه عن الدين.

وكان أبو الصبي قد هبط إلى السافلة واستقر فيها، فكانت لصاحب العالية عادة أن يزوره مرة في كل سنة. وكان إذا أقبل لم يقبل وحده، ولم يقبل في نفر قليل، وإنما أقبل في جيش ضخم؛ إن لم يبلغ المائة فليس ينحط عنها إلا قليلًا. ولم يكن يتخذ قطر السكة الحديدية ولا سفن النيل، وإنما كان يتخذ الجياد والبغال والحمير، يسير ومن حوله أصحابه فيمرون بالقرى والدساكر، ينزلون ويرحلون في أبهة وضخامة، منتصرين حيث لا سلطان إلا لهم، متحدين حيث لخصومهم شيء من القوة. وكانوا إذا زاروا أسرة الصبي أقبلوا حتى ينزلوا، فإذا الشارع ممتلئ بهم وبخيلهم وبغالهم وحمرهم، قد أخذوه من القناة إلى أقصاه الجنوبي. وإذا الشّاءُ تذبح، وإذا السمط ممدودَةٌ في الشارع، وإذا هم إلى

---

44. أعلا و أسفل here refer to the upper and lower parts of the province.
45. Here again, the author's terms of reference can create some confusion. The protagonist of the novel is called throughout «صاحبنا», meaning "our friend." The word صاحب can also mean owner or boss, and here refers to the leaders of the Sufi orders.

طعامهم في شره لا يعدله شره، والشيخ جالس في المنظرة ومن حوله أصفياؤه وأولياؤه، وبين يديه صاحب البيت وأخصاؤه يأتمرون أمره. فإذا فرغوا من الغداء انصرفوا عنه فنام حيث هو ثم نهض فتوضأ. فانظر إلى الناس يستبقون ويختصمون أيهم يصب عليه الماء! فإذا فرغ فانظر إليهم يستبقون ويختصمون أيهم يصيب من وضوء الشيخ جرعة! والشيخ عنهم في شغل، يصلي فيطيل الصلاة، ويدعو فيطيل الدعاء. حتى إذا فرغ من هذا كله جلس للناس وهم يتقاطرون عليه؛ منهم من يقبل يده وينصرف خاشعًا، ومنهم من يتحدث إليه لحظة أو لحظات، ومنهم من يسأله حاجة، والشيخ يجيب أولئك وهؤلاء بألفاظ غريبة غامضة، يذهبون في فهمها وتأويلها المذاهب.

أدخل عليه الصبي فمسح رأسه وتلا قول الله تعالي: «وعَلَّمكَ مَالَمْ تَكُنْ تَعْلَمُ وَكَانَ فَضْلُ الله عَلَيْك عَظيمًا».[46] من ذلك اليوم اقتنع أبو الصبي بأن سيكون لابنه شأن. فإذا صليت المغرب مدَّت الموائد وأكل الناس، ثم تصلي العشاء، ثم ينصب المجلس.

Comprehension Questions

١. كيف انقسم أهالي المدينة في ولائهم لشيوخ الصوفية؟

____

____

٢. أي شيخ من الشيوخ كان والدا صاحبنا يتبعانه؟

____

____

46. The Qur'an 4:113.

٣. لماذا كان أصحاب الطرق يسافرون حول الأقاليم؟

____

____

٤. كم شخصًا كان يرافق الشيخ الصوفي خلال زياراته إلى القرية؟

____

____

٥. لماذا أعتقد أبو الصبي أن ابنه سيصبح مهمًا؟

____

____

VI

ونصب المجلس عبارة عن اجتماع الناس إلى حلقة الذكر، يذكرون الله قاعدين ساكنين، ثم تتحرك رءوسهم وترتفع أصواتهم قليلاً، ثم تتحرك أنصافهم وترتفع أصواتهم قليلا، ثم تنبث في أجسامهم رعدة فإذا هم جميعًا وقوف؛ قد دفعوا في الهواء كأنما حركهم لولب، وقد انبثّ في الحلقة شيوخ ينشدون شعر ابن الفارض وما يشبهه من الشعر. وكان لهذا الشيخ خاصة كلفٌ بقصيدة معروفة، فيها ذكر الإسراء والمعراج، أولها:

من مكة والبيت الأمجد   للقدس سري ليلاً أحمد

كان الشيوخ يرتلونها ترتيلًا، وكان الذاكرون يحركون أجسامهم على هذا الترتيل، ينحنون ويستقيمون كأنما يرقصهم هؤلاء الشيوخ ترقيصًا.

ومهما ينس الصبي فلن ينسى ليلة غلط فيها أحد المنشدين فوضع لفظًا مكان لفظ من القصيدة، وإذا الشيخ قد ثار وفار، وأرغى وأزبد، وصاح بملء صوته: يا بني الكلاب! لعن الله آباءكم وآباء آبائكم وآباء آبائكم إلى آدم! أتريدون أن تخربوا بيت الرجل!

ومهما ينس الصبي فلن ينسى تأثير هذه الغضبة في نفوس الذاكرين، وفي نفوس الناس من حولهم، وكان الناس قد اقتنعوا بأن الغلط في هذه القصيدة مصدر شؤم لا يشبهه شؤم. وأظهر أبو الصبي تأثيرًا وفزعًا، ثم اطمئنانًا وهدوءًا. فلما انصرف الشيخ من الغد وتذاكرت الأسرة ما كان من أمره، وما كان من قصته مع الذاكرين والمنشدين، ضحك صاحب البيت ضحكة لم يشك الصبي بعدها في أن إيمان أبيه بهذا الشيخ لم يكن خالصًا من الشك والازدراء ... نعم من الشك والازدراء! فقد كان طمع الشيخ وحرصه أظهر من أن ينخدع بهما من له حظ من أناة وتفكير.

وكان من أشد الناس مقتًا للشيخ وسخطًا عليه أمُّ الصبي. كانت تكره زيارته، وتستثقل ظله، وتؤدي ما تؤدي، وتعدّ ما تعدّ وهي كارهة ساخطة؛ لا تكاد تمسك لسانها إلا في مشقة وعناء؛ ذلك لأن زيارة الشيخ كانت ثقيلة على هذه الأسرة التي كانت تعيش من سعة، ولكنها كانت فقيرة على كل حال.

كانت زيارة الشيخ تستهلك كثيرًا من القمح والسمن والعسل وما إلى ذلك، وكانت تكلف صاحب البيت الاقتراض لشراء ما لا بد منه من الضأن والمعز، وكان الشيخ لا يلم بهذه الأسرة إلا ارتحل من غده وقد أخذ شيئًا راقه وأعجبه. يأخذ في هذه المرة بساطًا، وفي هذه شالًا من الكشمير، وعلى هذا النحو.

كانت زيارة هذا الشيخ وأصحابه شيئًا ترغب فيه الأسرة رغبة شديدة، لأنه يمكنها من الفخر ورفع الرأس، ومناوأة الأشباه والنظائر، وتكرهه كرهًا شديدًا لأنه يكلفها ما يكلفها من المال والمشقة. كانت شرًّا لا بد منه جرت به العادة، وصادف هوى في الناس.

Comprehension Questions

١. ماذا كان الناس يفعلون خلال حلقة الذكر؟

٢. لماذا غضب الشيخ على المنشدين في الذكر؟

٣. كيف أثر غضب الشيخ على الذاكرين؟

٤. ماذا كان رأي أم صاحبنا في هذا الشيخ؟

٥. لماذا كانت زيارة الشيخ صعبة على الأسرة؟

Comprehension Exercise

Are the following statements true (صحيح) or false (خطأ) and why?

١. انكشف خداع صاحبنا لأن أباه كان يعرف نص الألفية جيدًا.

---

٢. تدخلت الأم بين صاحبنا وأخيه لحمايته من غضب الأب.

---

٣. تمتع المتعلمون في القرية باحترام أكبر من الذين يسكنون في العاصمة.

---

٤. كاتب المحكمة حصل على منصبه بفضل نجاحه في دروسه في جامعة الأزهر.

---

٥. كاتب المحكمة منع الشاب الأزهري من الصعود الى المنبر لأنه كان يعتبره صغيرًا في السن.

---

٦. معظم "حملة كتاب الله" كانوا مكفوفين.

---

٧. تتميز العلاقات بين طرق الصوفية بالتعاون.

---

٨. الشيخ الصوفي الذي زار بيت صاحبنا معروف بالتواضع والاعتدال.

---

٩. ترك غضب الشيخ الصوفي أثرًا قويًا على أهل القرية ومن بينهم صاحبنا.

---

١٠. على الرغم من أن أم صاحبنا كانت تكره الشيخ الصوفي، الا أنها كانت تسمح بزياراته.

Interpreting the Text

A. Answer the following questions in complete Arabic sentences, based on your interpretation of what you have read so far:

١. لماذا لم يستطع الصبي التقدم في دراسته لقواعد اللغة من كتاب الألفية في رأيكم؟

---

٢. ما الذي كشفه خداع صاحبنا عن مستوى تعليم أبيه؟

٣. لماذا كان احترام أهل الريف للعلماء يزيد عن مثيله في العاصمة؟

٤. من من علماء القرية يبدو جديرًا بالاحترام في نظر أهلها؟ ولماذا؟

٥. كيف يشعر الراوي حيال شيوخ الصوفية ودورهم الاجتماعي بصورة عامة؟

B. Taking stock of the story: By now, you have seen a number of interesting characters, all of whom display their own particularities. In a few sentences, discuss the differences and similarities between the pair of characters given:

١. سيدنا – الشيخ الصوفي

____

____

٢. أم صاحبنا – أبو صاحبنا

____

____

٣. كاتب المحكمة – إمام المسجد

____

____

٤. صاحبنا – أخوه الأزهري

____

____

٥. اختاروا الشخصيتين الأكثر تشابهًا في نظركم.

____

____

٦. اختارو الشخصيتين الأكثر اختلافًا في نظركم.

____

____

Cultural and Historical Background

1. The author refers to a number of positions traditionally held by religious scholars (علماء). The *imam* of the mosque will be the most familiar. Officially the prayer leader, a Sunni imam is the leader of the mosque community, similar to a Christian pastor. The other familiar position is the judge, or *qadi*, who runs the Islamic court. As many functions of family law fell under the purview of the religious court, the *qadi* played an important role in the community. The *katib* is technically a scribe, but in modern usage serves as a clerk or low-level bureaucrat.
2. Leaders of Sufi orders, or *tariqa*s, held as much influence in traditional communities as official religious functionaries. They may or may not have formal religious education, as is the case with those the author mentions. "Sheikh" is traditionally a title for a Sufi leader, which causes confusion here due to the author's use of the term for numerous different characters. The ceremony that the Sufis perform here, the *dhikr*, usually involves group chanting of the name of God and other religious sayings, such as the poem mentioned in this story.
3. Sunni Islam traditionally recognizes four main schools of law, although many others have existed. All four are considered acceptable in most Sunni communities, and many teaching mosques were designed with four wings, to accommodate the teaching of all four schools. The Maliki school, most popular

in North Africa, and the Shafi'i, dominant in part of southern Egypt, are both mentioned as popular in the village in this story. The court *katib* boasts of his Hanifi background, representing the official *madhhab* of the Ottoman Empire, which had ruled Egypt in practice until the nineteenth century.

Analyzing Elements of Literature

Setting (مكان وزمن القصة)

كل قصة تدور أحداثها في بيئة معينة، ويخلق المؤلف تلك البيئة — الموقع، والأشخاص، والفترة التاريخية — من أجل إنشاء سياق يؤدي بشكل طبيعي إلى فهم الأحداث والشخصيات. في الواقع، قد يكون المؤلف مهتمًا إلى حد كبير بالتعليق على هذه البيئة كهدف رئيسي لكتابته. في هذه الرواية، انتقد طه حسين بيئة التعليم في هذه القرية، والتي تشكل نموذجًا لحال القرى المصرية، في حملته الجادة لإصلاح التعليم على جميع المستويات. وكان معظم قرائه على دراية بقضايا التعليم التي يصفها طه حسين.

Answer the following questions about the setting of this novel. Many of the answers will come from previous sections of the book:

١. ما هي الحدود الجغرافية للبيئة التي تركز عليها هذه الرواية؟ بالإضافة إلى القرية نفسها، هل هناك أماكن أخرى مذكورة فيها؟

___

___

٢. هل نعرف الكثير من التفاصيل عن وضع هذه القرية، مثل اسمها، أو موقعها أو اقتصادها وغير ذلك؟

____

____

٣. لماذا يقدم المؤلف بعض المعلومات ويخفي غيرها في رأيكم؟

____

____

٤. ما هي أوضح وأبرز الصفات التي تميز هذه القرية في السرد؟

____

____

٥. كيف يبدو المناخ الاجتماعي في القرية؟ ما هي أبرز صفات سكانها؟

____

____

٦. إلى أي حد تعتقدون أن المكان والبيئة أثرا على مسيرة الصبي وفرصه؟

____

____

Themes

الدين الشعبي

Taha Hussein was no less critical of the religious institutions of his day than he was of the educational systems. Indeed, his treatment of religion would cause him more difficulties than his critiques of education. The corrupt, exploitative nature of religious structures is well illustrated by the portrayal of the Sufi sheikhs in this section. With this in mind, please prepare a one- to two-page brief to address the following question:

كيف يصور المؤلف المجموعات الدينية الشعبية كتشكيل فاسد ومنظم وواسع في نطاقه وقوي في تأثيره؟

Vocabulary Items

The following words are particularly useful in following Taha Hussein's narrative in this section:

bored, weary, overburdened	مُتَثاقِل
to mediate, intercede	شَفَعَ، يَشْفَع، شَفاعَة
memorable	مَشْهُود
apprehensive silence	وُجُوم
(in this case refers to a section or division of a book)	باب، أَبْوَاب
awe	مَهابَة

to create	فَطَرَ، يَفْطُر، فَطْر مِن
rough	غَليظ، غِلاظ
inside of the mouth, cheek	شِدْق، أَشْداق
to disparage	ذَمَّ، يَذُمّ، ذَمّ
to denigrate	غَضَّ، يَغَضّ، غَضاضَة
cunning	ماكِر، مَكَرَة
resentment	مَوْجِدَة
to be made null and void	بَطَلَ، يَبْطُل، بُطل
admiration	إِكْبار
to devote oneself to	انْقَطَعَ، يَنْقَطِع، انْقِطاع إلى
scattered	مُنْبَثّ
mystic, imparted by God	لَدُني
orphans	يَتيم، يَتامَى
(here) connection	سَبَب، أَسْباب
interpretation	تَأْويل

(here) to visit often	اخْتَلَفَ، يَخْتَلِف، اخْتِلاف
does not refuse, refrain from	لا يَأْبَى، أَبَى، إِباء
deception, cunning	كَيْد، كِياد
wickedness, greed	لُؤْم
troop, group	نَفَر، أَنْفار
small villages	دَسْكَرَة، دَساكِر
to prepare, set up	سَمَطَ، يَسْمُط، سَمْط
gluttony	شَرَه
spring, screw	لَوْلَب، لَوالِب
a way of reciting the Qur'an or other verses	تَرْتِيل
curse, bad luck	شُؤْم
hatred	مَقْت

Unit Seven

Preparation for Reading

Author's Background

عاد طه حسين إلى مصر بعد حصوله على الدكتوراه الثانية في فرنسا في عام ١٩١٩، ليصبح أستاذًا بالجامعة المصرية والتي تحمل اسم جامعة القاهرة الآن، ومن ثم بدأ سلسلة من الكتابات الجدلية تصدرها بكتابه عن شعر الجاهلية عام ١٩٢٦، وتضمنت مجموعة من التساؤلات النقدية عن التواريخ المقبولة لشبه الجزيرة العربية قبل الإسلام ومدى موثوقية القرآن كمصدر للمعلومات التاريخية، ولهذا واجه معارضة قوية من التيار الديني، وخاصة من مؤسسة الأزهر، والذي نجح في إجبار جامعة القاهرة على فصله من منصبه. في مثل هذه الظروف بالتحديد نشرت هذه الرواية، "الأيام"، والتي تفسر لنا في كثير من جوانبها أسباب كراهية طه حسين للنظم التقليدية، وبالتالي مسيرته النضالية الطويلة من أجل تقدم الحرية الأكاديمية والفكرية في مصر.

Reading

I

وكان اتصال الأسرة بهذا البيت من بيوت الطريق قويًا متينًا، ترك فيها آثارًا باقية من الأخبار والقصص، وأحاديث الكرامات والمعجزات. وكانت أم الصبي وأبوه يجدان لذة في أن يتحدثا إلى أبنائهما بهذه الأخبار والأحاديث. ولم تكن أمّ الصبي تدع فرصة إلا قصت فيها هذه القصة: «حج أبي ومعه جدتي مع الشيخ خالد مرة، وكان الشيخ قد حج ثلاث مرات تبعه فيها أبي، واصطحب أمه في هذه المرة. فلما فرغوا

من الحج وانصرفوا إلى المدينة، وقعت الشيخة في بعض الطريق من الرحل، فانحطم ظهرها انحطامًا، وعجزت عن المشي والحركة، وأخذ ابنها يحملها وينقلها من مكان إلى مكان، ويجد في ذلك من المشقة والعناء ما شكاه إلى الشيخ ذات يوم، فقال له الشيخ: ألست تزعم أنها شريفة من نسل الحسن بن علي؟ قال: بلى. قال: فهي ذاهبة إلى جدها، فإذا انتهيت بها إلى المسجد النبوي فضعها في ناحية منه، وخل بينها وبين جدها يصنع بها ما يشاء. وكذلك فعل الرجل: وضع أمه في ناحية من نواحي المسجد، وقال لها في لغة الفلاح الجافية يملؤها مع جفوتها الحب والإشفاق: أنت وجدك، فليس لي بكما شأن. ثم تركها وتبع شيخه يريد أن يطوف بقبر النبي. قال الرجل: فوالله ما خطوت خطوات حتى سمعت أمي تناديني، فالتفت فإذا هي قائمة تسعى، وأبيت أن أعود إليها، فإذا هي تعدو من ورائي عدوًا، وإذا هي تسبقني إلى الشيخ وتطوف مع الطائفين».

وكان أبو الصبي لا يدع فرصة إلا ذكر فيها عن الشيخ هذه القصة: ذكر أمامه أن الغزالي[47] قال في بعض كتبه: إن النبي لا يمكن أن يرى فيما يرى النائم.[48] فغضب الشيخ وقال: والله ما هكذا كان الأمل فيك[49] يا غزالي، لقد رأيته بعيني رأسي هذا راكبًا بغلته. وذكر له ذلك مرة أخرى فقال: والله ما هكذا كان الأمل فيك يا غزالي، لقد رأيته بعيني رأسي هذا راكبًا ناقته. وكان أبو الصبي يستنبط من ذلك أن الغزالي قد أخطأ، وأن عامة الناس يستطيعون أن يروا النبي فيما يرى النائم، وأن الأولياء والصالحين يستطيعون أن يروه وهم أيقاظ وكان أبو الصبي يثبت هذا بحديث يرويه كلما ذكر هذه القصة، وهو:

«من رآني في المنام فقد رآني حقًا فإن الشيطان لا يتمثل بي».[50]

وعلى هذا النحو حفظ الصبي ألوانًا من أخبار الكرامات والمعجزات وأسرار الصوفية، وكان إذا أراد أن يتحدث بشيء من ذلك إلى أترابه

47. Abu Hamid al-Ghazali, a Medieval scholar of Islamic Law and one of the foremost authorities in Sufism.
48. فيما يرى النائم – i.e., in a dream.
49. An expression meaning "I had hoped for better from you," i.e., "you disappoint me."
50. A Hadith of the Prophet.

ورفاقه في الكُتّاب قصوا عليه أمثاله؛ يضيفونه إلى صاحب السافلة ويؤمنون به إيمانًا شديدًا.

كانت لأهل الريف شيوخهم وشبّانهم وصبيانهم ونسائهم عقلية خاصة فيها سذاجة وتصوّف وغفلة، وكان أكبر الأثر في تكوين هذه العقلية لأهل الطريق.

Comprehension Questions

١. في القصة التي رويتها أم صاحبنا، كيف جرحت الحاجة العجوز؟

____

____

٢. بم نصح الشيخ خالد (الشيخ الصوفي) الرجل بأن يفعل مع أمه؟

____

____

٣. كيف برر الشيخ هذه النصيحة؟

____

____

٤. في قصة أبي صاحبنا، ماذا قال الغزالي؟

____

____

٥. لماذا لم يتفق الشيخ خالد مع رأي الغزالي؟

____

____

II

على أن صبينا لم يلبث أن أضاف إلى هذه الألوان من العلم لونًا آخر جديدًا، وهو علم السحر والطلاسم، فقد كان باعة الكتب يتنقلون في القرى والمدن بخليط من الأسفار؛ لعله أصدق مثل لعقيدة الريف في ذلك العهد. كانوا يحملون في حقائبهم مناقب الصالحين، وأخبار الفتوح والغزوات، وقصة القط والفأر، وحوار السلك والوابور،[51] وشمس المعارف الكبرى في السحر، وكتابًا آخر لست أدري كيف كان يسمى، ولكنه كان يعرف بكتاب «الديربي»، ثم أورادًا مختلفة، ثم قصص المولد النبوي، ثم مجموعات من الشعر الصوفي، ثم كتبًا في الوعظ والإرشاد، وأخرى في المحاضرات وعجائب الأخبار، ثم قصص الأبطال من الهلاليين والزناتيين، وعنترة، والظاهر بيبرس، وسيف بن ذي يزن،[52] ثم القرآن الكريم مع هذا كله. وكان الناس يشترون الكتب كلها، ويلتهمون ما فيها التهامًا، وكانت عقليتهم تتكوّن من خلاصته كما تتكون أجسامهم من خلاصة ما كانوا يأكلون ويشربون.

وقد قرئَ لصاحبنا من هذا كله، فحفظ منه الشيء الكثير. ولكنه عني بشيئين عناية خاصة: عني بالسحر، وعني بالتصوف. ولم يكن في الجمع بين هذين اللونين من العلم شيء من الغرابة ولا من العسر، فإن التناقض الذي يظهر بينهما ليس إلاّ صوريًا في حقيقة الأمر. أليس الصوفي يزعم لنفسه وللناس أنه يخترق حجب الغيب، وينبئُ بما كان وما سيكون، كما أنه يتعدى حدود القوانين الطبيعية ويأتي بضروب الخوارق والكرامات؟ والساحر ماذا يصنع؟ أليس يزعم لنفسه القدرة على الإخبار بالغيب، وتجاوز حدود القوانين الطبيعية أيضًا، والاتصال

51. These are famous stories or genres of literature.
52. The Hilalites and Zanatines are famous tribes; Antar, Baybars, and Sayf Ibn Zy Yazan are heroes about whom epic poems were written.

بعالم الأرواح؟ ... بلى! كل ما يوجد من الفرق بين الساحر والصوفي هو أن هذا يتصل بالملائكة وذلك يتصل بالشياطين. ولكن يجب أن نقرأ ابن خلدون[53] وأمثاله لنصل إلى تحقيق مثل هذا الفرق، ونرتب عليه نتائجه الطبيعية من تحريم السحر والترغيب عنه، وتحبيب التصوف والترغيب فيه.

وما كان أبعد صبينا وأترابه عن ابن خلدون وأمثال ابن خلدون! إنما كانت تقع في أيديهم كتب السحر ومناقب الصالحين وكرامات الأولياء، فيقرأون ويتأثرون ثم لا يلبثون أن يتجاوزوا القراءة والإعجاب إلى الاقتداء والتجربة. وإذا هم يسلكون مناهج الصوفية، ويأتون ما يأتيه السحرة من ضروب الفن، وكثيرًا ما يختلط في عقولهم السحر والتصوف، فيصبح كلاهما شيئًا واحدًا، غايته تيسير الحياة والتقرب إلى الله.

وكذلك كان الأمر في نفس صاحبنا، فقد كان يتصوّف ويتكلف السحر، وهو واثق بأنه سيرضي الله، ويظفر من الحياة بأحب لذاتها إليه.

Comprehension Questions

١. من أين تعرف صاحبنا على فن السحر؟

____

____

٢. ما هي بعض مواضيع الكتب التي تباع في القرى؟

____

____

53. Ibn Khaldun—an eminent classical historian and philosopher with highly nuanced ideas on science, magic, and religion.

٣. هل اعتقد صاحبنا أن تجاربه في السحر ستسيء إلى الله؟

____

____

٤. لماذا اعتبر الصبي أن السحر مثل التصوف؟

____

____

٥. هل اقتصرت معرفة صبينا وأصدقائه بالسحر على القراءة فقط؟

____

____

III

وكان من القصص التي تكثر في أيدي الصبيان يحملها إليهم باعة الكتب، قصة اقتطعت من «ألف ليلة وليلة»[54] وتعرف بقصة «حسن البصري».[55] في هذه القصة أخبار ذلك المجوسي الذي كان يحول النحاس ذهبًا. وأخبار ذلك القصر الذي كان يقوم من وراء الجبل على عمد شاهقة في الهواء، وتقيم فيه بنات سبع من بنات الجن، والذي أوى إليه حسن البصري، ثم أخبار حسن هذا وما كان من رحلته الطويلة الشاقة إلى دور الجن. وبين هذه الأخبار خبر ملأ الصبي إعجابًا؛ وهو أن قضيبًا أهدي إلى حسن هذا في بعض رحلته وكان من خواص هذا القضيب أن تضرب به الأرض فتنشق ويخرج منها تسعة نفر يأتمرون

54. *A Thousand and One Nights*, i.e., *The Arabian Nights* stories.

55. Hassan al-Basri (642–728), a famous mystic and ascetic, one of the founders of Sufism.

أمر صاحب القضيب، وهم بالطبع من الجن أقوياء خفاف يطيرون ويعدون، ويحملون الأثقال، ويقتلعون الجبال، ويأتون من عجيب الأمر ما لا حدّ له.

فتن الصبي بهذه العصا، ورغب في أن يظفر بها رغبة شديدة قوية أرَّقت ليله ونغصت يومه. فأخذ يقرأ كتب السحر والتصوف، يلتمس عند السحرة والمتصوفين وسيلة تمكنه من هذه العصا.

وكان له قريب صبي مثله يرافقه إلى الكُتّاب، فكان أشد منه كلفًا بهذه العصا. وما هي إلا أن جدَّ الصبيَّان في البحث حتى انتهيا إلى وسيلة يسيرة تمكنهما مما يريدان. وجداها في كتاب الديربي، وهي أن يخلو الفتى إلى نفسه وقد تطهَّر ووضع بين يديه نارًا ومقدارًا من الطيب ثم يأخذ في ترديد هذا الاسم من أسماء الله «يا لطيف يا لطيف» ملقيًا في النار شيئًا من الطيب من حين إلى حين، فيمضي في ترديد هذه الكلمة وتحريق هذا الطيب، حتى تدور به الأرض، وينشق أمامه الحائط ويمثل أمامه خادم من الجن موكل بهذا الاسم من أسماء الله، فيطلب إليه ما يريده، والحاجة مقضية من غير شك.

ظفر الصبيَّان بهذه الوسيلة فاعتزما أن يستخدماها. وما هي إلا أن اشتريا ضروبًا من الطيب، وخلا صبينا إلى نفسه في المنظرة، أغلق بابها من دونه ووضع بين يديه قطعًا من النار وأخذ يلقي فيها الطيب، ويردّد: «يا لطيف! يا لطيف!» وطال به هذا وهو ينتظر أنٍ تدور به الأرض وينشق له الحائط ويمثل الخادم بين يديه، ولكن شيئًا من ذلك لم يكن. وهنا تحوّل صبيُّنا الساحر المتصوف إلى نصَّاب.

خرج من المنظرة مضطربًا يمسك رأسه بيديه ولا يكاد لسانه ينطلق بحرف واحد، فتلقاه صاحبه الصبي يسأله: هل لقيٍ الخادم؟ وهل طلب إليه العصا؟ وصاحبنا لا يجيب إلا مضطربًا مرتجفًا، تصطك أسنانه اصطكاكًا، حتى روّع رفيقه الصبي. وبعد لأي أخذ صاحبنا يهدأ ويجيب في ألفاظ متقطعة، وبصوت متهدج: «لقد دًارت بي الأرض حتى كدت أسقط، وانشق الحائط وسمعت صوتًا ملأ الحجرة من جميع نواحيها، ثم أغمي عليّ، ثم أفقت فخرجت مسرعًا!!»

سمع الصبي هذا! فامتلأ فرحًا وإعجابًا بصاحبه، وقال له: هوّن عليك، فقد أصابك الرعب وملك الخوف عليك أمرك، فلنبحثن في الكتاب عن شيء يؤمنك ويشجعك على أن تثبت للخادم وتطلب منه ما تشاء.

واستأنفا البحث في الكتاب. وانتهى بهما البحث إلى أنّ صاحب الخلوة يجب أن يصلي ركعتين قبل أن يجلس إلى النار ويأخذ في ترديد هذا الاسم. وكذلك فعل الصبي من غده، وأخذ يلقي الطيب في النار ويردد دعاء «اللطيف» ينتظر أن تدور به الأرض، وينشق له الحائط، ويمثل الخادم بين يديه. ولكن شيئًا من ذلك لم يكن. وخرج الصبي إلى صاحبه هادئًا مطمئنًا، فأخبره أن قد دارت الأرض وانشق الحائط ومثل الخادم بين يديه وسمع منه حاجته، ولكنه لم يشأ أن يجيبه إليها حتى يمرن على هذه الخلوة ويكثر من الصلاة وإطلاق البخور وذكر الله، وضرب له موعدًا لقضاء هذه الحاجة شهرًا كاملًا يأتي فيه هذا الأمر في نظام، فإن فسد هذا النظام فلا بد من استئناف الأمر شهرًا كاملًا آخر. وصدّق الصبي صاحبه، وأخذ يلحّ عليه في كل يوم أن يخلو إلى النار ويردّد الدعاء، وأخذ الصبي يستغل من صاحبه هذا الضعف، ويكلفه ما شاء من مشقة وعناء فإن أبى أو أظهر الإباء أعلن إليه صاحبه أنه لن يخلو إلى النار، ولن يدعو «اللطيف» ولن يلتمس العصا؛ فيذعن إذعانًا سريعًا.

Comprehension Questions

١. من أي مجموعة جاءت قصة "حسن البصري"؟

____

____

٢. ماذا كانت قدرة المجوسي في القصص؟

____

____

٣. ماذا يفعل القضيب السحري لصاحبه حسب القصة؟

____

____

٤. ما النتيجة التي توقعها صاحبنا بعد القيام بالطقوس السحرية؟

____

____

٥. هل نجحت الطقوس في إعطاء الصبي ما يريده؟

____

____

IV

على أن صاحبنا لم يكن يميل وحده إلى السحر والتصوف، وإنما كان يدفع إلى ذلك دفعًا، يدفعه إليه أبوه؛ ذلك أن الشيخ كان كثير الحاجات عند الله. كان له أبناء كثيرون، وكان يحرص على تعليمهم وتهذيبهم، وكان فقيرًا لا يستطيع أن يؤدي نفقات ذلك التعليم، وكان يستدين من حين إلى حين ويثقل عليه أداء الدين، وكان يطمع في أن يزاد راتبه من حين إلى حين، وكان يطمع في أن يتقدم درجة وينتقل من عمل إلى عمل، وكان يلتمس هذا كله عند الله بالصلاة والدعاء والاستخارة، وكان أحب وسائل الالتماس إليه «عدية يس»[56] وكان يطلب «عدية يس» هذه إلى ابنه الصبي، لأنه صبي ولأنه مكفوف، وهو بهاتين المزيتين أثير

56. Reciting Sura Yaa Siin (the thirty-sixth sura of the Qur'an)

عند الله رفيع المكانة عنده، وهل يرضى الله أن يرد صبيًا مكفوفًا حين يطلب إليه أمرًا من الأمور متوسلا بقراءة القرآن؟

وكانت «عدية يس» مراتب: أولها أن يخلو الإنسان إلى نفسه فيقرأ هذه السورة من سور القرآن أربع مرات ثم يطلب ما يشاء وينصرف. والثانية أن يخلو إلى نفسه فيتلو هذه السورة سبع مرات، ثم يطلب ما يشاء وينصرف. والثالثة أن يخلو إلى نفسه فيتلو هذه السورة إحدى وأربعين مرة لا يفرغ من قراءتها مرة حتى يتبعها بدعاء يس: «يا عصبة الخير بخير الملل»، فإذا أتم القراءة طلب ما شاء وانصرف. والبخور محتوم في هذه المرتبة الثالثة. وكان الشيخ يكلف ابنه العدّية الصغرى في صغار الأمور، والوسطى في الأمور الهامة، والكبرى في الأمور التي تمس حياة الأسرة كلها. فإذا سعى في أن يدخل أحد أبنائه في المدرسة مجانًا فالعدّية الصغرى. وإذا التمس إلى الله أداء دين ثقيل فالعدّية الوسطى. وإذا رغب في أن ينتقل من عمل إلى عمل وأن يزاد راتبه جنيهًا أو بعض الجنيه فالعدّية الكبرى. وكان لكل عدّية أجر: فأما العدية الصغرى فأجرها قطعة من السكر أو الحلوى، وأما العدية الوسطى فأجرها خمسة مليمات، وأما العدية الكبرى فأجرها عشرة. وكثيرًا ما خلا الصبي إلى نفسه وقرأ سورة يس أربعًا أو سبعًا أو إحدى وأربعين. ومن عجيب الأمر أن الحاجات كانت تقضى دائمًا! وما هي إلا أن تم اقتناع الشيخ بأن ابنه مبارك، وبأنه أثير عند الله.

ولم يكن أمر السحر والتصوف مقصورًا على قضاء الحاجات والتنبؤ بما سينجلي عنه الغيب، وإنما كان يتجاوز هذا كله إلى دفع المكروه واتقاء النكبات. وقد نسي الصبي أشياء كثيرة، ولكنه لم ينس هذا الرعب الذي ملأ قلوب الناس جميعًا في المدينة وما حولها من القري؛ حين وصلت إليهم الأخبار من القاهرة بأن نجمًا ذا ذنب سيظهر في السماء بعد أيام؛ حتى إذا كانت الساعة الثانية بعد الظهر مسّ الأرض بطرف من ذنبه فإذا هي هشيم تذروه الرياح. فأما النساء وعامة الناس فلم يحفلوا بهذا أو لم يكادوا يحفلون به، وإنما كانوا يشعرون بشيء من الرعب كلما تحدثوا بهذه النازلة أو سمعوا الحديث عنها، ثم لا يلبثون أن ينصرفوا إلى ما هم فيه من حياة عملية. وأما المتفقهون في الدين وحملة القرآن وأصحاب الطرق وتلاميذهم فكانوا هلعين حقًا مروّعين، لا تكاد تستقر قلوبهم بين جنوبهم، وكانوا يتحاورون في ذلك تحاورًا

متصلاً، فمنهم من يزعم أن هذه الكارثة لن تقع، لأنها مخالفة لما عرف من أشراط الساعة. وما كان للأرض أن تفنى قبل أن تظهر الدابة والنار والدَّجال، وقبل أن يهبط المسيح إلى الأرض فيملأها عدلاً بعد أن ملئت جورًا. ومنهم من كان يظن أن الكارثة من أشراط الساعة.[57] ومنهم من كان يتحدث بأن هذه الكارثة قد تقع فتصيب الأرض بشيء من التدمير دون أن تأتي عليها جميعًا. كانوا يتحاورون طول النهار، حتى إذا أقبل الليل وصليت المغرب اجتمعوا حلقًا في المسجد وأمام الدور، وأخذوا يُرددون هذه الكلمة: «أزفت الآزفة ليس لها من دون الله كاشفة»[58] حتى تصلى العشاء. وانقضت الأيام، وجاءت الساعة المحتومة، ولم يظهر في السماء نجم ذو ذنب ولم يصب الأرض دمار قليل ولا كثير. فانقسم المتفقهون في الدين وحملة القرآن وأصحاب الطرق، فأما أهل العلم الذين يستمدون علمهم من الكتب وينتمون إلى الأزهر فانتصروا، وقالوا: «ألم نقل لكم: إن هذه الكارثة لا يمكن أن تقع قبل أن تظهر أشراط الساعة؟ ألم ندعكم إلى تكذيب المنجمين؟» وأما حملة القرآن فقالوا: «كلا، لقد كادت تقع الكارثة لولا أن لطف الله بالرضَّع والحوامل والبهائم، وسمع لدعاء الداعين، وتضرع المتضرعين.» وأما أهل التصوف والعلم اللدني فقالوا: «كلا لقد كادت تقع الكارثة لولا أن توسط القطب المتولي[59] بين الناس والله، فصرف عن الناس هذا البلاء، واحتمل عنهم أوزارهم».

Comprehension Questions

١. لماذا اعتقد الأب أن صلاة ابنه لها قوة خاصة؟

____

____

57. The signs of the Day of Judgment.
58. The Qur'an 53:57–58; these verses are from the Sura "The Star" and refer to the coming judgment.
59. A famous Sufi mystic believed to live in old Cairo and watch over Sufis.

٢. كيف قرر الأب نوع (أو مستوى) المساعدة التي يأمر الصبي بطلبها؟

---

٣. لماذا كانت القرية بأكملها في حالة رعب بعد سماع الأخبار القادمة من القاهرة؟

---

٤. لماذا لم تحدث كارثة حسب الصوفية؟

---

٥. كيف شرح القادة الدينيون المثقفون عدم وقوع الكارثة؟

V

وأنت تستطيع أن تقول: إن هذا الدافع الذي كان يدفع الناس إلى التحصن من الخماسين[60] كان سحرًا أو تصوفًا. أما أنا فلا أستطيع إلا أن أحدثك بما يذكر الصبي من أن الأيام التي كانت تسبق أيام شم

60. The Khamasin are the dust storms that affect Egypt in the spring.

النسيم[61] كانت أيامًا غريبة؛ يخالط فيها قلوب النساء والصبيان وحملة القرآن شيء من الفرح والخوف. كانوا إذا أظلهم يوم الجمعة أسرفوا في الأكل وفي ألوان خاصة من الطعام، حتى إذا كان يوم السبت أسرفوا في أكل البيض الملوّن. وكان الفقهاء قد استعدوا لهذا اليوم استعدادًا خاصًا فاشتروا ورقًا أبيض صقيلًا، وقطعوه قطعًا صغارًا دقاقًا وكتبوا على كل قطعة «ا ل م ص» ثم يطوون هذه القطع ويملئون بها جيوبهم. حتى إذا كان يوم السبت ألموا بالدّور التي كانوا يتصلون بها ففرقوا هذه القطع من الورق على أهلها، وطلبوا إلى كل واحد أن يبتلع منها أربعًا قبل أن يلم بطعام أو شراب. وكانوا يزعمون للناس أن ابتلاع هذه القطع من الورق يصرف عنهم ما تأتي به الخماسين من المكروه، ويصرف عنهم الرمد بنوع خاص. وكان الناس يصدقونهم ويبتلعون هذا الورق ويؤدون إلى الفقهاء ثمنه بيضًا أحمر وأصفر. وليس يدري الصبي ماذا كان يصنع سيدنا بما كان يجتمع له من البيض في يوم سبت النور؟ فقد كان كثيرًا يتجاوز المئات. على أن استعداد الفقهاء لهذا اليوم لم يكن يقف عند إعداد هذه القطع من الورق، وإنما كان يتجاوز ذلك إلى شيء آخر! كانوا يشترون الورق الأبيض الصقيل، ويقطعونه قطعًا طويلة عريضة بعض العرض، ويكتبون عليها مخلفات النبي:

مخلف طه[62] سبحتان ومصحف ومكحلة سجادتان رحى عصا

حتى إذا فرغوا من هذه المخلفات أضافوا إليها دعاءً آخر يبتدئ بهذه الكلمات التي كان الفقهاء يقولون إنها سريانية: «دنبد دنبي، كرى كرندي، سرى سرندي، سبر سبربتونا، واحبسوا البعيد عنا لا يأتينا، والقريب منا لا يؤذينا ...» إلخ ثم يطوون هذه الأوراق على أنها حجب وتمائم، يفرقونها في البيوت على النساء والصبيان، ويتقاضون أثمانها دراهم وخبزًا وفطيرًا وضروبًا من الحلوى، ويزعمون للناس أن اتخاذ هذه التمائم والحجب يدفع عنهم أذي هذه الشياطين التي تحملها رياح الخماسين. وكان النساء يتلقين هذه الحجب مطمئنات إليها، ولكن ذلك

61. Shamm al-Nasim, an Egyptian holiday marking the beginning of spring.
62. That is, the Prophet.

لم يكن يمنعهن من اتقاء العفاريت يوم شم النسيم بشق البصل وتعليقه على أبواب الدور، وأكل الفول النابت دون غيره من ألوان الطعام في هذا اليوم.

Comprehension Questions

١. كيف كان الناس يشعرون قبل شم النسيم؟

____

____

٢. ماذا كانوا يأكلون في يوم السبت قبل شم النسيم؟

____

____

٣. لماذا أمر الفقهاء الشعب بابتلاع قطع الأوراق التي كتبوا عليها؟

____

____

٤. كيف دفع أهل القرية ثمن قطع الأوراق للفقهاء؟

____

____

٥. كيف كان بعض الناس يتقي شر العفاريت في يوم شم النسيم؟

____

____

Comprehension Exercise

Are the following statements true (صحيح) or false (خطأ) and why?

١. أظهرت قصة الشيخ خالد في المدينة أنه رجل كثير الصبر والرحمة.

____

٢. أحب والدا الشاب سرد القصص عن مشايخ الصوفية.

____

٣. أصر صاحبنا على الفرق الواضح بين السحر والتصوف.

____

٤. يعتبر المؤلف موضوعات الكتب التي كان القرويون يشترونها خرافات.

____

٥. كان الصبي يرغب في الحصول على قضيب سحري لاستخدامه في طقوس سحرية.

____

٦. رأى صاحبنا الخادم السحري في الحقيقة.

____

٧. استغل صاحبنا ثقة وسذاجة صديقه.

____

٨. كان الأب يكلف ابنه بالصلاة نيابة عنه لأنه أعمى.

____

٩. بعد ظهور النجم المذنب ضربت القرية كارثة طبيعية هائلة.

____

١٠. اتخذ أهل القرية إجراءات احتياطية كثيرة للاحتماء من عواصف "الخماسين".

____

Interpreting the Text

A. Answer the following questions in complete Arabic sentences, based on your interpretation of what you have read so far:

١. ما الرسالة التي تحملها قصة أم صاحبنا عن الشيخ خالد في رأيكم؟ ولماذا كانت أمه تحب هذه القصة؟

____

____

٢. كيف عكست محاولة الصبي لمساعدة والده باستخدام السحر مستوى الإيمان بالخرافات في القرية ؟

____

____

٣. ما معنى قول المؤلف إن الصبي وأصدقائه لم يقرؤوا أفكار ابن خلدون في السحر والتصوف، بل الكتب المباعة في القرية فقط؟

____

____

٤. لماذا لجأ صاحبنا إلى السحر للحصول على ما يريده؟ بالنظر إلى خلط الصبي بين الدين والسحر، هل تظنون أن هناك نقد للدين الشعبي هنا؟

____

____

٥. لماذا روى الكاتب تجارب صاحبنا مع الطقوس السحرية قبل تجاربه مع "عدية يس" مباشرة؟ ما هو تأثير هذا الترتيب؟

____

____

B. Predicting the direction of the story: This section of the novel has revealed more facts about the main character and some of the events of his life. Based on what you have read, what can you conclude about the hero's life and what do you expect will happen as the story progresses?

١. هل تعتقدون أن إيمان الصبي بالمؤسسات الدينية سيزداد في المستقبل، أم سينخفض؟

____

____

٢. هل سيجد صاحبنا تناقضًا بين السحر والدين في المستقبل؟

____

____

٣. أي توجه سيفضله صاحبنا، الصوفية أم الفقه الإسلامي أم غيرهما؟

____

____

٤. هل سيكون عمى صاحبنا عقبة أمام متابعة تعليمه أم سيتغلب عليها؟

---

٥. هل تتوقعون أن يستمر اهتمامه بالسحر؟

Cultural and Historical Background

1. In the Hajj story related in Section I, the group led by Sheikh Khalid has completed the Hajj to Mecca and is continuing on to Medina, where the mosque and the tomb of the Prophet are located. While not officially part of the Hajj, this visit is typically added to Hajj itineraries after completing the rituals in Mecca. The sheikh is in a hurry to complete the ritual circling *(tawaf)* of the tomb of the Prophet.
2. Descendants of the Prophet, referred to as *Sharif*s or *Sayyid*s, are accorded special status in Islam, the specifics of which differ from country to country. In all cases their treatment is intended as a sign of reverence and respect. In this story, however, the Sheikh is using the woman's status as an excuse for abandoning her so he can carry out rituals ostensibly honoring the Prophet, and this is thus another indication of his hypocrisy and selfishness.
3. The recitation of Surat Yaa Siin (Qur'an 36) that the father has his son carry out is based on a Hadith of the Prophet that states: "If anyone recites Yaa Siin at the beginning of the day, their

needs for that day will be fulfilled." Thus it is a common practice to recite the sura at the beginning of each day. In another Hadith, this sura is called "the heart of the Qur'an." Here, the author is drawing an obvious comparison between the magic ritual the boys practice and the religious ritual of reciting Yaa Siin.

4. The evil star referred to in section IV is an astrological prediction that God would visit judgment on the Earth. The Qur'anic verses that the people repeat are from the sura of *al-Najm* (the Star), which describes previous judgments that God has brought, such as Sodom and Gomorrah and the flood of Noah, and predicts a coming judgment. The reactions to this prediction are the kind of confused mix of beliefs and superstitions that Taha Hussein wishes to point out, including Christian Messianic references and Sufi beliefs in a mystic saint interceding for the people.
5. Shamm al-Nasim, the holiday described in section V, is derived from ancient Egyptian spring celebrations. With the coming of Christianity, it became associated with Easter. It is now celebrated by both Christians and Muslims. The tradition of dyeing and eating colored eggs is similar to Easter traditions in the west.

Analyzing Elements of Literature

Genre (جنس أدبي)

الجنس العربي يشير إلى نوع الأدب بصورة عامة. تعود مفاهيمنا عن النوع الأدبي إلى الإغريق القدماء. كانت الأنواع الرئيسية الثلاثة النثر(prose)، الشعر (poetry)، والمسرح (drama)، ويمكننا أن نقسم هذه الأنواع الثلاثة إلى عدد غير محدود من الأنواع الثانوية. ومع أن جنس الرواية (the novel) كان سائدًا في أوروبا منذ قرنين، إلا أنه كان جديدًا في العالم العربي في ذلك الوقت. في بداية القرن العشرين قدم كثير من الأدباء العرب الذين درسوا في أوروبا شكل الرواية، ومن بينهم طه حسين. كتاب "الأيام" فيه العديد من خصائص السيرة الذاتية

(autobiography) ولكنـه يتميـز أيضًـا بخصائـص الروايـة. فـي الحقيقـة، يعـود الكثيـر مـن جاذبيـة الكتـاب إلـى امتـزاج النوعـين. علـى سـبيل المثـال، يسـمي المؤلف بطـل القصـة "صاحبنـا"، بالرغـم مـن أنـه مسـتلهم مـن قصـة حيـاة طـه حسـين نفسـه، ولكـن لـم يعطـه اسـم معـين لتأسـيس هويـة مسـتقلة لـه، منفصلـة عـن هويـة المؤلـف. إنـه موجـود فـي مـكان مـا بـين الحالتـين.

١. كيف يطمس استخدام "صاحبنا" في الإشارة إلى بطل الكتاب، بدلا من الاسم أو ضمير المتكلم، الخط الفاصل بين جنسي الرواية والسيرة الذاتية؟

____

____

٢. كيف يعطي جنس الرواية للمؤلف حرية في التعبير عن آرائه حول حياته وتجاربه غير موجودة في السيرة ذاتية؟

____

____

٣. هل من الممكن أن تكون الرواية أقرب إلى الحقيقة من السيرة الذاتية؟ كيف هذا؟

____

____

Themes

الخرافة

In the view of reformers like Taha Hussein, superstition was as much a cause of the backwardness of society as the deficiencies in education and widespread corruption. In particular, he believed religious organizations were infused with popular folk superstitions. In these sections above, this critique is especially pronounced. Based on your reading so far, prepare a three- to four-minute presentation on the following question:

في رأي المؤلف، خلط أهل القرية بين السحر والدين وفضلوا السحر على العلم لحل مشاكلهم. كيف أظهرت أحداث هذه الرواية الآثار السلبية للخرافات (ومنها الخرافات الدينية) على تفكير القرويين؟

Vocabulary Items

The following words are particularly useful in following Taha Hussein's narrative in this section:

saddle	رَحْل، رِحال
descendant of the Prophet	شَرِيف، شُرَفاء
descendants, line of descent	نَسْل، أَنْسال
to refuse	أَبَى، يَبَى، إِباء
female mule	بَغْلَة، بَغْلات
female camel	ناقَة، نُوق

to deduce or infer	اِسْتَنْبَطَ، يَسْتَنْبِط، اِسْتِنْباط
talismans, spells	طِلَسْم، طَلاسِم
tomes, books	سِفْر، أَسْفار
sermon, preaching	وَعَظَ، يَعِظ، وَعْظ
virtues, deeds	مَنْقَبة، مَناقِب
superficial, in appearance only	صُورِي
to reveal, foretell	أَنْبَأَ، يُنْبِئ، إِنْباء
to overstep, go beyond	تَعَدَّى، يَتَعَدَّى، تَعَدٍّ
angel	مَلاك، مَلائِكة
magicians, Magi	مَجُوس
lofty, towering	شاهِق، شَواهِق
rod	قَضِيب، قُضْبان
soldier, troop	نَفَر، أَنْفار
incense	طِيب، طِيُوب
trickster, deceiver	نَصّاب

to chatter one's teeth	اصْطَكَّ، يَصْطَكّ، اصْطِكاك
seclusion	خَلْوَة
to submit, to yield	أَذْعَنَ، يُذْعِن، إِذْعان
to borrow, go into debt	اسْتَدان، يَسْتَدِين، اسْتِدانة
ritual repetition, recitation	عَدِّيَة
to seek God's guidance	اسْتَخارَ، يَسْتَخِير، اسْتِخارَة
to become manifest	انْجَلَى، يَنْجَلِي، انْجِلاء
to ward off, protect from	اتَّقَى، يَتَّقِي، اتِّقاء
chaff	هَشِيم
to disperse, blow away	ذَرَا ، يَذْرُو
to despair	هَلِعَ، يَهْلَع، هَلَع
to draw near	أَزِفَ، يَأْزَف، أَزَف
sin, burden	وِزْر، أَوْزار
to swallow	ابْتَلَع، يَبْتَلِع، ابْتِلاع
(here) to consume food or drink	لَمَّ، يَلُمّ، لَمّ

string of prayer beads سُبْحَة، سُبْحات

Syriac سُرِيانِيَة

Unit Eight

Preparation for Reading

Author's Background

في سنة ١٩٣٨ كتب طه حسين واحدًا من أهم كتبه وأكثرها تأثيرًا وهو "مستقبل الثقافة في مصر"، وفيه، شجع على أهمية بناء مصر المستقلة، وتركيز الجهود على تأسيس جيش مستقل وقوي وتعليم حرّ ومجاني لكل المصريين. وأضاف فيه أيضا إن مصر كانت وما زالت جزء من الحضارة الغربية وليست الشرقية، وان مصادر الثقافة المصرية كانت يونانية ورومانية، وعلى هذا الأساس اعترض على حركات الوحدة العربية وشجع على أهمية التعلّم من أوروبا. وقد كان لمثل هذا الكتاب وعموم أفكاره في التعليم أثرًا واضحًا في تنصيبه وزيرًا للمعارف (وهذه الوزارة تسمى الآن التربية والتعليم).

Reading

I

وأراد الله أن يشقي سيدنا بتلميذه شقاءً غير قليل. فلم تكفه تلك الحوادث التي كانت تحدث من حين إلى حين عندما كان الشيخ يمتحن الصبي، ولم تكفه هذه النكبات المتصلة التي نشأت عن عناية الصبي بحفظ "الألفية" وغيرها من المتون، وجعلت الصبي ثقيلًا سمجًا يتعالى على أترابه وعلى سيده، ويرى لنفسه مكانة العلماء، ويعصي أوامر العريف. لم يكفه هذا كله، بل كانت نكبة أخرى لم يكن الرجل ينتظرها حقا، وكانت أشد عليه من كل النكبات الأخرى، لأنها مسته في صناعته، ذلك أن رجلا من أهل القاهرة هبط إلى المدينة في يوم من الأيام

على أنه مفتش للطريق الزراعية. وكان هذا الرجل في متوسط عمره. وكان مطربشا يتكلم الفرنسية، وكان يقول: إنه تخرج في مدرسة الفنون والصنائع. وكان خفيف الظل جذابا. فما لبث أن أحبه الناس ودعوه إلى دورهم ومجالسهم. وما لبث أن اتصلت المودة بينه وبين أبي الصبي. وكان قد رتب سيدنا في بيته يقرأ له سورة من القرآن في كل يوم، وجعل له عشرة قروش في كل شهر، وهو الأجر المرتفع الذي كان يدفعه وجوه الناس. فكان سيدنا محبًا لهذا الرجل مثنيًا عليه. ولكن رمضان أقبل، وكان الناس يجتمعون في ليالي رمضان عند رجل من أهل المدينة وجيه يعمل في التجارة. وكان سيدنا يقرأ القرآن عند هذا الرجل طوال الشهر. وكان الصبي يرافق سيدنا ويريحه من حين إلى حين بقراءة سورة أو جزء مكانه. فقرأ ذات ليلة وسمعه هذا المفتش، فقال لأبيه: إن ابنك لشديد الحاجة إلى تجويد القرآن.

قال الشيخ: سيجوده متى ذهب إلى القاهرة على شيخ من شيوخ الأزهر.

قال المفتش: فأنا أستطيع أن أجود له القرآن على قراءة حفص،[63] حتى إذا ذهب إلى الأزهر كان قد ألم بأصول التجويد، وسهل عليه أن يفرغ للقراءات السبع أو العشر أو الأربع عشرة.

قال الشيخ: وهل أنت من حملة القرآن؟

قال المفتش: ومن المجودين، ولولا أني مشغول لاستطعت أن أقرئ ابنك القرآن على الروايات جميعًا، ولكني أحب أن أخصص له ساعة في كل يوم فأقرئه رواية حفص، وأدرس له أصول الفن، وأعده بذلك للأزهر إعدادًا صحيحًا.

قال القوم: وكيف لمطربش يتكلم الفرنسية بحفظ القرآن ورواية القراءات؟

قال المفتش: أنا أزهري تقدمت في دراسة العلوم الدينية إلى مدى بعيد، ثم انصرفت عنها إلى المدارس، فتخرجت من مدرسة الفنون والصنائع.

قالوا: فاقرأ لنا شيئًا. فنزع الرجل نعليه وتربع ورتّل لهم سورة هود[64] ترتيلًا ما سمعوا مثله. فلا تسل عن إعجابهم به وإكبارهم إياه،

63. Hafs is the most common style of Qur'anic intonation in Egypt.
64. The eleventh sura of the Qur'an.

ولا تسل عما أصاب سيدنا من الحزن والغيظ، فقد قضى الرجل ليلته كأنه مصعوق.

Comprehension Questions

١. كيف وصف المفتش الذي جاء إلى القرية؟

____

____

٢. كيف تغيرت شخصية صاحبنا نتيجة لدراسته الألفية والكتب الأخرى؟

____

____

٣. كيف تعلم المفتش تجويد القرآن؟

____

____

٤. ماذا اقترح المفتش على أبي الصبي؟

____

____

٥. كيف أثر ترتيل المفتش على سيدنا؟

____

____

II

وأصبح الشيخ فأمر ابنه بأن يختلف إلى بيت المفتش في كل يوم. وفرح الصبي بهذا فرحًا شديدًا، فأعاده على أترابه في الكُتّاب وتحدث به الصبيان. ولا تسل عن مقدار ما كان يترك هذا الحديث في نفس سيدنا من الحزن، فقد نهر الصبي وأمره ألا يذكر اسم المفتش مرة في الكُتّاب.

وذهب الصبي إلى بيت المفتش واتصل ذهابه إلى هذا البيت وأقرأه المفتش «تحفة الأطفال» وشرح له أصول التجويد.

علّمه المدّ والغن والإخفاء والإدغام[65] وما يتصل بهذا كله. وكان الصبي معجبا بهذا العلم، وكان يتحدث به إلى أترابه في الكُتّاب، وكان يبين لهم أن سيدنا لا يحسن المدّ ولا يتقن الغنَّ، ولا يعرف الفرق بين المد الكلمي والحرفي، ولا بين المد المثقل والمخفّف، وكانت أصداء هذا كله تصل إلى سيدنا فتغمه وتحزنه وتخرجه أحيانًا عن طوره.

وأخذ الصبي يقرأ القرآن على المفتش من أوله، وأخذ المفتش يعلمه مواضع الوقف والوصل، وأخذ الصبي يقلد المفتش في ترتيله ويحاكي نغمه، وأخذ يقرأ القرآن على هذا النحو في الكُتّاب، وجعل أبوه يمتحنه. فإذا سمعه يقرأ على هذا النحو الجديد أعجب وطرب وأثنى على المفتش. وما كان شيء يغيظ سيدنا مثل ما كان يغيظه هذا الثناء.

وقضى الصبي سنة كاملة يتردد على هذا البيت ويقرأ القرآن على المفتش، حتى أتقن التجويد برواية حفص، وكاد يبدأ في رواية ورش[66] لولا أن حدثت حوادث وسافر الصبي إلى القاهرة.

أكان الصبي يحب الاختلاف إلى هذا البيت لأنه كان يعجب بالمفتش ولأنه كان يحرص على إتقان القرآن وتجويده وعلى أن يغيظ سيدنا

---

65. المد والغن والإخفاء والإدغام – specific elements of Qur'anic recitation.
66. Like حفص, another popular style of reciting the Qur'an.

ويظهـر التفـوق علـى أترابـه؟ نعـم! فـي الشـهرين الأولـين مـن هـذه السـنة. فأمَّـا بعـد هذيـن الشـهرين فقـد كان يجذبـه إلـى بيـت المفتـش ويحببـه فيـه شـيء آخـر ...

Comprehension Questions

١. إلى أين أرسل الشيخ ابنه؟

___

___

٢. لماذا غضب سيدنا؟

___

___

٣. بماذا أمر سيدنا صاحبنا؟

___

___

٤. ماذا قال الصبي لزملائه عن تجويد سيدنا؟

___

___

٥. لماذا لم يبدأ صاحبنا تعلم رواية ورش في بيت المفتش؟

____

____

III

كان المفتش متوسط العمر قد بلغ الأربعين إن لم يكن قد جاوزها، وكان قد تزوج من فتاة لم تبلغ السادسة عشرة، ولم يكن له ولد، ولم يكن يعمر بيته الكبير إلا هذه الفتاة وجدَّة لها قد جاوزت الخمسين، فأما حين بدأ الصبي يختلف إلى هذه الدار فقد كان يذهب ويعود دون أن يلتفت إليه أحد غير المفتش. وما هي إلا أن كثر تردد الصبي حتى أخذت الفتاة تتحدث إليه وتسأله عن نفسه وعن أمه وعن إخوته وعن داره، وأخذ الصبي يجيبها مستحييًا، ثم متبسطًا، ثم مطمئنًا، واتصلت بين هذه الفتاة وهذا الصبي مودة ساذجة كانت حلوة في نفس الصبي لذيذة الموقع في قلبه، وكانت ثقيلة على نفس هذه الشيخة، وكان المفتش يجهلها جهلًا تامًا.

وأخذ الصبي يذهب إلى دار المفتش قبل الميعاد ليظفر بساعة أو بعض ساعة يتحدث فيها إلى هذه الفتاة، وأخذت الفتاة تنتظره، حتى إذا أقبل أخذته إلى غرفتها، فجلست وأجلسته وتحدثا، وما هي إلا أن استحال الحديث إلى لعب، إلى لعب كلعب الصبيان لا أكثر ولا أقل، ولكنه كان لعبًا لذيذًا. وقص الصبي هذا كله على أمه، فضحكت ورثت للفتاة قائلة لأخت الصبي: طفلة زوجت من هذا الشيخ لا تعرف أحدًا ولا يعرفها أحد فهي ضيقة الصدر في حاجة إلى اللهو والعبث.

ومن ذلك اليوم سعت أم الصبي في التعرف إلى هذه الفتاة ودعتها إلى البيت وإلى أن تكثر التردد عليها.

Comprehension Questions

١. كم الفرق بين عمر المفتش وعمر زوجته؟

٢. من يسكن في البيت مع المفتش وزوجته؟

٣. كيف قضى صاحبنا وقته مع زوجة المفتش؟

٤. كيف فسرت أم صاحبنا الصداقة بين ابنها وزوجة المفتش؟

٥. كيف حاولت الأم أن تساعد الزوجة في التكيف مع الحياة في القرية؟

IV

وكذلك اتصلت أيام الصبي بين البيت والكُتّاب والمحكمة والمسجد وبيت المفتش ومجالس العلماء وحلقات الذكر، لا هي بالحلوة ولا هي بالمرَّة، ولكنها تحلو حينًا وتمر حينًا آخر، وتمضي فيما بين ذلك فاترة سخيفة. حتى كان يوم من الأيام ذاق الصبي فيه الألم حقا، وعرف منذ ذلك أن تلك الآلام التي كان يشقى بها ويكره من أجلها الحياة لم تكن شيئًا، وأن الدهر قادر على أن يؤلم الناس ويؤذيهم ويحبب إليهم الحياة ويهون من أمرها على نفوسهم في وقت واحد. كانت للصبي أخت هي صغرى أبناء الأسرة، كانت في الرابعة من عمرها. كانت خفيفة الروح طلقة الوجه فصيحة اللسان عذبة الحديث قوية الخيال، كانت لهو الأسرة كلها، كانت تخلو إلى نفسها ساعات طوالاً في لهو وعبث، تجلس إلى الحائط فتتحدث إليه كما تتحدث أمها إلى زائرتها، وتبعث في كل اللعب التي كانت بين يديها روحًا قويًا وتسبغ عليها شخصية. فهذه اللعبة امرأة وهذه اللعبة رجل، وهذه اللعبة فتى، وهذه اللعبة فتاة، والطفلة بين هؤلاء الأشخاص جميعًا تذهب وتجيء، وتصل بينها الأحاديث مرة في لهو وعبث، وأخرى في غيظ وغضب، ومرة ثالثة في هدوء واطمئنان. وكانت الأسرة كلها تجد لذة قوية في الاستماع إلى هذه الأحاديث والنظر إلى هذه الألوان من اللعب دون أن ترى الطفلة، أو تسمع، أو تحس أن أحدًا يرقبها.

فما هي إلا أن أقبلت بوادر عيد الأضحى في سنة من السنين، وأخذت أمّ الصبي تستعد لهذا العيد تهيئ له الدار وتعد له الخبز وألوان الفطير، وأخذ إخوة الصبي يستعدون لهذا العيد، يختلف كبارهم إلى الخياط حينًا، وإلى الحذاء حينًا آخر، ويلهو صغارهم بهذه الحركة الطارئة على الدار، فينظر صبينا إلى أولئك وهؤلاء في شيء من الفلسفة كان قد تعوَّده. فلم يكن في حاجة إلى أن يختلف إلى خيّاط أو حذاء، وما كان ميالا إلى اللهو بمثل هذه الحركات الطارئة، وإنما كان يخلو إلى نفسه ويعيش في عالم من الخيال يستمده من هذه القصص والكتب المختلفة التي كان يقرؤها فيسرف في قراءتها.

أقبلت بوادر هذا العيد، وأصبحت الطفلة ذات يوم في شيء من الفتور والهمود لم يكد يلتفت إليه أحد، والأطفال في القرى ومدن الأقاليم معرضون لهذا النوع من الإهمال، ولا سيما إذا كانت الأسرة

كثيـرة العـدد، وربـة البيـت كثيـرة العمـل. ولنسـاء القـرى ومـدن الأقاليـم فلسـفة آثمـة وعلـم ليـس أقـل منهـا إثمًـا. يشـكو الطفـل، وقلمـا تعنـي بـه أمـه ... وأي طفـل لا يشـكو! إنمـا هـو يـوم وليلـة ثـم يفيـق ويُبـلّ. فـإن عنيـت بـه أمـه فهـي تـزدري الطبيـب أو تجهلـه، وهـي تعتمـد علـى هـذا العلـم الآثـم، علـم النسـاء وأشـباه النسـاء. وعلـى هـذا النحـو فقـد صبينـا عينيـه؛ أصابـه الرمـد فأهمـل أيامًـا، ثـم دعـي الحـلاق فعالجـه علاجـا ذهـب بعينيـه. وعلـى هـذا النحـو فقـدت هـذه الطفلـة الحيـاة؛ ظلـت فاتـرة هامـدة محمومـة يومًـا ويومًـا ويومًـا، وهـي ملقـاة علـى فراشـها فـي ناحيـة مـن نواحـي الـدار، تعنـى بهـا أمهـا أو أختهـا مـن حـين إلـى حـين، تدفـع إليهـا شـيئا مـن الغـذاء، اللـه يعلـم أكان جيـدًا أم رديئـا؟ والحركـة متصلـة فـي البيـت: يهيـأ الخبـز والفطيـر فـي ناحيـة، وتنظـف المنظـرة وحجـرة الاسـتقبال فـي ناحيـة أخـرى، والصبيـان فـي لهوهـم وعبثهـم، والشـبان فـي ثيابهـم وأحذيتهـم، والشـيخ يغـدو ويـروح ويجلـس إلـى أصحابـه آخـر النهـار وأول الليـل.

Comprehension Questions

١. كيف وصف الكاتب حياة الصبي قبل مرض أخته؟

____

____

٢. لماذا كانت البنت الصغيرة مصدر فرح للعائلة كلها؟

____

____

٣. بماذا كانت تشتغل الأم في الأيام قبل مرض البنت؟

---

٤. لماذا شعرت الأم بضغط رأي القرية لإستعداد للعيد؟

---

٥. كيف فقد صاحبنا بصره؟

V

حتى إذا كان عصر اليوم الرابع وقف هذا كله فجأة. وقف وعرفت أم الصبي أن شبحًا مخيفًا يحلق على هذه الدار. ولم يكن الموت قد دخل هذه الدار من قبل، ولم تكن هذه الأمّ الحنون قد ذاقت لذع الألم الصحيح. نعم! كانت في عملها وإذا الطفلة تصيح صياحًا منكرًا، فتدع أمها كل شيء وتسرع إليها، والصياح يتصل ويزداد، فتدع أخوات الطفلة كل شيء ويسرعن إليها، والصياح يتصل ويشتد، والطفلة تتلوى وتضطرب بين ذراعي أمّها، فيدع الشيخ أصحابه ويسرع إليها. والصياح يتصل ويشتد، والطفلة ترتعد ارتعادًا منكرًا ويتقبض وجهها ويتصبب العرق عليه، فينصرف الصبيان والشبان عما هم فيه من لهو وحديث ويسرعون إليها. ولكن الصياح لا يزداد إلا شدة، وإذا هذه الأسرة كلها واجمة مبهوتة محيطة بالطفلة لا تدري ماذا تصنع! ... ويتصل ذلك ساعة وساعة. فأما الشيخ فقد أخذه الضعف الذي

يأخذ الرجال في مثل هذه الحال فينصرف مهمهما بصلوات وآيات من القرآن يتوسل بها إلى الله. وأما الشبان والصبيان فيتسللون في شيء من الوجوم لا يكادون ينسون ما كانوا فيه من لهو وحديث ولا يكادون يستأنفونه. هم كذلك حيارى في الدار! وأمهم جالسة واجمة تحدق في ابنتها وتسقيها ألوانًا من الدواء لا أعرف ما هي. والصياح متصل مشتد، والاضطراب مستمر متزايد.

ما كنت أحسب أن في الأطفال ولما يتجاوزوا الرابعة قوة تعدل هذه القوة. وتأتي ساعة العشاء وقد مدت المائدة، مدتها كبرى أخوات الصبي، وأقبل الشيخ وبنوه فجلسوا إليها. ولكن صياح الطفلة متصل فلا تُمَدُّ يد إلى طعام، وإنما يتفرقون جميعا وترفع المائدة كما مدّت. والطفلة تصيح وتضطرب، وأمها تحدق إليها حينًا وتبسط يدها إلى السماء حينًا آخر، وقد كشفت عن رأسها وما كان من عادتها أن تفعل! ولكن أبواب السماء كانت قد أغلقت في ذلك اليوم، فقد سبق القضاء بما لا بد منه، فيستطيع الشيخ أن يتلو القرآن، وتستطيع هذه الأم أن تتضرع. ومن غريب الأمر أن أحدًا من هؤلاء الناس جميعًا لم يفكر في الطبيب. وتقدم الليل وأخذ صياح الفتاة يهدأ، وأخذ صوتها يخفت، وأخذ اضطرابها يخف، وخيل إلى هذه الأمّ التعسة أن قد سمع الله لها ولزوجها، وأن قد أخذت الأزمة تنحل. وفي الحق أنَّ الأزمة كانت قد أخذت تنحل، وأن الله كان قد رأف بهذه الطفلة، وأن خفوت الصوت وهدوء هذا الاضطراب كانا آيتي هذه الرأفة. تنظر الأم إلى ابنتها فيخيل إليها أنها ستنام، ثم تنظر فإذا هدوء متصل لا صوت ولا حركة، وإنما هو نفس خفيف شديد الخفة يتردَّد بين شفتين مفتحتين قليلا، ثم ينقطع هذا النفس وإذا الطفلة قد فارقت الحياة. ماذا كانت علتها؟ كيف ذهبت بحياتها هذه العلة؟ الله وحده يعلم هذا.

Comprehension Questions

١. ماذا حدث في اليوم الرابع وغير سلوك الأم تجاه ابنتها الصغرى؟

____

____

٢. كيف تعامل الأولاد مع مرض البنت؟

____

____

٣. هل فقدت هذه العائلة طفلًا قبل هذا؟

____

____

٤. كيف فسرت الأم هدوء الطفلة تدريجيًا؟

____

____

٥. ماذا كان السبب الحقيقي لهدوئها؟

____

____

Comprehension Exercise

Are the following statements true (صحيح) or false (خطأ) and why?

١. نشأت صداقة قوية بين سيدنا والمفتش.

____

٢. بالرغم من معرفته الجديدة، ظل صاحبنا متواضعًا.

____

٣. غضب سيدنا عندما أثنى أبو صاحبنا على المفتش.

____

٤. تتفوق مهارات سيدنا في التجويد على قدرات المفتش.

____

٥. نشأت بين الصبي وزوجة المفتش صداقة ساذجة.

____

٦. الاستعدادات للعيد كانت صعبة وثقيلة على نساء القرية.

____

٧. فقد صاحبنا بصره في حريق في البيت.

____

٨. ماتت أخت الصبي الصغيرة فجأة وبهدوء في نومها.

____

٩. كانت الأخت الصغيرة أول فرد في الأسرة يموت طفلًا.

____

١٠. أعتبر صاحبنا موت أخته رحمة من الله.

____

Interpreting the Text

A. Answer the following questions in complete Arabic sentences, based on your interpretation of what you have read so far:

١. لماذا كانت نتائج التعلم سلبية في حياة صاحبنا؟ ماذا افتقده في تعليمه؟

____

____

٢. ما هي أكبر دوافع صاحبنا لتعلم التجويد؟

____

____

٣. كيف أثر الزواج في سن مبكرة من رجل أكبر منها في العمر على حياة زوجة المفتش الاجتماعية؟

____

____

٤. ماذا كان رأي الناس في القرية في الطب والأطباء؟

____

____

٥. كيف حاولت العائلة فهم مرض وموت البنت؟ على أي أساس؟

____

____

B. How would you interpret the following lines from the text in terms of their implications and reflections?

١. قال القوم: وكيف لمطربش يتكلم الفرنسية بحفظ القرآن ورواية القراءات؟

____

____

٢. طفلة زوجت من هذا الشيخ لا تعرف أحدًا ولا يعرفها أحد، فهي ضيقة الصدر في حاجة إلى اللهو والعبث.

____

____

٣. وهي تعتمد على هذا العلم الآثم؛ علم النساء وأشباه النساء.

---

٤. ما كنت أحسب أن في الأطفال ولما يتجاوزوا الرابعة قوةً تعدل هذه القوة.

---

٥. ومن غريب الأمر أن أحدًا من هؤلاء الناس جميعًا لم يفكر في الطبيب.

---

٦. ماذا كانت علتها؟ كيف ذهبت بحياتها هذه العلة؟ الله وحده يعلم هذا.

Cultural and Historical Background

1. The "tarbush" hat that the inspector wears is the Egyptian name for the type of headgear more commonly known in the west as a *fez*. The Moroccan city name refers to the place where the red dye for the hats was manufactured, but it was the Ottoman Empire that popularized the fez. Replacing the traditional tur-

ban with the fez was part of modernizing reforms in the 1800s, and as such, a fez, or tarbush, was a sign of being an important official in Ottoman-controlled Egypt. Because of its association with the old elite, the tarbush was banned by Gamal Abd al-Nasser in 1958. The amazement of the guests in the first scene at the inspector's knowledge of the Qur'an is due to the association of the tarbush with the modern, more secular elite. As the inspector explains, he has had both a traditional religious and a modern technical education.

2. The "readings" (قراءات) of the Qur'an that the inspector is teaching the boy refer to the sets of rules for pronouncing the Qur'an, including such things as intonation, pauses, elongation of sounds. There are ten recognized schools of reciting, of which that of Hafs 'an 'Asim ('Hafs the student of 'Asim,' 706–96), the first one that the inspector teaches, is by the far the most popular. The most popular text of the Qur'an is the 1924 Cairo edition, containing additional symbols for guiding intonation according to the Hafs recitation. The second version that the inspector planned to teach him was that of Warsh 'an Naafi' (Warsh, the student of Naafi'), a contemporary of Hafs from Egypt. The Warsh reading is most popular in Africa and Yemen. Differences between them are very slight, and by the implication of the youth's criticism, not well known by "Our Master."
3. The operation that blinded the youth was carried out by the local barber to reduce swelling on his eyes. This was a common practice in the early twentieth century, as the barber would be the person skilled with knives. In many parts of Africa and the Middle East, barbers still perform "surgery," often with disastrous results. Female circumcision, or genital mutilation, was often done by barbers.

Analyzing Elements of Literature

Fiction (الأدب الروائي)

يصعب تعريف مفهوم "fiction" بأي لغة. في اللغة العربية، يمكن تسمية هذا النوع من الأدب بالأدب القصصي أو الأدب الروائي. لكن الأدب الروائي قد يعتمد بشكل كبير على تصوير الواقع. على سبيل المثال، قال الكاتب صنع الله إبراهيم إن الرواية التي كتبها عن بناء السد العالي كانت فيها من الحقيقة أكثر من المقالات التي كتبها عن نفس الموضوع في الصحف الحكومية. من سمات "fiction" أنه مفتوح للتأويل وأن المؤلف لا يدعي تقديم الحقيقة فقط. كانت رواية "الأيام" من أول وأهم الكتب التي تطمس الخط الفاصل بين الخيال والسيرة الذاتية.

١. ما هي توقّعاتك من قراءة رواية، وكيف تختلف هذه التوقّعات من قراءة سيرة ذاتية؟

____

____

٢. هل تعتقد أن كل الكتابات غير الروائية (non-fiction) أقرب عن الحقيقة من الأدب الروائي؟

____

____

٣. ما هي بعض إيجابيات اختيار كتابة قصة حياة في إطار روائي (fiction) بدلا من إطار غير روائي (non-fiction)؟

____

____

Themes

الطب

الطب هو واحد من أبرز المواضيع التي يستعملها طه حسين لتوضيح مشكلة الجهل في الريف المصري. منذ قرون كان العرب رواد العلوم الطبية، لكن في بداية القرن عشرين ظلت أساليبهم عالقة في العصور القديمة. رأى طه حسين الأضرار التي سببها الجهل بالعلوم الطبية إشارة إلى نتائج العمق في التقاليد في المجتمع الريفي.

Based on what you have read in this section, please prepare a two- to three-minute presentation on Taha Hussein's use of medical issues to highlight the adherence to tradition and custom instead of science as a problem in rural development:

كيف كشفت الأزمات الصحية في هذه القرية وردود الأفعال عليها عن رؤية مغلوطة للطب والصحة؟

Vocabulary Items

The following words are particularly useful in following Taha Hussein's narrative in this section:

to make miserable, humiliate	شَقَى، يَشْقُو، شَقْو
text	مَتْن، مُتُون
ugly, disgusting	سَمُجَ، يَسْمُج، سَمْج
one who wears the tarbush (a fez hat); a sign of importance	مُطَرْبَش

chant in a musical manner	رَتَّلَ، يُرَتِّل، تَرْتيل
rage, anger	غَيْظ
to scold, rebuke	نَهَرَ، يَنْهَر، نَهْر
echo	صَدى، أَصْدَاء
to pain, cause grief	غَمَّ، يَغُمّ، غَمّ
to praise	أَثْنَى، يُثْنِي
with awkwardness, shyness	مُسْتَحَيِيًا
at length, in detail	مُتَبَسِّطًا
to pity	رَثَى، يَرْثُو، رَثْو
languid, lazy	فاتِر
simple, empty	سَخِيف، سِخاف
the passage of time	دَهْر، دُهور
to amuse, delight	لَها، يَلْهُو، لَهْو
to clothe, imbue (with)	أَسْبَغَ، يُسْبِغ، إِسْباغ
to do something to excess	أَسْرَفَ، يُسْرِف، إِسْراف

criminal, wicked	آثِم، أَثَمَة
ophthalmia, inflammation of the eyes	الرَّمَد
lifeless, still	هامِد
bad	رَدِيء
tenderhearted	حَنُون
to tremble	ارْتَعَدَ، يَرْتَعِد، ارْتِعاد
stunned, shocked	واجِم
perplexed, aghast	مَبْهُوت
to mumble, murmur	هَمْهَمَ، يُهَمْهِم، هَمْهَمَة
confused (plural)	حَيْران، حَيارَى
to plead, beg	تَضَرَّعَ، يَتَضَرَّع، تَضَرُّع
defect, complaint	عِلَّة

Unit Nine

Preparation for Reading

Author's Background

كتب طه حسين خلال حياته أكثر من ستين كتابًا، ستة فقط منها كانت روايات، بما في ذلك "الأيام". وترجم الأعمال الأدبية من الفرنسية واليونانية إلى العربية. ولم تقتصر أعماله على الأدب والترجمة فقط وإنما قام بتحرير عدة صحف ونشر أكثر من ألف مقال. وعلى الرغم من أنه لم يفز بجائزة نوبل، إلا أنه رشح لها أكثر من مرة. ولقد أكسبته كل هذه الإنجازات، إلى جانب عمله عميدًا لكلية الآداب، لقب "عميد الأدب العربي" المرموق.

Reading

I

وهنا يرتفع صياح آخر ويتصل ويشتد. وهنا يظهر اضطراب آخر ويتصل ويشتد. ولكنه ليس صياح الطفلة ولا اضطرابها، وإنما هو صياح هذه الأم وقد رأت الموت، واضطرابها وقد أحست الثكل. وإذا الشبان والصبيان قد فزعوا إلى أمّهم وسبقهم إليها الشيخ. وإذا هي في جزع وهلع ينطق لسانها بألفاظ لا صلة بينها ويقطع الدمع صوتها تقطيعًا، وإذا هي تلطم خديها في عنف متصل، وزوجها ماثل أمامها لا ينطق لسانه بحرف وإنما تنهمر دموعه انهمارًا. وإذا الجارات والجيران قد سمعوا هذا الصياح فأقبلوا مسرعين. فأما الشيخ فينصرف إلى الرجال يتقبل عزاءهم في قوة وجلد. وأما الشبان والصبيان فيتفرقون في الدار، قد قست قلوب بعضهم فنام، ورقّت قلوب بعضهم فسهر. وأما

الأم ففيما هي فيه من جزع وهلع! أمامها ابنتها هامدة جامدة، تولول وتخمش وجهها وتصك صدرها، ومن حولها بناتها وجاراتها يصنعن صنيعها يولولن ويخمشن الوجوه ويصككن الصدور حتى ينقضي الليل كله.

وما أشد نكر هذه الساعة التي أقبل فيها بعض الناس واحتملوا الطفلة ومضوا بها إلى حيث لا تعود. كان ذلك اليوم يوم الأضحى، وكانت الدار قد هيئت للعيد. وكانت الضحايا قد أعدت. فياله من يوم! ويا لها من ضحايا! ويا نكرها من ساعة حين عاد الشيخ إلى داره مع الظهر وقد وارى ابنته في التراب!

منذ ذلك اليوم اتصلت الأواصر بين الحزن وبين هذه الأسرة. فما هي إلا أشهر حتى فقد الشيخ أباه الهرم. وما هي إلا أشهر أخرى حتى فقدت أم الصبي أمّها الفانية. إنما هو حداد متصل وألم يقفو بعضه بعضا، منه اللاذع ومنه الهادئ. حتى كان هذا اليوم المنكر الذي لم تعرف الأسرة يومًا مثله، والذي طبع حياتها بطابع من الحزن لم يفارقها، والذي ابيض له شعر الأبوين جميعًا، والذي قضى على هذه الأم أن تلبس السواد إلى آخر أيامها، وألا تذوق للفرح طعمًا، ولا تضحك إلاّ بكت إثر ضحكها، ولا تنام حتى تريق بعض الدموع، ولا تفيق من نومها حتى تريق دموعا أخرى، ولا تطعم فاكهة حتى تطعم منها الفقراء والصبيان، ولا تبتسم لعيد، ولا تستقبل يوم سرور إلا وهي كارهة راغمة.

كان هذا اليوم يوم ٢١ أغسطس من سنة ١٩٠٢. وكان الصيف منكرًا في هذه السنة. وكان وباء الكوليرا قد هبط إلى مصر ففتك بأهلها فتكا ذريعًا: ودمر مدنًا وقرى، ومحا أسرًا كاملة، وكان سيدنا قد أكثر من الحجب وكتابة المخلفات، وكانت المدارس والكتاتيب قد أقفلت، وكان الأطباء ورسل مصلحة الصحة قد انبثوا في الأرض ومعهم أدواتهم وخيامهم يحجزون فيها المرضى، وكان الهلع قد ملأ النفوس واستأثر بالقلوب، وكانت الحياة قد هانت على الناس، وكانت كل أسرة تتحدث بما أصاب الأسر الأخرى وتنتظر حظها من المصيبة، وكانت أمّ الصبي في هلع مستمر، وكانت تسأل نفسها ألف مرة في كل يوم بمن تنزل النازلة من أبنائها وبناتها! وكان لها ابن في الثامنة عشرة جميل المنظر رائع الطلعة، نجيب ذكي القلب، وكان أنجب الأسرة وأذكاها وأرقها

قلبا، وأصفاها طبعا، وأبرَّها بأمّه، وأرأفها بأبيه، وأرفقها بصغار إخوته وأخواته، وكان مبتهجًا أبدًا. وكان قد ظفر بشهادة البكالوريا وانتسب إلى مدرسة الطب وأخذ ينتظر آخر الصيف ليذهب إلى القاهرة، فلما كان هذا الوباء، اتصل بطبيب المدينة وأخذ يرافقه، ويقول إنه يتمرن على صناعته، حتى كان يوم ٢٠ أغسطس.

Comprehension Questions

١. كيف عبرت الأم والنساء عن حزنهن إثر موت البنت؟

____

____

٢. من مات في الأسرة بعد البنت الصغيرة؟

____

____

٣. كيف تغيرت حياة الأم اليومية بعد وفاة ابنتها؟

____

____

٤. ماذا كانت الأزمة الكبيرة في صيف ١٩٠٢؟

____

____

٥. لماذا بدأ الابن مرافقة الطبيب في عمله؟

____

____

II

أقبل الشاب آخر هذا اليوم كعادته باسمًا، فلاطف أمه وداعبها وهدأ من روعها وقال: لم تصب المدينة اليوم بأكثر من عشرين إصابة وقد أخذت وطأة الوباء تخف. ولكنه مع ذلك شكا من بعض الغثيان وخرج إلى أبيه فجلس إليه وحدثه كعادته، ثم ذهب إلى أصحابه فرافقهم إلى حيث كان يذهب معهم في كل يوم عند شاطئ الإبراهيمية. فلما كان أول الليل عاد وقضى ساعة في ضحك وعبث مع إخوته، وفي هذه الليلة زعم لأهل البيت جميعًا أن في أكل الثوم وقاية من الكوليرا، وأكل الثوم وأخذ كبار إخوته وصغارهم بالأكل منه وحاول أن يقنع أبويه بذلك فلم يوفق.

وكانت الدار هادئة مغرقة في النوم كبارها وصغارها وحيوانها عندما انتصف الليل. ولكن صيحة غريبة ملأت هذا الجو الهادئ، فهبّ لها القوم جميعًا. فأمَّا الشيخ وزوجته فكانا في هذا الدهليز المنبسط الذي تظله السماء يدعوان ابنهما باسمه. وأما الشبان من أهل الدار فكانوا يثبون من فراشهم مسرعين إلى حيث الصوت. وأما الصبيان فكانوا يجلسون يحكون أعينهم بأيديهم يحاولون أن يتبينوا في شيء من الهلع من أين يأتي الصوت وماذا كانت الحركة الغريبة!

وكان مصدر هذا كله صوت هذا الفتى وهو يعالج القيء، وكان الفتى قد قضى ساعة أو ساعتين يخرج من الحجرة على أطراف قدميه ويمضي إلى الخلاء ليقيء مجتهدا ألا يوقظ أحدًا. حتى إذا بلغت العلة منه أقصاها لم يملك نفسه ولم يستطع أن يقيء في لطف، فسمع أبواه هذه الحشرجة ففزعا لها، وفزع معهما أهل الدار جميعًا.

إذن فقد أصيب الشاب ووجد الوباء طريقه إلى الدار، وعرفت أمّ الفتى بأي أبنائها تنزل النازلة. لقد كان الشيخ في تلك الليلة خليقًا بالإعجاب حقًا. كان هادئًا رزينًا مروّعًا مع ذلك، ولكنه يملك نفسه

وكان في صوته شيء يدل على أن قلبه مفطور، وعلى أنه مع ذلك جلد مستعد لاحتمال النازلة. آوى ابنه إلى حجرته وأمر بالفصل بينه وبين بقية إخوته، وخرج مسرعًا فدعا جارين من جيرانه، وما هي إلا ساعة حتى عاد ومعه الطبيب.

وفي أثناء ذلك كانت أمّ الفتى مروّعة جلدة مؤمنة تعنى بابنها، حتى إذا أمهله القيء خرجت إلى الدهليز فرفعت يدها ووجهها إلى السماء وفنيت في الدعاء والصلاة، حتى تسمع حشرجة القيء فتسرع إلى ابنها تسنده إلى صدرها وتأخذ رأسه بين يديها، ولسانها مع ذلك لا يكف عن الدعاء والابتهال.

ولم تستطع أن تحول بين الصبيان والشبان وبين المريض، فملأوا عليه الحجرة وأحاطوا به واجمين، وهو يداعب أمّه كلما أمهله القيء، ويعبث مع صغار إخوته، حتى إذا جاء الطبيب فوصف ما وصف وأمر بما أمر وانصرف على أن يعود مع الصبح، لزمت أم الفتى حجرة ابنها وجلس الشيخ قريبًا من هذه الحجرة واجمًا لا يدعو ولا يصلي ولا يجيب أحدًا من الذين كانوا يتحدثون إليه.

Comprehension Questions

١. كيف دخل المرض بيت العائلة؟

____

____

٢. ماذا وصف الشاب للوقاية من الكوليرا؟

____

____

٣. ما هي أولى أعراض مرض الشاب؟

____

____

٤. كيف أمضت الأم وقتها في أثناء مرض ابنها؟

____

____

٥. لماذا كان من الصعب إبعاد الشاب المريض عن باقي أفراد الأسرة؟

____

____

III

وأقبل الصبح بعد لأي، وأخذ الفتى يشكو ألما في ساقيه. وأقبلت إليه أخواته يدلكن له ساقيه، وهو يشكو صائحا مرة كاتما ألمه مرة أخرى، القيء يجهده ويخلع في الوقت نفسه قلب أبويه. وقضت الأسرة كلها صباحًا لم تقض مثله قط: صباحًا واجمًا مظلمًا فيه شيء مفزع مروع. فأما خارج الدار فكان يزدحم بالناس أقبلوا إلى الشيخ يواسونه. وأما داخل الدار فكان يزدحم بالنساء أقبلن يواسين أمَّ الفتى. وكان الشيخ وزوجه عن أولئك وهؤلاء في شغل. وكان الطبيب يتردد بين ساعة وساعة. وكان الفتى قد طلب أن يبرق إلى أخيه الأزهري في القاهرة وإلى عمه في أعلى الإقليم. وكان يطلب الساعة من حين إلى حين ينظر فيها كأنه يتعجل الوقت، وكأنه يشفق أن يموت دون أن يرى أخاه الشاب وعمه الشيخ. يا لها من ساعة منكرة، هذه الساعة الثالثة من الخميس ٢١ أغسطس سنة ١٩٠٢.

انصرف الطبيب من الحجرة يائسًا، وكأنه قد أسرَّ إلى رجلين من أقرب أصحاب الشيخ إليه بأن الفتى يحتضر، فأقبل الرجلان حتى دخلا الحجرة على الفتى ومعه أمه. ظهرت في هذا اليوم لأول مرة في حياتها أمام الرجال.

والفتى في سريره يتضور: يقف ثم يلقي بنفسه، ثم يجلس ثم يطلب الساعة، ثم يعالج القيء، وأمه واجمة، والرجلان يواسيانه وهو يجيبهما: لست خيرًا من النبي. أليس النبي قد مات! ويدعو أباه يريد أن يواسيه فلا يجيبه الشيخ. وهو يقوم ويقعد ويلقي نفسه في السرير مرة ومن دون السرير مرة أخرى، وصبينا منزوٍ في ناحية من هذه الحجرة، واجم كئيب دهش يمزق الحزن قلبه تمزيقًا.

ثم ألقى الفتى نفسه على السرير وعجز عن الحركة، وأخذ يئن أنينًا يخفت من حين إلى حين. وكان صوت هذا الأنين يبعد شيئًا فشيئًا. وإن الصبي لينسى كل شيء قبل أن ينسى هذه الأنّة الأخيرة التي أرسلها الفتى نحيلة ضئيلة طويلة ثم سكت.

في هذه اللحظة نهضت أم الفتى وقد انتهى صبرها ووهى جلدها، فلم تكد تقف حتى هوت أو كادت، وأسندها الرجلان فتمالكت نفسها وخرجت من الحجرة مطرقة ساعية في هدوء، حتى إذا جاوزتها انبعثت من صدرها شكاة، لا يذكرها الصبي إلا انخلع لها قلبه انخلاعا. واضطرب الفتى قليلًا ومرّت في جسمه رعدة تبعها سكوت الموت. وأقبل الرجلان إليه فهيآه وعصباه وألقيا على وجهه لثامًا، وخرجا إلى الشيخ. ثم ذكر أن الصبي منزو في ناحية من نواحي الحجرة، فعاد أحدهما إليه فجذبه جذبًا وهو ذاهل حتى انتهى به إلى مكان بين الناس فوضعه فيه كما يوضع الشيء.

Comprehension Questions

١. ماذا طلب الشاب قبل وفاته؟

____

____

٢. كيف قضى صاحبنا وقت موت أخيه؟

---

٣. كيف حضّر صديقا الأب جثة الشاب للدفن؟

---

٤. ماذا قال الشاب عن الموت قبل وفاته؟

---

٥. ماذا فعل الرجل بعد أن تذكر أن الصبي يجلس في الحجرة؟

IV

وما هي إلا ساعة أو بعض ساعة حتى هيئ الفتى للدفن وخرج الرجال به على أعناقهم.

فيا للقضاء! ما كادوا يبلغون به باب الدار حتى كان أول من لقي النعش هذا العم الشيخ الذي كان الفتى يتمهل الموت دقائق ليراه.

من ذلك اليوم استقر الحزن العميق في هذه الدار وأصبح إظهار الابتهاج أو السرور بأي حادث من الحوادث شيئا ينبغي أن يتجنبه الشبان والأطفال جميعًا.

من ذلك اليوم تعود الشيخ ألاّ يجلس إلى غدائه ولا إلى عشائه حتى يذكر ابنه ويبكيه ساعة أو بعض ساعة وأمامه امرأته تعينه على البكاء، ومن حوله أبناؤه وبناته يحاولون تعزية هذين الأبوين فلا يبلغون منهما شيئا فيجهشون جميعًا بالبكاء.

من ذلك اليوم تعودت هذه الأسرة أن تعبر النيل إلى مقر الموتى من حين إلى حين، وكانت من قبل ذلك تعيب الذين يزورون الموتى.

ومن ذلك اليوم تغيرت نفسية صبينا تغيرًا تامًا. عرف الله حقًا. وحرص على أن يتقرب إليه بكل ألوان التقرب: بالصدقة حينًا وبالصلاة حينًا آخر وبتلاوة القرآن مرة ثالثة. ولقد شهد الله ما كان يدفعه إلى ذلك خوف ولا إشفاق ولا إيثار للحياة، ولكنه كان يعلم أن أخاه الشاب كان من أبناء المدارس، وكان يقصر في أداء واجباته الدينية، فكان الصبي يأتي ما يأتي من ضروب العبادة يريد أن يحط عن أخيه بعض السيئات. كان أخوه في الثامنة عشرة من عمره، وكان الصبي قد سمع من الشيوخ أن الصلاة والصوم فرض على الإنسان متى بلغ الخامسة عشرة. فقدّر الصبي في نفسه أن أخاه مدين لله بالصوم والصلاة ثلاثة أعوام كاملة، وفرض الصبي على نفسه ليصلين الخمس في كل يوم مرتين: مرة لنفسه ومرة لأخيه! وليصومنّ من السنة شهرين: شهرًا لنفسه وشهرًا لأخيه، وليكتمن ذلك عن أهله جميعا وليجعلن ذلك عهدًا بينه وبين الله خاصة، وليطعمن فقيرًا أو يتيمًا مما تصل إليه يده من طعام أو فاكهة قبل أن يأخذ بحظه منه. وشهد الله لقد وفى الصبي بهذا العهد أشهرًا، وما غيرّ سيرته هذه إلا حين ذهب إلى الأزهر.

Comprehension Questions

١. ماذا أصبحت عادة الأب قبل كل وجبة بعد وفاة ابنه؟

____

____

٢. كيف تغيرت الحالة النفسية للأسرة بعد فقدان الشاب؟

---

٣. كيف تغير أداء صاحبنا لواجباته الدينية بعد وفاة أخيه؟

---

٤. في رأي صاحبنا، لماذا أهمل أخوه فروضه الدينية؟

---

٥. كيف حسب الصبي دين صلاة وصيام أخيه؟

V

من ذلك اليوم عرف الصبي أرق الليل. فكم أنفق سواد الليل كاملًا يفكر في أخيه أو يقرأ سورة الإخلاص آلاف المرات ثم يهب ذلك كله لأخيه، أو ينظم شعرًا على نحو هذا الشعر الذي كان يقرؤه في كتب القصص يذكر فيه حزنه وألمه لفقد أخيه، معنيًا بألا يفرغ من قصيدة حتى يصلي في آخرها على النبي، واهبًا ثواب هذه الصلاة لأخيه.

نعم! ومن ذلك اليوم عرف الصبي الأحلام المروعة، فقد كانت علة أخيه تتمثل له في كل ليلة، واستمرت الحال كذلك أعوامًا. ثم تقدمت به السن وعمل فيه الأزهر عمله، فأخذت علة أخيه تتمثل له من حين إلى حين، وأصبح فتًى ورجلًا، وتقلبت به أطوار الحياة، وإنه لعلى ما هو عليه من وفاء لهذا الأخ، يذكره ويراه فيما يرى النائم مرة في الأسبوع على أقل تقدير.

ولقد تعزى عن هذا الفتى إخوته وأخواته، ونسيه من نسيه من أصحابه وأترابه، وأخذت ذكراه لا تزور أباه الشيخ إلا لمامًا، ولكن اثنين يذكرانه أبدًا وسيذكرانه أبدًا أول الليل من كل يوم، هما: أمُّه وهذا الصبي.

Comprehension Questions

١. هل كان الصبي ينام جيدًا بعد وفاة أخيه؟

____

____

٢. كيف حافظ صاحبنا على ذكرى أخيه المرحوم؟

____

____

٣. ماذا رأى صاحبنا في أحلامه؟

____

____

٤. أين تعلم الصبي أنواع الشعر التي كتبها بعد موت أخيه؟

____

____

٥. كم شخصًا استمر في ذكر الأخ لسنوات بعد موته؟

____

____

Comprehension Exercise

Are the following statements true (صحيح) or false (خطأ) and why?

١. بعد وفاة أخته الصغيرة، عادت الحياة في أسرة الصبي إلى طبيعتها كما كانت من قبل.

____

٢. دمر الوباء مدن وقرى كاملة في مصر.

____

٣. كان الأخ الأكبر يخشى مرافقة الطبيب في زياراته عبر القرية بسبب المرض.

____

٤. ظل الأب والأم هادئان وسعيدان أثناء مرض ابنهما.

___

٥. ساعد بعض أصدقاء الأب الأسرة خلال وفاة الابن وبعدها.

___

٦. ترك الناس صاحبنا في الحجرة وحده عندما خرجوا للاستعداد للدفن.

___

٧. أهمل صاحبنا واجباته الدينية بعد وفاة أخيه.

___

٨. ساد حزن ثقيل ودائم على بيت صاحبنا إثر موت الابن.

___

٩. بعد أن ذهب إلى الأزهر، نسي صاحبنا أخاه المرحوم.

___

١٠. تغيرت حياة الأم بعد فقدان ابنها أكثر من حياة الأب، كما يبدو في هذا النص.

___

Interpreting the text

A. Answer the following questions in complete Arabic sentences, based on your interpretation of what you have read so far:

١. ما هو مستوى الوعي الطبي حتى بين المتخصصين في هذا الوقت؟ كيف يعكس مصير الشاب هذا؟

____

____

٢. ما هي العبادات الدينية الجديدة التي بدأ الصبي يمارسها؟ ما هو موقف الراوي منها؟

____

____

٣. في رأيكم كيف عكس رد فعل الصبي على الوباء معتقداته حول المرض والموت؟

____

____

٤. لماذا أثّر موت الشاب على الأسرة بشكل مختلف عن موت الفتاة الصغيرة؟

____

____

٥. لماذا ظل صاحبنا أكثر تضررًا من وفاة أخيه من أفراد أسرته الآخرين؟ ماذا يمكن أن نستنتج عنه؟

____

____

B. What are the implications of the following lines from the text in terms of the overall themes?

١. ما كان يدفعه إلى ذلك [الواجبات الدينية] خوف ولا إشفاق ولا إيثار للحياة، ولكنه كان يعلم أن أخاه الشاب كان من أبناء المدارس، وكان يقصر في أداء واجباته الدينية؛

____

____

٢. وكان سيدنا قد أكثر من الحجب وكتابة المخلفات،

____

____

٣. لست خيرًا من النبي، أليس النبي قد مات!

____

____

٤. فيا للقضاء! ما كادوا يبلغون به باب الدار حتى كان أول من لقي النعش هذا العم الشيخ الذي كان الفتى يتمهل الموت دقائق ليراه.

____

____

٥. من ذلك اليوم تعودت هذه الأسرة أن تعبر النيل إلى مقر الموتى من حين إلى حين، وكانت من قبل ذلك تعيب الذين يزورون الموتى.

____

____

Cultural and Historical Background

1. The epidemic referred to in the story is the 1902 cholera epidemic (part of the 1899–1923 pandemic), which affected over two thousand cities and villages in Egypt and killed approximately 35,000 people. It was the sixth cholera outbreak in Egypt since the mid 1800s. Egypt was especially vulnerable due to its reliance on a single source of water (the Nile) and extensive irrigation. Modern sanitation has largely eliminated cholera, but using unclean water sources can still spread it. This serves for Taha Hussein as another example of lack of education being the cause of suffering.
2. The immediate burial that follows the son's death differs from western customs that may involve several days of "viewing" the body in a casket before burial. The purpose of the quick burial is to avoid embalming the body, which is *haram* in Islam. This is avoided if the body is buried on the day of death. Cremation is

also prohibited in Islam. In an epidemic like the one described in this scene, quick burial is even more urgent as the body carries disease.

3. The sura that the youth repeats thousands of times in the last section is Surat al-Ikhlas, the 112th sura of the Qur'an. Although it is only four *ayat* (verses), it is said in a Hadith to be worth a third of the Qur'an because it is the most succinct statement of God's oneness. Repeating Surat al-Ikhlas is believed by many Muslims to rid one's house of suffering.

Analyzing Elements of Literature

Plot (الحبكة)

حبكة القصة من أهم عواملها. هذا المصطلح يشير إلى أحداث القصة وترتيبها، وهذا يختلف عن السرد الذي يشير إلى كيفية رواية الأحداث. عادة ما تكون الحبكة عبارة عن سلسلة متصلة من الأحداث ذات بنية منطقية لبناء العواطف أو الإثارة أو لتعليم درس. في العديد من القصص، وخاصة القصص الحداثية، هناك فرق كبير بين الحبكة والسرد. تميل القصص "الواقعية" إلى قلة الاختلافات بين هذين العنصرين. في بعض القصص تكون الشخصية والزمان والمكان والموضوعات أكثر أهمية من تسلسل الأحداث.

Having now read a great deal of this novel, answer the following questions about the role of "plot" in *The Days*:

١. كيف تتناسب أهمية الحبكة في هذه الرواية مع العناصر الأخرى (الشخصية، المكان والزمان، والموضوع، وما إلى ذلك)؟

___

___

٢. هل تتوقعون أن تكونٍ الحبكة في عمل يتناول سيرة ذاتية مثل هذه الرواية أكثر تسلسلًا من القصص الخيالية أم أقل؟ لماذا؟

____

____

٣. ما هو التحول أو التغيير الرئيسي الذي يحدث على مدار الرواية؟ كيف تشكل الأحداث هذا التغيير؟

____

____

٤. هل هناك أحداث مهمة في القصة كانت مفاجئة لكم؟ ما هو تأثير هذا؟

____

____

٥. في أحيان كثيرة، تحتوي الحبكة الأدبية على سؤال مركزي يجب الإجابة عليه من خلال أحداث القصة. ما هو السؤال الرئيسي لهذه القصة في رأيكم؟

____

____

Themes

الشعور بالذنب

ترتبط أحداث الوباء بالشعور الذنب بين أفراد العائلة والقرية كلها وخاصة في وجدان صاحبنا. هذا الشعور لا يعود إلى أخطاء طبية أو صحية ارتكبها الشخص وأدت إلى انتشار المرض، بل إن هذا الشعور بالذنب نابع من أسباب دينية وتصور التقصير في الواجبات الدينية.

Based on what you have read and your knowledge of the author's positions on education, health and tradition, prepare a one- to two-page response to the following question:

كيف يعكس شعور الصبي بالذنب وإسناد اللوم في وفاة أخيه الأفكار التقليدية عن السبب والنتيجة؟ كمصلح مهتم بإصلاح الصحة والتعليم، كيف استخدم طه حسين هذه العوامل من أجل نقد مجتمعه؟

Vocabulary Items

The following words are particularly useful in following Taha Hussein's narrative in this section:

the loss of a child (esp. by a mother)	ثَكَل، ثُكْل
to slap	لَطَمَ، يَلْطِم، لَطْم
to be poured out (tears)	انْهَمَرَ، يَنْهَمِر، انْهِمار
to soften	رَقَّ، يَرِقّ، رِقَّة
to scratch	خَمَشَ، يَخْمِش، خَمْش

relationship	آصِرة، أَوَاصِر
stinging, burning	لاذِع
cholera	الكُولِيرا
to annihilate	فَتَكَ، يَفْتُك، فَتْك
to prosper	أَكْثَرَ، يُكْثِر، إِكْثار
amulets	حِجاب، حُجُب
nausea, sickness	غَثَيان
prevention	وِقايَة
foyer, anteroom	دِهْلِيز، دَهالِيز
rattling in the throat	حَشْرَجَة
split, broken	مَفْطُور
supplication to God	ابْتِهال
(here) to separate, keep apart	حالَ، يَحول، حال
(here) to send a telegram	أَبْرَقَ، يُبْرِق، إِبْراق
(used in the passive) to die	أُحْتُضِرَ، يُحْتَضَر
to groan	أَنَّ، يَئِنّ، أَنِين

to collapse	هَوَى، يَهْوِي، هُوِي
to be emitted, sent out	انْبَعَثَ، يَنْبَعِث، انْبِعاث
veil	لِثام
to bandage	عَصَبَ، يَعْصِب، عَصْب
dazed, distracted	ذاهِل
fate	القَضاء
to sob	أَجْهَشَ، يُجْهِش، إِجْهاش
to find fault with	عابَ، يَعِيب، عَيْب
to reduce, lessen	حَطَّ، يَحُطّ، حَطّ
indebted	مَدِين، مَدِينُون
insomnia	أَرَق
occasionally, infrequently	لِمامًا

Unit Ten

Preparation for Reading

Author's Background

في عـام ١٩٤٧، قـام طـه حسـين بترجمـة سلسـلة مـن المقـالات المؤثـرة للفيلسـوف الفرنسـي Jean-Paul Sartre فـي موضـوع "la litterature engagée" مؤكـدًا علـى فكـرة أن واجـب المؤلـف أن يكتـب مـن أجـل العدالـة الاجتماعيـة وليـس مـن أجـل الفـن فقـط، وقـام علـى أساسـها بصياغـة مصطلحـي "التـزام الأديـب" و"الأدب الملتـزم" الـذي أصبـح مـن الأشـكال الأدبيـة المهيمنـة فـي منتصـف القـرن العشـرين، خاصـة فـي مصـر مـع تزامن الثـورة الاشـتراكية. ومـع أنـه كان رائـدًا فـي هـذا النـوع مـن الأدب القائـم علـى نظريـة الالتـزام، إلا أنـه رفـض التقيـد الصـارم بمفهـوم "واجـب" أو "التـزام" الكاتـب، وأصـر علـى بقائـه حـرًا. وتظـل روايتـه "الأيـام" فـي ضـوء مـا تقـدم مـن بـين أهـم الأمثلـة علـى الأدب الـذي يهـدف إلـى تحقيـق العدالـة والإصـلاح الاجتماعـي.

Reading

I

أمـا فـي هـذه المـرة فسـتذهب إلـى القاهـرة مـع أخيـك، وسـتصبح مجـاورًا، وسـتجتهد فـي طلـب العلـم، وأنـا أرجـو أن أعيـش حتـى أرى أخـاك قاضيـا وأراك مـن علمـاء الأزهـر، قـد جلسـت إلـى أحـد أعمدتـه ومـن حولـك حلقـة واسـعة بعيـدة المـدى.

قـال الشـيخ ذلـك لابنـه آخـر النهـار فـي يـوم مـن خريـف سـنة ١٩٠٢، وسـمع الصبـي هـذا الكـلام فلـم يصـدِّق ولـم يكـذِّب، ولكنـه آثـر أن ينتظـر

تصديق الأيام أو تكذيبها له، فكثيرا ما قال له أبوه مثل هذا الكلام، وكثيرا ما وعده أخوه الأزهري مثل هذا الوعد، ثم سافر الأزهري إلى القاهرة، ولبث الصبي في المدينة يتردد بين البيت والكُتّاب والمحكمة ومجالس الشيوخ.

وفي الحق أنه لم يفهم لماذا صدّق وعد أبيه في هذه السنة، فقد أخبر الصبي ذات يوم أنه مسافر بعد أيام. وأقبل يوم الخميس، فإذا الصبي يرى نفسه يتأهب للسفر حقًا، وإذا هو يرى نفسه في المحطة ولما تشرق الشمس. وهو يرى نفسه جالسًا القرفصاء منكس الرأس كئيبًا محزونًا، ويسمع أكبر إخوته ينهره في لطف قائلاً له: لاتنكس رأسك هكذا، ولا تأخذ هذا الوجه الحزين فتحزن أخاك. ويسمع أباه يشجعه في لطف قائلاً: ماذا يحزنك؟ ألست رجلا؟ ألست قادرا على أن تفارق أمك؟ أم أنت تريد أن تلعب؟ ألم يكفك هذا اللعب الطويل؟

شهد الله ما كان الصبي حزينًا لفراق أمه، وما كان الصبي حزينًا لأنه لن يلعب، إنما كان يذكر هذا الذي ينام هنالك من وراء النيل. كان يذكره، وكان يذكر أنه كثيرًا ما فكر في أنه سيكون معهما في القاهرة تلميذا في مدرسة الطب. كان يذكر هذا كله فيحزن، ولكنه لم يقل شيئا ولم يظهر حزنًا، وإنما تكلّف الابتسام. ولو قد أرسل نفسه مع طبيعتها لبكى ولأبكى من حوله أباه وأخويه.

وانطلق القطار ومضت ساعات ورأى صاحبنا نفسه في القاهرة بين جماعة من المجاورين قد أقبلوا إلى أخيه فحيوه وأكلوا ما كان قد احتمله لهم من طعام.

انقضى هذا اليوم. وكان يومُ الجمعة، وإذا الصبي يرى نفسه في الأزهر للصلاة. وإذا هو يسمع الخطيب شيخًا ضخم الصوت عاليه، فخم الراءات والقافات،[67] لا فرق بينه وبين خطيب المدينة إلا في هذا. فأما الخطبة فهي ما كان تعوّد أن يسمع في المدينة. وأما الحديث فهو هو. وأما النعت فهو هو. وأما الصلاة فهي هي ليست أطول من صلاة المدينة ولا أقصر.

67. Referring to his pronunciation of the letters *ray* and *qaaf*.

Comprehension Questions

١. لماذا لم يصدق صاحبنا وعد الأب بأنه ذاهب للأزهر؟

---

٢. لماذا حذره شقيقه من الظهور بمظهر حزين؟

---

٣. كيف قضى يومه الثاني في القاهرة؟

---

٤. ما هو السبب الحقيقي لحزن الصبي على الرحيل؟

---

٥. ماذا كانت خطة صاحبنا للدراسة في القاهرة قبل وفاة شقيقه؟

II

وعاد الصبي إلى بيته أو قل إلى حجرة أخيه خائب الظن بعض الشيء. وسأله أخوه: ما رأيك في تجويد القرآن ودرس القراءات؟

قال الصبي: لست في حاجة إلى شيء من هذا، فأما التجويد فأنا أتقنه، وأما القراءات فلست في حاجة إليها، وهل درست أنت القراءات؟ أليس يكفيني أن أكون مثلك؟ إنما أنا في حاجة إلى العلم، أريد أن أدرس الفقه والنحو والمنطق والتوحيد.

قال أخوه: حسبك! يكفي أن تدرس الفقه والنحو في هذه السنة.

وكان يوم السبت، فاستيقظ الصبي مع الفجر، وتوضأ وصلّى، ونهض أخوه فتوضأ وصلى كذلك، ثم قال له: ستذهب معي الآن إلى مسجد كذا، وستحضر درسا ليس لك وإنما هو لي، حتى إذا فرغنا من هذا الدرس ذهبت بك إلى الأزهر فالتمست لك شيخا من أصحابنا تختلف إليه وتأخذ عنه مبادئ العلم.

قال الصبي: وما هذا الدرس الذي سأحضره؟

قال أخوه ضاحكا: هو درس الفقه وهو ابن عابدين على الدرّ. قال ذلك يملأ به فمه.

قال الصبي: ومَن الشيخ؟

قال أخوه: هو الشيخ ...

وكان الصبي قد سمع اسم الشيخ ... ألف مرة ومرة. فقد كان أبوه يذكر هذا الاسم ويفتخر بأنه عرف الشيخ حين كان قاضيا للإقليم. وكانت أمّه تذكر هذا الاسم، وتذكر أنها عرفت امرأته فتاة هوجاء جلفة، تتكلف زي أهل المدينة وما هي من زيّ أهل المدن في شي، وكان أبو الصبي يسأل ابنه الأزهري كلما عاد من القاهرة عن الشيخ ودروسه وعدد طلابه.

وكان ابنه الأزهري يحدثه عن الشيخ ومكانته في المحكمة العليا وحلقته التي تعد بالمئات. وكان أبو الصبي يلح على ابنه الأزهري في أن يقرأ كما كان يقرأ الشيخ، فيحاول الفتى تقليده فيضحك أبوه في إعجاب وإكبار. وكان أبو الصبي يسأل ابنه: أيعرفك الشيخ؟

فيجيب الفتى: وكيف لا! وأنا ورفاقي من أخص تلاميذه وآثرهم عنده، نحضر درسه العام ثم نحضر عليه درسًا خاصًا في بيته، وكثيرًا ما نتغدى لنعمل معه بعد ذلك في كتبه الكثيرة التي يؤلفها. ثم يمضي

الفتى في وصف بيت الشيخ وحجرة استقباله ودار كتبه، وأبوه يسمع ذلك معجبًا، حتى إذا خرج إلى أصحابه قص عليهم ما سمع من ابنه في شيء من التيه والفخار.

كان الصبي إذًا يعرف الشيخ، وكان سعيدًا بالذهاب إلى حلقته والاستماع له. وكم كان مبتهجًا حين خلع نعليه عند باب المسجد ومشى على الحصير ثم على الرخام ثم على هذا البساط الرقيق الذي فرش به المسجد. وكم كان سعيدًا حين أخذ مكانه في الحلقة على هذا البساط إلى جانب عمود من الرخام، لمسه فأحب ملاسته ونعومته، وأطال التفكير في قول أبيه: إني لأرجو أن أعيش حتى أرى أخاك قاضيا وأراك صاحب عمود في الأزهر. وفيما هو يفكر في هذا ويتمنى أن يمس أعمدة الأزهر ليرى أهي كأعمدة هذا المسجد، وللطلاب من حوله دويّ غريب، أحس أن هذا الدويّ يخفت ثم ينقطع، وغمزه أخوه بيده قائلًا في صوت خافت: لقد أقبل الشيخ. اجتمعت شخصية الصبي كلها حينئذ في أذنيه وأنصت. ماذا يسمع؟ يسمع صوتًا خافتًا هادئًا رزينًا ملؤه شيء قل إنه الكبر، أو قل إنه الجلال، أو قل إنه ما شئت، ولكنه شيء غريب لم يحبه الصبي. ولبث الصبي دقائق لا يميز مما يقول الشيخ حرفا، حتى إذا تعودت أذناه صوت الشيخ وصدى المكان سمع وتبين وفهم. وقد أقسم لي بعد ذلك أنه احتقر العلم منذ ذلك اليوم.

سمع الشيخ يقول: «ولو قال لها أنت طلاق أو أنت ظلام أو أنت طلال أو أنت طلاة،[68] وقع الطلاق ولا عبرة بتغيير اللفظ.» يقول ذلك متغنيا به مرتلًا له ترتيلًا في صوت لا يخلو من حشرجة، ولكن صاحبه يحتال أن يجعله عذبًا، ثم يختم هذا الغناء بهذه الكلمة التي أعادها طوال الدرس: «فاهم يا أدع.» وأخذ الصبي يسأل نفسه عن «الأدع» هذا ما هو؟ حتى إذا انصرف عن الدرس سأل أخاه: ما الأدع؟ فقهقه أخوه وقال: الأدع الجدع في لغة الشيخ.

ومضى به بعد ذلك إلى الأزهر فقدمه إلى أستاذه الذي علمه مبادئ الفقه والنحو سنة كاملة.

68. Mispronunciations of "divorced."

Comprehension Questions

١. أين سكن الصبي في القاهرة؟

٢. ماذا أراد صاحبنا من دراسته في الأزهر؟

٣. كيف عرف الأب الشيخ الذي درس في الأزهر؟

٤. لماذا أراد الأخ أن يأخذ الصبي للقاء زملائه؟

٥. كيف أثر صوت الشيخ على صاحبنا؟

III

إنك يا ابنتي لساذجة سليمة القلب طيبة النفس. أنت في التاسعة من عمرك، في هذه السن التي يعجب فيها الأطفال بآبائهم وأمهاتهم، ويتخذونهم مثلا عليا في الحياة: يتأثرونهم في القول والعمل، ويحاولون أن يكونوا مثلهم في كل شيء، ويفاخرون بهم إذا تحدثوا إلى أقرانهم أثناء اللعب، ويخيل إليهم أنهم كانوا أثناء طفولتهم كما هم الآن مثلاً عليا يصلحون أن يكونوا قدوة حسنة وأسوة صالحة.

أليس الأمر كما أقول؟ ألست ترين أن أباك خير الرجال وأكرمهم؟ ألست ترين أنه قد كان كذلك خير الأطفال وأنبلهم؟ ألست مقتنعة أنه كان يعيش كما تعيشين أو خيرًا مما تعيشين؟ ألست تحبين أن تعيشي الآن كما كان يعيش أبوك حين كان في الثامنة من عمره؟ ومع ذلك فإن أباك يبذل من الجهد ما يملك، ويتكلف من المشقة ما يطيق وما لا يطيق، ليجنبك حياته حين كان صبيًا.

لقد عرفته يا ابنتي في هذا الطور من أطوار حياته. ولو أني حدثتك بما كان عليه حينئذ لكذّبت كثيرًا من ظنك، ولخيبت كثيرًا من أملك، ولفتحت إلى قلبك الساذج ونفسك الحلوة بابًا من أبواب الحزن؛ حرام أن يفتح إليهما وأنت في هذا الطور اللذيذ من الحياة. ولكني لن أحدثك بشيء مما كان عليه أبوك في ذلك الطور الآن. لن أحدثك بشيء من هذا حتى تتقدم بك السن قليلا فتستطيعين أن تقرئي وتفهمي وتحكمي، ويومئذ تستطيعين أن تعرفي أن أباك أحبك حقًا، وجدّ في إسعادك حقًا، ووفق بعض التوفيق إلى أن يجنبك طفولته وصباه.

نعم يا ابنتي لقد عرفت أباك في هذا الطور من حياته. وإني لأعرف أن في قلبك رقة ولينًا، وإني لأخشى لو حدثتك بما عرفت من أمر أبيك حينئذ أن يملكك الإشفاق وتأخذك الرأفة فتجهشي بالبكاء.

Comprehension Questions

١. إلى من يتكلم الراوي في هذا القسم؟

____

____

٢. في رأي الراوي، كيف ينظر الأطفال في هذا العمر إلى والديهم؟

____

____

٣. لماذا قرر الراوي عدم إعلام البنت بكل تفاصيل حياة أبيها في هذا الوقت؟

____

____

٤. بالنسبة للراوي، ماذا كان هدف أبي البنت في إرشادها خلال طفولتها؟

____

____

٥. كيف يتوقع الراوي أن البنت سرد على أحوال أبيه لو عرفت الحقيقة؟

____

____

IV

لقد رأيتك ذات يوم جالسة على حجر أبيك وهو يقص عليك قصة «أوديب ملكًا»،[69] وقد خرج من قصره بعد أن فقأ عينيه لا يدري كيف يسير، وأقبلت ابنته «أنتيجون»[70] فقادته وأرشدته. رأيتك ذلك اليوم تسمعين هذه القصة مبتهجة من أولها، ثم أخذ لونك يتغير قليلاً قليلاً، وأخذت جبهتك

69. *Oedipus Rex.*
70. *Antigone.*

السمحة تربدّ شيئًا فشيئًا، وما هي إلاَّ أن أجهشت بالبكاء وانكببت على أبيك لثمًا وتقبيلا، وأقبلت أمّك فانتزعتك من بين ذراعيه، وما زالت بك حتى هدأ روعك، وفهمت أمّك وفهم أبوك وفهمت أنا أيضًا أنك إنما بكيت لأنك رأيت أوديب الملك كأبيك مكفوفًا لا يبصر ولا يستطيع أن يهتدي وحده. فبكيت لأبيك كما بكيت «لأوديب».

نعم! وإني لأعرف أن فيك عبث الأطفال وميلهم إلى اللهو والضحك وشيئًا من قسوتهم، وإني لأخشى يا ابنتي إن حدّثتك بما كان عليه أبوك في بعض أطوار صباه أن تضحكي منه قاسية لاهية، وما أحب أن يضحك طفل من أبيه، وما أحب أن يلهو به أو يقسو عليه. ومع ذلك فقد عرفت أباك في طور من أطوار حياته أستطيع أن أحدثك به دون أن أثير في نفسك حزنًا، ودون أن أغريك بالضحك أو اللهو.

عرفته في الثالثة عشرة من عمره حين أرسل إلى القاهرة ليختلف إلى دروس العلم في الأزهر؛ إن كان في ذلك الوقت لصبي جد وعمل. كان نحيفًا شاحب اللون مهمل الزيّ أقرب إلى الفقر منه إلى الغنى، تقتحمه العين اقتحامًا في عباءته القذرة وطاقيته التي استحال بياضها إلى سواد قاتم، وفي هذا القميص الذي يبين إثناء عباءته وقد اتخذ ألوانًا مختلفة من كثرة ما سقط عليه من الطعام، ومن نعليه الباليتين المرقعتين. تقتحمه العين في هذا كله، ولكنها تبتسم له حين تراه على ما هو عليه من حال رثة وبصر مكفوف، واضح الجبين مبتسم الثغر مسرعًا مع قائده إلى الأزهر، لا تختلف خطاه ولا يتردّد في مشيته، ولا تظهر على وجهه هذه الظلمة التي تغشى عادة وجوه المكفوفين. تقتحمه العين ولكنها تبتسم له وتلحظه في شيء من الرفق، حين تراه في حلقة الدرس مصغيًا كله إلى الشيخ يلتهم كلامه التهامًا، مبتسمًا مع ذلك لا متألمًا ولا متبرمًا ولا مظهرًا ميلا إلى لهو، على حين يلهو الصبيان من حوله أو يشرئبون إلى اللهو، عرفته يا ابنتي في هذا الطور، وكم أحب لو تعرفينه كما عرفته. إذًا تقدرين ما بينك وبينه من فرق، ولكن أنّى لك هذا وأنت في التاسعة من عمرك ترين الحياة كلها نعيمًا وصفوًا!

Comprehension Questions

١. لماذا حزنت البنت لسماع قصة أوديب؟

____

____

٢. ماذا يخشى الراوي من ردة فعل البنت عند سماع قصة والدها؟

____

____

٣. كيف كانت حال ملابس صاحبنا؟

____

____

٤. كيف اختلف صاحبنا عن غيره من المكفوفين؟

____

____

٥. كيف اختلف سلوكه في الدروس عن غيره من الأطفال في سنه؟

____

____

V

عرفته ينفق اليوم والأسبوع والشهر والسنة لا يأكل إلا لونًا واحدًا، يأخذ منه حظه في الصباح ويأخذ منه حظه في المساء، لا شاكيًا ولا متبرمًا ولا متجلدًا، ولا مفكرًا في أن حاله خليقة بالشكوى. ولو أخذت يا ابنتي من هذا اللون حظًا قليلاً في يوم واحد لأشفقت أمّك ولقدمت إليك قدحًا من الماء المعدني، ولانتظرت أن تدعو الطبيب.

لقد كان أبوك ينفق الأسبوع والشهر لا يعيش إلا على خبز الأزهر، وويل للأزهريين من خبز الأزهر؛ إن كانوا ليجدون فيه ضروبًا من القش وألوانًا من الحصى وفنونًا من الحشرات.

وكان ينفق الأسبوع والشهر والأشهر لا يغمس هذا الخبز إلا في العسل الأسود، وأنت لا تعرفين العسل الأسود، وخير لك ألا تعرفيه.

كذلك كان يعيش أبوك جادًا مبتسمًا للحياة والدرس، محرومًا لا يكاد يشعر بالحرمان. حتى إذا انقضت السنة وعاد إلى أبويه وأقبلا عليه يسألانه كيف يأكل؟ وكيف يعيش؟ أخذ ينظم لهما الأكاذيب كما تعود أن ينظم لك القصص، فيحدثهما بحياة يحياها كلها رغد ونعيم. وما كان يدفعه إلى هذا الكذب حب الكذب. إنما كان يرفق بهذين الشيخين ويكره أن ينبئهما بما هو فيه من حرمان، وكان يرفق بأخيه الأزهري، ويكره أن يعلم أبواه أنه يستأثر دونه بقليل من اللبن. كذلك كانت حياة أبيك في الثالثة عشرة من عمره.

فإن سألتني كيف انتهى إلى حيث هو الآن؟ وكيف أصبح شكله مقبولاً لا تقتحمه العين ولا تزدريه؟ وكيف استطاع أن يهيئ لك ولأخيك ما أنتما فيه من حياة راضية؟ وكيف استطاع أن يثير في نفوس كثير من الناس ما يثير من حسد وحقد وضغينة، وأن يثير في نفوس ناس آخرين ما يثير من رضًا عنه وإكرام له وتشجيع؟ إن سألت كيف انتقل من تلك الحال إلى هذه الحال، فلست أستطيع أن أجيبك! وإنما هناك شخص آخر هو الذي يستطيع هذا الجواب، فسليه ينبئك.

أتعرفينه؟ انظري إليه! هو هذا الملك القائم الذي يحنو على سريرك إذا أمسيت لتستقبلي الليل في هدوء ونوم لذيذ، ويحنو على سريرك إذا أصبحت لتستقبلي النهار في سرور وابتهاج. ألست مدينة لهذا الملك بما أنت فيه من هدوء الليل وبهجة النهار!

لقد حنا يا ابنتي هذا الملك على أبيك، فبدّله من البؤس نعيمًا، ومن اليأس أملًا، ومن الفقر غنى، ومن الشقاء سعادة وصفوًا.

ليس دين أبيك لهذا الملك بأقل من دينك. فلتتعاونا يا ابنتي على أداء هذا الدين. وما أنتما ببالغين من ذلك بعض ما تريدان.

طه حسين

Comprehension Questions

١. كيف يصف الراوي نظام طعام صاحبنا في الأزهر؟

____

____

٢. ما هي حالة الخبز الذي كان يأكله طلاب الأزهر؟

____

____

٣. لماذا كذب الصبي بخصوص ظروف معيشته في الأزهر؟

____

____

٤. من المسؤول عن نجاح صاحبنا رغم بداياته الفقيرة؟

____

____

٥. لمن تدين البنت ووالدها حسب الراوي؟

Comprehension Exercise

Are the following statements true (صحيح) or false (خطأ) and why?

١. كان يأمل الصبي أن يدرس في كلية الطب مثل أخيه المرحوم.

---

٢. وجد صاحبنا أن الخطبة في مسجد الأزهر تختلف عن الخطبة في القرية اختلافًا كبيرًا.

---

٣. يفتخر الأب بأن ابنه درس في الأزهر مع شيخ عرفه من الماضي.

---

٤. لم يرغب صاحبنا في دراسة التجويد وتلاوة القرآن، بل أراد الانتقال مباشرة إلى مواضيع أكثر تقدمًا مثل الفقه والمنطق.

---

٥. كشف الراوي في نهاية القصة أنه كان يرويها إلى بنت صاحبنا.

---

٦. بعدما صار صاحبنا أبًا كان لا يريد أن تعيش ابنته حياة مثل التي عاشها.

____

٧. تميز صاحبنا في الأزهر بنظافته واهتمامه بملابسه.

____

٨. كان صاحبنا طالبًا مجتهدًا جدًا في الأزهر.

____

٩. كطالب في الأزهر، اتبع صاحبنا نظامًا غذائيًا صحيًا للغاية.

____

١٠. يعتقد الراوي أن ملاك هو المسؤول عن نجاحه.

____

Interpreting the Text

A. Answer the following questions in complete Arabic sentences, based on your interpretation of what you have read so far:

١. هل يبدو أن صاحبنا يظهر التواضع والصبر في خططه للدراسة؟ لماذا تعتقدون أن هذا هو الحال؟

____

____

٢. ما مدى أهمية العلاقات الشخصية بين الطلاب وبين الطلاب والمعلمين في نظام التعليم في الأزهر؟

____

____

٣. ما هي العلاقة الفعلية بين البنت (المستمعة للقصة) والراوي وصاحبنا؟ كيف يختلف عرض العلاقة عن الواقع؟

____

____

٤. في القسم الأخير من الرواية يترك المؤلف للقارئ (ابنته) العديد من الأسئلة. ما رأيكم في الهدف من هذه الأسئلة التي لم تتم الإجابة عليها؟

____

____

٥. ما هي الجوانب من حياة الراوي التي لا يريد للبنت أن تجربها بنفسها؟

____

____

B. Analyzing the story: Having now read the entire novel, you can reflect back on your earlier predictions and expectations. Based on all you've read, answer the following questions:

١. كيف تغيرت شخصية صاحبنا منذ بداية الرواية إلى الشخص الذي نراه كطالب في الأزهر؟

____

____

٢. ما هي التجربة التي كان لها التأثير الأكبر في أن يصبح كما هو موصوف في المشاهد الأخيرة في رأيكم؟

____

____

٣. بالنظر إلى موقفه من السحر والخرافات، لماذا ينسب الراوي نجاح صاحبنا إلى "ملاك"؟

____

____

٤. هل تتوقعون أن تستمر سعادة صاحبنا في الأزهر طويلاً؟

____

____

٥. ما هي التجارب التي يريد صاحبنا حماية أطفاله منها؟

____

____

Cultural and Historical Background

1. The study circle described above reflects the traditional format of instruction in mosque schools, where students would form in semi-circles around the teacher. From this arrangement came the terms حلقة ('circle')—to refer to a study or discussion group—and صف ('row')—for a class or cohort of students, the most senior or preferred sitting closest. The pillar of the mosque marks the place where the sheikh would sit. Thus, the youth's father envisions him one day being "the owner of a pillar (صاحب عمود)," that is to say, a prominent teacher for whom a space is set aside to teach.
2. In the final sections, the author makes reference to the Greek tragedies *Oedipus Rex* and *Antigone*. Taha Hussein not only translated classical Greek works but was a strong advocate of Greek culture as an essential part of the Egyptian identity. He asserted—against trends like pan-Arabism and Orientalism—that Egypt belonged in the "western" cultural sphere, rather than the eastern, and the Greek and Roman influences were among

his primary evidence for this belief. The image of the author teaching *Oedipus* to his young children, while otherwise wanting to spare them from sadness, reinforces the importance he places on this as a foundation of their cultural identity.

Analyzing Elements of Literature

Narrator (الراوي، السارد)

حتى هذه النقطة من القصة، ظلت هوية الراوي غامضة عمدًا. رغم التشابه الواضح مع حياة طه حسين إلا أنه لم يتم التعرف على هوية الصوت الراوي، حتى إذا كان هذا الصوت يخص شخصًا معينًا أو إذا كان لهذا الشخص أي علاقة بالشخصية الرئيسية. فقط قرب نهاية القصة يعرف الراوي نفسه على أنه بطل القصة، وذلك بشكل غير مباشر فقط. هذا أيضًا هو المكان الذي يحدد فيه الشخص الذي تروى له القصة ولماذا. وبذلك لا يظهر الكتاب كسيرة ذاتية عادية في معظمه، حيث يتم تقديم السرد في نمط رواية. جعل هذا من "الأيام" عملًا مبتكرًا في الأدب المصري في ذلك الوقت وساعد في تقديم نوع الرواية. وجدير بالذكر أن هذه الرواية نشرت في سلسلة من الأجزاء في جريدة وقرأها القراء بدون معرفة هوية الراوي حتى آخر جزء.

Based on your reading, answer the following questions about the role of the narrator in *The Days*:

١. هل تغير شعوركم تجاه القصة الآن بعد أن تم الكشف عن هوية الراوي (إلى حد كبير)؟

____

____

٢. كيف يؤثر هذا الكشف على رؤيتنا لشخصية الصبي، وخاصة صفاته السلبية؟

____

____

٣. في ظل هذه المعرفة، كيف يمكن تفسير استخدام الراوي وصف "صاحبنا" للشخصية الرئيسية؟

____

____

٤. إذا كانت القصة تروى لابنة الراوي كما يزعم هنا، فماذا سيكون تأثير سماعها لها وكأن القصة عن شخص ثالث (غيرها وغير أبيها)؟

____

____

Themes

واجب الأب

Taha Hussein ends the novel with an emotional expression of his desire as a parent to spare his children from the miseries he suffered. Most of those miseries, we have seen, are due to failings in the education, health, and social systems under which he lived. As his life bears out, the author also felt the responsibility to ensure a better life for the next generation, applied to Egypt as a nation. In a one- to two-page paper in Arabic, address the following question:

نظـرًا للمشـاكل الجوهريـة فـي المجتمـع المصـري التـي كشـفت فـي هـذه الروايـة، مـا هـي بعـض الاصلاحـات التـي تشـير إليها تجـارب صاحبنـا فـي طفولتـه فـي القريـة؟

Final Project

Congratulations on completing your reading of *The Days* by Taha Hussein. To bring together all that you have learned over the course of the ten units, please complete one of the final projects below. We hope these will help you reflect on your study of the novel and its place in Egyptian literary history.

Writing Projects

Please prepare a five- to seven-page essay in Arabic on one of the following questions. In your answer, include quotations from the text of the novel, and reference to at least three of the elements of literature that you studied in the units:

ا. كيف تغيرت شخصية صاحبنا خلال القصة؟ هل تعتبر تغيراته تطوّرًا إيجابيًا؟ ما هي أسباب هذه التغيرات؟ كيف استخدم الكاتب العناصر الأدبية لرسم هذه التغيرات؟

ب. هل تعتبر شخصية صاحبنا رمزًا لمجتمعه أو جزء من هذا المجتمع؟ كيف تعكس تجاربه تجارب ذلك المجتمع؟ ما هي أهم الموضوعات (themes) في سياق تطوره وتطور المجتمع؟

ج. هذه القصة تقع على الحد الفاصل بين جنسي الرواية والسيرة الذاتية. هل تشعرون أن القصة تعززها عناصر الرواية؟ إذا كان الأمر كذلك، كيف يمكن أن تكون القصة أكثر فعالية من سيرة ذاتية عادية؟

Speaking Projects

Please prepare a three- to five-minute presentation, with visual aids if appropriate, on one of the following questions. In your answer, discuss at least three of the elements of literature you studied.

١. طه حسين سيصبح لاحقًا من أعظم المصلحين في المجتمع المصري وخاصة في مجال التعليم. كيف تظهر شخصية صاحبنا صفات المصلح المستقبلي؟

٢. شخصية الراوي في هذه القصة هي أحد عناصرها الأكثر إبداعًا. ماذا يمثل لكم هذا الصوت؟ ما مدى أهمية العلاقة بين الراوي وصاحبنا والبنت في نهاية القصة لرسالتها؟

٣. ما تزال رواية "الأيام" من أكثر الروايات العربية المؤثرة والمعروفة. لماذا تركت هذه القصة انطباعًا قويًا في المجتمع المصري وخارجه في رأيكم؟

Vocabulary Items

The following words are particularly useful in following Taha Hussein's narrative in this section:

squatting	قُرْفُصاء
to hang one's head	نَكَسَ، يَنْكُس، نَكْس اَلْرَّأْس
to intensify	فَخَّمَ، يُفَخِّم، تَفْخِيم
to look for, search for	الْتَمَسَ، يَلْتَمِس، الْتِماس
boorish, uncultured	جِلْف، أَجْلاف
foolish	هَوْجاء
admiration	إِكْبار
most favored	آثَر
mat	حَصِير، حُصُر
rug	بِساط، أَبْسِطَة
to hum, buzz	دَوِيَ، يَدَى، دَوِي
to signal	غَمَزَ، يَغْمِز، غَمْز
serious, serene	رَزِين

young fellow	جَذَع، جِذْعان
to follow one's example, emulate	تَأَثَّرَ، يَتَأَثَّر، تَأَثُّر
model, exemplar	قُدْوَة
to be capable of, to endure	طاقَ، يَطُوق، طَوْق
lap	حِجْر
to poke out an eye	فَقَأَ، يَفْقَأ، فَقْء
to assume a glowering expression	أَرْبَدَ، يُرْبِد، إِرْباد
to prostrate, lean against	انْكَبَّ، يَنْكَبّ، انْكِباب
ragged	رَثَّة
to cover	غَشَا، يَغْشُو، غَشْو
annoyed	مُتَبَرِّمًا
portion	حَظّ، حُظُوظ
(here) to be worried about	أَشْفَقَ، يُشْفِق، إِشْفاق
distress, affliction	وَيْل

straw	قَشّ
pebbles	حَصَى
rancor, resentment	ضَغِينَة، ضَغائِن